MISSING SOMMER

NORA SOMMER CARIBBEAN SUSPENSE - BOOK EIGHT

NICHOLAS HARVEY

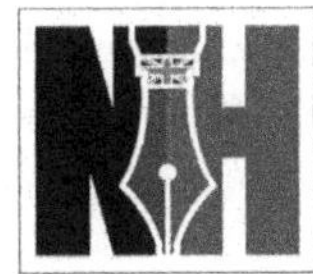

For our God son, Niki Niemela
May he always enjoy the exciting times after sleep.

PROLOGUE

In her eleven and three-quarter years, Chloe had been scared plenty of times. But nothing compared to this.

Bound at her wrists and ankles, the drawstring of a hood pulled snug around her throat, and a gag and earplugs firmly taped in place. The heat was stifling. Oppressive and stale. Choking back the terror, she instinctively knew that unless she calmed herself, she'd soon pass out. But maybe that would be okay. She was being taken away from everything she knew. Away from help.

How long would it be before anyone noticed she was gone? Too long. Besides, she'd been incredibly sneaky. So smart. She'd thought. Chloe now realised how well Grey Eyes had played her. Lured her, and arranged everything so perfectly. Not even her best friend knew exactly where she'd been going or who she'd been seeing.

Her parents' boring lectures echoed in her head. The reminders given at school every term and their frustratingly annoying procedures and rules about pickups. None of it seemed so trivial and pointless now.

Chloe's senses spun in confusion and nausea began consuming her. A rocking movement combined with her terror raised bile in her throat, which she fought back in whimpers and sobs. She'd heard about people choking on their own vomit. That disgusting boy, Freddie, had tried to show her a video of weird ways people had died. The first one had been a rock star who'd thrown up, passed out, and died because he couldn't breathe. She shivered at the memory and willed herself not to puke.

Something changed. Without sight or sound, her only indication was movement, and although Chloe felt disorientated, she was sure they'd started moving. She'd been laid down on something soft, like a mattress, but her shoulder nudged against a hard surface, and vibrations and bumps transferred to her body despite not being able to hear what caused them. Grey Eyes was moving around nearby.

An odour slowly made its way through the heavy material of the hood. It smelled like the noisy trimmers and cutters the gardener, Kyle, used. Without the grass smell. Just the horrible exhaust and oily part. Kyle usually worked in a tank top and sweat gleamed from his muscles. It made his dark skin shimmer. On several occasions, Chloe had caught her mother watching Kyle as he worked in their garden. Sometimes she'd go out to the pool house and watch from there, oblivious of her daughter observing everything. But that was typical. Her father was too busy with work and her mother absorbed in her own life.

They were moving a little faster now, bumping and rocking along. Occasionally, a bigger jolt rolled her to one side or the other. Chloe sweated from the heat and she wondered how long this ordeal would last. *Part of her begged for the journey to end, but then what would happen?* Maybe travelling blindly towards an unknown fate was better than what waited ahead.

She was lying on her left side, perpendicular to the direction of travel. She could tell because when they slowed and the front dipped, she was rolled more onto her back. It was then Chloe realised her balance seemed to be improving and her sense of movement heightened. Last term, they'd watched a presentation in one of her classes about people with various disabilities and how they adapted. It had been fascinating how a blind person focused more acutely on sounds, smells, and motion to navigate their surroundings. Chloe wondered if she'd ever see her classroom again. Her mum and dad. Her best friend, Emma.

Would Emma have kept the secret she made her swear to never tell? She hoped not. If her friend didn't say anything, then no one would know what happened. Not that Emma knew who or where she'd been going, but enough to alert people to begin searching. Surely the school would alert her mum and dad. Who would freak out and call the police. She'd be grounded until she was eighteen. If she lived to be twelve.

Her feeling of panic ebbed and flowed with the movement all around her until eventually Chloe relaxed into a state of resigned tension. They'd been travelling for what felt like hours when the engine note changed and she sensed the deceleration. *Where were they now?* The ordeal had scrambled her internal clock, such as it was. Grand Cayman wasn't a big island. Only 26 miles from end to end. At some point, the alarm would be raised and the search would begin at her school. Unless they'd travelled in circles for a reason Chloe couldn't imagine, she was now nowhere even close to school. She'd never be found. News reports talked about children going missing without a trace. But that was in England, not here in the Cayman Islands.

From the sharp bumps, she knew they'd stopped, and a few moments later the vibration from the engine went away. Having talked herself into being better off travelling than reaching their destination, the unbridled terror quickly returned.

Chloe screamed into her gag when her body was abruptly grabbed and picked up. She could feel arms clutching her under her shoulders and knees. Was it still Grey Eyes? Or had she been passed on to a stranger? Sold. Traded. But the touch felt the same.

Her head banged against a solid surface, and she silently yelped. This was it. The nausea rose again as panic and dread seized her petite body. *Was she about to be thrown into a deep, dark hole to die alone?* Or simply dropped into the water, tethered to an anchor. *How long would it take to drown?* Not long. But long enough to know she was dying with no one to save her.

She and Emma had played around in the pool, seeing how long they could hold their breath on the bottom. Chloe recalled the fear and panic she'd felt when it didn't seem like she could hold her breath a moment longer, but she didn't want to lose the game. *Was that what this would feel like?* No, this would be very different. Far worse. In the pool, all she had to do was push off the bottom to reach the air only three feet above her. The danger was all in her mind. This was all too real.

She felt a breeze across her bare legs and realised her school uniform skirt had ridden up her thighs. Exposed, a new fear gripped her mind. Chloe had never even kissed a boy. The thought of being sexually molested brought another level of horror she'd not yet contemplated. Her body jolted and a new heat struck her skin. It felt like the familiar scorching rays of the Caribbean sun.

By the rise and fall of the motion, Chloe knew she was still being carried. Possibly down a path or along something straight, as she couldn't feel them turning. There was a fresh smell. Sweet and slightly citrusy. Chloe was familiar with the odour, but couldn't place from where.

Her own breathing echoed in her head while the world around remained muted. Her mind returned to playing tricks, throwing ghastly images of ghouls and those orc creatures from the *Lord of the Rings* movies. Her parents had warned her not to watch the films, but she and Emma had done it anyway. Now those images fed her overactive imagination, while her logic, fed by the usual senses, was unable to keep them at bay.

Chloe jerked her bound legs as a grotesque hand swiped at her tiny form, a jagged fingernail scratching her bare flesh above her sock. She began convulsing, fighting for gulps of air as terror consumed her. She writhed in Grey Eyes' arms, her efforts countered by a tightened grip on her body. Their movement halted and Chloe imagined the creatures gathering all around to devour the meat from her bones. She could no longer draw air into her lungs and her head throbbed. Dizziness swamped her mind and all she could think about was forcing a breath before she suffocated.

A moment later, her feet bashed against something solid and she rocked in the arms of Grey Eyes, her crazed imaginary world vanishing with the new environment. Guessing she was now indoors, Chloe expected the cooling wave of air conditioning, but none came. The flowery smell had gone, replaced with a damp, stale odour like an old shed. Struggling with her bound wrists, she tugged and pulled on her skirt until it covered her thighs once more.

Lowered, she felt her backside land in a chair with a curved rail against her back. A hand tugged on the cord cinching the hood around her throat and she held her breath again. The hood pulled clear and Chloe blinked against the yellowish light from a single bulb dangling from a wire in the ceiling.

The room was small, dingy, and empty apart from the chair. No windows, or at least none she could see, but she was facing a closed door. If there was a window, it was covered over. *Or was it night-time already? Had it been that long? And where was Grey Eyes?* She couldn't see anyone or hear anything with the earplugs still in place. She looked left and right. The walls were pale blue painted concrete with water stains spreading down in rough elliptical beige blotches. The skirting boards were bubbled and speckled with mould.

Chloe startled as someone moved from behind her and knelt down in front of the chair. Shivering in fear, she stared into the grey eyes which had seemed so full of excitement and truth before today. Her little secret. A naughty but harmless escape from the boring everyday drudgery of school, and a home in which her parents pretended everything. Pretended to love each other. Pretended to care about their daughter when they were both too consumed in their own lives. Buying her things to win her over for when the inevitable happened and everything would be divided.

Those grey eyes held no excitement now.

Just a cold, resolute stare.

1

SCOTS, FINNS, AND POLES

Fy faen. It would only be a matter of time before the girl across the room recognised me. I knew her. She got her dumb arse nicked for solicitation and possession. I didn't arrest her, but I was on the team who ran the raids in the shitty hotel where her pimp ran his operation. I looked different now with a brunette wig over my Scandinavian blonde hair and makeup on my face, but she kept staring at me, so I knew what was coming.

I couldn't make too much fuss. Sitting in a suite at the Ritz-Carlton, a third girl was currently being interviewed in the bedroom while we waited our turn. Music played, drowning out the voices, or whatever else was going on, so there was no way to know when one of the three men would walk back in.

"I know you, don't I?" the girl asked, chomping her chewing gum and waggling a finger at me.

I couldn't recall from her arrest, but I knew she had to be older than eighteen. Probably not by much. Certainly no older than twenty-one. She was pale and spoke with an English accent, so I wondered how she'd swung a work permit to stay on the island. Probably a bartender or some other bullshit job to get her paperwork.

"You don't," I replied. "I'm not from here," I added, accentuating my accent.

"Where you from?" the girl asked.

"Finland," I lied, giving her the country we'd used as my cover.

No one spoke Finnish, except the Finnish, so I was unlikely to run into anyone who'd test me. It was a unique and difficult language to learn, so no one bothered unless they had to. My native Norwegian was very similar to Swedish, and somewhat close to Danish, so I'd be able to bumble my way by, but my Norwegian accent would give me away. So we chose Finnish. I'd only run into one Finn on the island in the several years I'd been in Grand Cayman. He was a divemaster and instructor with one of the local ops, so I was unlikely to come across him while undercover on this case. Divemasters couldn't afford to pay for high-class strippers.

"I swear you look really familiar," the girl persisted.

This was going to be a problem. Violet Blaze. That was her name. I remembered now. We all thought it had to be her porn name, but she had it on every piece of ID. I got up from my chair and walked over, sitting next to her on the couch. She smiled at me and leaned closer, like we were about to become buddies. We weren't.

"You have two options," I explained. "One is much better than the other."

She lost the smile. "Fuck…"

"Yeah. We've met before. How come you weren't deported?"

"Case is still pending trial," she replied, studying my face. "You changed something."

"No shit. I'm undercover. Which, if you blow, you'll beg to be deported."

"I need this gig," she hissed. "I'm skint and I can't work with this stupid charge hanging over me."

"Then get the gig," I replied. "But if you compromise me, you're getting locked up, understand? All you have to do is play along."

"Then you'll nick me when you nick them," she complained.

"So walk out now and don't say a word," I offered.

"I need the fucking money," she groaned.

"Then you play along, and I'll keep you out of the bust."

"How can I trust you?" she said, frowning at me. "I always get screwed."

"You're a hooker. Your job is to get screwed."

"Fuck you. I quit all that," she snapped.

"Right, and you're here applying for the maid's position."

She groaned. "I was told this is just stripping. No touching."

I raised an eyebrow. "They all start with just stripping."

She groaned again. "True."

"So, are you walking away now, or playing along?" I asked.

"Or telling them who you are," she said, and grinned. "My third option. Bet they'd pay me pretty well to narc on you."

"Yup, they'll be tripping over themselves to PayPal you from jail. RCIPS firearms squad will be through that door within ten seconds if you snitch. This whole place is wired."

Violet looked at the door to the suite. "Fuck."

"Walk or play along?" I repeated.

"What happens if I walk?"

I thought for a second before replying, trying to decide what was best for my cover.

"You don't make any money and we don't help you with your current charges."

She swore again. "But I'd be helping you!"

I shrugged my shoulders. "You'd be not hurting us. That's different."

Violet looked at me, then the door, and finally back to me. "If I stay and help you, you'll get my current charge dropped?"

"Not my call, but I'll try."

She rolled her eyes. "You can screw me and there's nothing I can do about it."

"You're not my type."

Violet laughed sarcastically. "I think you already screwed me."

The music turned down, and the door opened to the bedroom. The girl came out first, buttoning up her glittery halter top. She was a pretty, dark-skinned woman. Older than I'd first thought, now I could see she wasn't smiling and hopeful.

"Remember. Not a word," the man who'd introduced himself as Ness said, opening the door for her to leave.

She nodded, stuffed a wad of cash into her purse, and hurried out, glancing nervously back before Ness closed the door behind her.

Ness. Not Mr Ness, or James Ness. Just Ness. He looked at me.

"You're next," he said with a slight Scottish accent.

I stood, taking Violet's hand as I did. Squeezing, I smiled at her.

"Wish me luck, babe."

She forced a smile in return. "Break a leg."

That didn't seem like a very nice way of wishing someone luck, but Ness didn't flinch, so I followed him into the bedroom, hoping Violet wouldn't rat me out. I had a feeling she wouldn't. Unless they got out the pliers, and then she'd sing like a parrot before they ever touched a fingernail.

A shiny, brass-coloured pole was tensioned between the tile floor and the ceiling in the room, and two other men stood by the window with drinks in their hands. Like Ness, they both wore suits. Maybe expensive Italian custom tailored, or off the rack at a discount shop. I could never tell until I saw them up close.

"Where have you danced before?" Ness asked, closing the door.

"Finland. Some in Germany."

"What are you doing here in the Cayman Islands?" he asked, sitting on the edge of the bed.

I hoped he didn't expect me to join him there.

"I teach freediving," I replied.

"Freediving?" he questioned, laughing and looking at the other two men. "Like that shit where you hold your breath for ages and swim around underwater?"

"*Joo*," I replied, using the little Finnish I knew.

"Then let's see if you can take our breath away," he laughed, and nodded to one of the others.

The man turned the music up. It was some annoying electronic dance music. Ness gesticulated to the pole.

"What's your name?" he asked.

"Viivi," I replied. "Viivi Piironen."

If they had enough reach to check work permits, they'd find my fake identity with a valid work permit and visa. The Royal Cayman Islands Police Service couldn't swing a Finnish passport, but we hoped their background research didn't go that far. After all, they were hiring strippers in a country where strip clubs of any sort were forbidden, not school teachers.

"One more very important question, Viivi," Ness said as I walked to the pole. "Are you a copper?"

I laughed. "How would a twenty-year-old from Finland become a policewoman on a Caribbean Island?"

Before he could answer, I gripped the metal pole and swung, hooking a foot around the base and letting the long, brunette wig stream behind me as I spun. The other two moved in closer, and I kicked a silvery high-heeled pump off my foot, which the chubby, bearded one caught and laughed.

I hoped they'd forgotten about the question I'd evaded, as our entire operation and all the effort we'd put in rested on that detail. If I lied, everything would be thrown out of court for entrapment. I'd exaggerated to Violet about guys with guns waiting to knock the door down. We had the head of the firearms group outside, Sergeant Williams, sitting in a car with Detective Vincent Weatherford, but if things went melon shaped, that was all the backup I had. The part about the room being wired was true, and I hoped the stupid music wasn't drowning out the conversation, otherwise they could say I lied about being a cop. It would be their word against mine. Three to one. We needed the recording, and for these three men to forget about police and laws and trouble. So I slid from the pole to my knees and pulled my metallic red tank top over my head. That seemed to get their attention.

Five minutes later, one of them turned the music down and all three applauded.

I picked my clothes up off the floor and started dressing. "When can I start?"

"You're assuming you got the gig," Ness replied with a grin.

I pointed to the crotch of Chubby Beard. "Looks like I won over the audience."

The man turned sideways and his cheeks blushed. I winked at him.

"I got the gig."

Ness laughed. "Maree there gets excited when his mother walks around the house without a bra."

The third man chuckled grimly, and Maree punched his arm.

"Screw you guys. She's fucking hot," he said, pointing at me. He was Scottish, too.

"Alright, lassie. So, can you start this week?" Ness asked. "We take you out on Friday afternoon and bring you back around one or two in the morning. You'll be on our weekend shift, so we'll repeat on Saturday and Sunday."

"Take me where?" I asked, as though I didn't know.

"You don't get seasick, do you?"

"I grew up on boats," I replied, which was one of the few truths I'd shared.

"Good. We take you to a private yacht in international waters. Means it's all legal."

I doubted that. We knew their luxury yacht, *Manannán*, was registered in Sint Maarten, where strip clubs were legal. Which meant, under international maritime law, it was governed by its flag country's rules, but we wouldn't be going to all this trouble if we thought they were completely legit.

"Can you be gone each evening over the weekend?" he asked.

"Sure. I can move my clients to later in the mornings. As long as the pay's worth it."

"The pay's a grand a night," Ness replied. "Plus fifty percent of tips."

I frowned at him. "Only half the tips?"

"This isn't like a regular peeler joint, lassie. Your clients will be high-rolling big spenders. We're guaranteeing you a grand a night and I bet you'll pull in that again from your split in tips. That's six grand for a weekend. You making that holding your breath underwater?"

I shook my head. "No, but I don't have a bunch of ancient perverts slobbering on me while I'm naked. How do you keep the girls safe?"

Ness nodded towards the third man. "Lomond handles security. We don't have any trouble."

He'd just given me the third name, but it wouldn't do us any good. I'd thought it odd the second man was called Mary, but now I'd figured it out. They were using code names taken from Scottish lochs. I knew Ness and Lomond. Now I realised the way he'd pronounced Mar-ee wasn't the woman's name. At least not in English.

"And we check before we bring you back," Lomond said. He was a lean, muscular man, going by the way his suit hung from his frame and his severe jawline. He wasn't Scottish. Northern English. "Try keeping tip money from us, and you don't come home."

I tried to look shocked, but I was shit at making my face do the acting things. I probably looked more like I had gas pains.

"For six grand a weekend, I plan on working for you for a while."

"We'll see," Ness said, in what now sounded like a pleasant tone compared to his mate, Lomond. "We'll be here for a few weeks. You'll make a lot of money if the clients like you."

"Where do I meet you Friday?" I asked.

"George Town harbour at four o'clock. Don't be late. Bring a selection of outfits."

He walked to the door and paused. I'd followed him and now stopped. I was standing closer to the man than I'd been so far. His eyes were hazel and quite captivating. Not menacing. But I'd fallen for that *trust me* look before and found the evil hiding underneath. I'd happily lock all three of these men up.

"And bring makeup, but don't put any on," he said, and there it was. The evil poking its head up to say hi.

"You want me to look younger?" I asked playfully.

He nodded.

"How young?"

He grinned. "Like you just walked off the playground, lassie."

2

LIFE'S UNWAVERING ROAD MAP

I wasn't a hugger. But I detoured on my way out of the hotel suite to put my arms around Violet. She reciprocated. Stiffly.

"They like young. Play along and I'll help you," I whispered in her ear.

She relaxed a little and squeezed me. "Okay."

I left and resisted looking back as I walked down the hall to the lifts. Walking across the lobby, I noticed a lot of eyes on me. I was wearing a shiny red tank top, a white miniskirt, and high heels. If it was dark outside, no one would notice, but it was three o'clock in the afternoon, so a little early to be heading to the clubs. A man moved from behind the reception counter and aimed to intercept me before I reached the revolving entry doors. He oozed underpaid security guard vibes.

"Ma'am, may we have a word?" he asked when he approached.

"*Nei*," I replied, and veered to exit through the regular door to the left.

"Ma'am?" he persisted, but I let the door close behind me.

I heard him chase me outside, but he stopped and didn't say anything more. We'd avoided involving anyone at the hotel beyond the manager for fear of a leak as more people became involved. We needed access to the suite for the bugs, otherwise we wouldn't have even told the manager. I was now on security's watch list, but it shouldn't matter. I doubted I'd be returning to the hotel.

It felt silly, getting into a piece of crap little rusty car in my stripper-clubbing-hooker outfit, but we'd borrowed an unclaimed car from the pound to complete my cover. I drove south on West Bay Road and took every turn I could to the bypass before using the next exit to return to the main road behind Seven Mile Beach. Once I was certain I hadn't been tailed, I parked behind the central police station on Elgin Road and entered the building from the rear entrance.

"Can I help you?" an officer asked.

"*Nei*," I replied and strode upstairs to Detective Whittaker's office.

Either the constable ended up recognising me or my confidence threw him as he didn't pursue me either.

"Sir," I said, entering my boss's office. Weatherford was already there.

Whittaker looked me over with an air of concern. "Any trouble?" he asked in his light Caymanian accent.

The lead detective for the western part of the island was a slim man in his fifties, tall, with a skin tone typical of the mixed racial heritage of the Cayman Islands. He wore glasses, and his greying goatee and hair were always meticulously groomed.

"*Nei*," I replied.

"Did they make you..." he stammered. "You know," he added, waving a hand up and down at my outfit.

"Strip, sir?"

He grunted like he'd stubbed his toe, then nodded.

"Of course."

Whittaker blew out a long breath. "I commend you for taking this on, Nora, but I'm going to say it one more time. I'm very uncomfortable with this operation."

I shrugged my shoulders. "It's fine, sir."

"The recording isn't perfect," Weatherford said, keen to move on as he'd been the one pushing for the undercover project. It had been his source in Jamaica who'd warned him the yacht was coming our way. "But it'll work. We can hear them clearly enough to hold up in court."

Weatherford was less well groomed. He was about the same height as our boss, but heavier, and always looked like he'd had a few minutes too little to get ready for the day. A decade or more younger than Whittaker, his skin tone was slightly darker, and he always had a light to heavy stubble on his face. Like he'd shaved the night before instead of in the morning. His local accent was slightly stronger, but still softened from conversing with so many non-islanders.

"Did they hire Violet?" I asked.

"They did, and she kept your cover," Weatherford confirmed, to my relief. "One guy asked if she knew you, and she said you'd just met."

"Good. She might be an asset," I said. "But she recognised me. I thought we were screwed."

"Not Violet Blaze?" Whittaker asked.

"*Ja,*" I confirmed.

"We couldn't hear what you said in the lounge," Weatherford said with a smile. "But good job winning her over."

"We'll need to go easy on her if she doesn't blow my cover," I replied, pulling the pins to my own hair, which held the wig in place. "I promised I'd try to help."

Short hair would be so much easier to deal with, but then I'd look like a fourteen-year-old choirboy. Which those men would like, but every filthy old man would be paying double to put their wrinkly willies in my one-way street. So far, the Scotsmen hadn't said anything about going any farther than stripping, and I hoped they wouldn't. I had a limit to where I was willing to go in my undercover adventures.

My friend AJ wore her hair down to her shoulders, which was more manageable and still just long enough to tie back and not get in her face when she was diving. But she had nice wavy hair. Mine fell dead straight. I'd look like a weirdo band member from the eighties.

I pulled the wig free and ruffled my own blonde hair, pulling it from the folds on top of my head.

"We'll keep it in mind," Whittaker promised.

"Sir, can you please search for famous lochs in Scotland?" I asked, and he tapped away on the keyboard.

"Loch Ness, obviously," he read from the screen. "Lomond is the largest."

"Those were code names," Weatherford said as he realised.

"One sound like Mary, sir?" I asked. "But more like mar-ee."

"Loch Maree," Whittaker replied. "Apparently it's known for its stunning scenery."

"This bloke isn't, that's for sure," I muttered. "The boss is Ness. Scottish. A hundred and eighty centimetres, maybe a little less. Eighty kilos. Forties. Hazel eyes. Dark brown hair with a few grey bits."

"Hang on a moment," Weatherford mumbled, and typed into his mobile. "That's about 5 foot 10 inches… and 175 lbs."

I forgot they needed the stupid imperial measurements. "Lomond is about the same size and age. My guess is former military. He's Northern English. Lighter brown hair."

"Could be they served together," Whittaker said. "We have someone shooting pictures of everyone going in and out of the hotel today, so we'll match photos to your description and have you verify them before we send them to immigration services. They should be able to ID them through facial recognition."

The room was booked under a company name from Sint Maarten, but we'd have a match from entry records before the Dutch-governed island country got back to us about the business.

"Third guy, Maree, he was dumpy, shorter, and younger," I continued. "Thick beard. Maybe thirties. He's either hired for a role or he's associated with Ness. There was a familiarity between them."

"Ness picked on him pretty good," Weatherford said, without

bringing up why and embarrassing our boss even more. "The only timing reference we heard was Ness talking about weeks."

"*Ja.* But he said I'd be on the weekend shift, so sounded like they have more girls working during the week. They hired me and Violet, so they could have more interviews, or just needed a couple of girls to fill in."

"I think they brought some along with them," Weatherford commented. "We caught more conversation after you left. They talked about making it work by adding the two of you."

"And they're looking for young," I added. "Violet has a baby face, but we know she's over eighteen. The girls they already have might not be."

Whittaker let out a sigh and thought about saying something to me, but turned to Weatherford instead. "We have no intel on who their guests may be?"

"No," Weatherford replied. "It's why we need someone on the boat, Roy. We figured they'd do less background checks on the girls, so one would be far easier to create and place than a client. We haven't even discovered how they're letting potential clients know."

Whittaker rubbed the neatly trimmed goatee on his chin. "But you think they have customers lined up already?"

"They must have. My contact in Jamaica told me they opened operations there on the day they moored. Of course, strip clubs are legal, but they still needed to stay in international waters to avoid permit and licence issues."

Detective Whittaker sat back and tapped a pen on the table. "We can't send Nora out to this yacht with absolutely no backup on site, Vincent. It's far too risky."

"We'll have two crews on standby within a few miles, Roy. I've lined up a pair of sport-fishing boats that'll outrun their yacht if need be."

"That won't help Nora if she's discovered," Whittaker protested. "And how will she communicate with you? She can hardly wear a wire when she'll have to… you know… end up with nowhere to hide one."

I accidentally snickered. Not that getting caught by a group of illicit floating strip club owners was amusing, but because my mentor's embarrassment at my nudity. He frowned at me.

"Sorry, sir. But I have an idea to take care of this."

I almost grinned again as his expression turned even more worried. I think he thought I was about to suggest a tricky and very personal location for a listening device.

"I'll disable the yacht," I continued. "They'll need to call out someone to work on it. We'll send Williams. I'm sure he can stretch it to stay overnight."

Weatherford couldn't hide his enthusiasm. "All we need is one illegal tie to the Cayman Islands and we'll have reason to bring them here. Once we can search the yacht, you know we'll find more. My Jamaican contact is convinced they're moving drugs."

"Proof?" Whittaker asked.

Weatherford shook his head. "Nothing concrete. But a drug cartel was one of their clients. Only customers for three straight days."

Whittaker stood and looked at his watch. "I have to be somewhere, so we'll pick this up tomorrow. It's Thursday. We have half a day tomorrow to come up with a solid plan that minimises Nora's exposure while on the yacht."

I looked away, but Weatherford was grinning at the lead detective's poor choice of words, which made me find it even funnier.

"Come on, you two, this is serious," Whittaker said, but he was trying not to laugh. "I must make a note to not put you both working together in the future. You encourage each other in the wrong way."

"Sorry, Roy. I promise I'm just as concerned about Nora's well-being as you are," Weatherford said. "We'll look into her idea of getting Williams aboard."

Whittaker took his jacket from the coat rack and picked up his satchel, sliding the strap over his shoulder.

"Let's speak again tomorrow morning, Vincent. Have a good night."

Weatherford led us out of our boss's office before turning into his own farther down the hall.

"Good work today, Nora," he said over his shoulder. "I'll see you tomorrow."

"Sir," I acknowledged, and continued down the stairs, with Whittaker behind me.

As I reached the bottom, he rested a hand on my shoulder and steered me to one side of the reception area. We were well away from anyone else, but he still lowered his voice.

"Are you certain you're okay with this, Nora? It has to bring up awful memories for you. This can't be easy."

He was referring to the year I'd spent in a gentlemen's private resort club here in Grand Cayman. It was a club to the members, but more like a compound to us, the girls who worked there. The people who owned and ran the place cleverly recruited young girls from around the Caribbean from difficult and sometimes abusive situations and offered us money and a new identity. I was a runaway, sailing around the islands, and doing whatever I needed to do to survive. They treated us like princesses, brainwashed us, and trained us to be escorts. At the end of the contracted year, we thought the girls left to begin their new lives with enough money to live on for years. Of course, it was all a lie. They were taking those who'd reached their one-year anniversary out to deep water and throwing them over with a weight around their ankle.

"It's worth it to nail these creeps. I'll be fine," I replied, because that's what I was telling myself.

Besides, I would never be fine. There were far too many awful memories of beatings and rape to ever be anywhere close to fine. Functioning was all I could hope for, and for the past few years, with a few falters and slips, I'd been functioning.

"You don't have to do this, Nora. Just remember that. You can pull the plug at any time."

"*Ja*," I replied, noticing more strange looks across the reception area. "You should get going, sir."

Whittaker looked around and faces quickly turned away. My precinct was West Bay, so although I'd spent time in Central Station in George Town, most officers and staff here didn't know me. They probably thought Detective Whittaker was having a very hushed and intimate conversation with a hooker. I didn't give a shit, but it might bother him.

"I'll see you tomorrow, Constable," he said loudly enough for most to hear, then walked towards the door.

I waited until he was outside, then followed. My Jeep was in the car park and I was ready to put a T-shirt on over this shiny red top before I drove home. When I stepped outside and shielded my eyes from the bright sunshine, I noticed several men gathered around Whittaker and his Range Rover. I paused. It was the Commissioner of Police and another high-ranking officer, but I couldn't remember his name. The conversation appeared slightly heated. I ran to my Jeep and pulled a T-shirt from a waterproof bag I left in the back. I'd hoped for one of my plain dark blue shirts with 'Police' written on the front to offset the miniskirt, but a black Mermaid Divers one would have to do. Losing the heels, I slipped into a pair of flip-flops and casually walked towards Whittaker's Range Rover.

"You know I have to take these things seriously, Roy, so let's get this over with," the commissioner was saying.

The man who'd encouraged me to join the police force, and made it possible, clicked the unlock on his key fob and took a step back.

"Be my guest, sir," he said.

Looking past the two men, he saw me slowly approaching and subtly shook his head. I paused, but didn't back up. I had no idea what was going on, but intuitively I knew it wasn't good. Nothing made sense. Why would the commissioner himself feel the need to search Detective Whittaker's vehicle?

"Good God," I heard the highest ranking policeman exclaim.

Whittaker peered into the back of his SUV. "They're just… What is that?"

"That is exactly what we were tipped off about, Roy," the commissioner said.

The other man took out his mobile and made a call. I heard him asking for immediate assistance.

"I've been set up, sir," Whittaker said in a defeated tone.

I have no choice in these circumstances," the commissioner replied. "We're required to investigate, Roy. You know that."

Whittaker glanced my way. "Nora, call Rosie for me, please. Ask her to contact our lawyer. It seems I'll need his services."

I stood there in disbelief. My instincts screamed at me to rush over and take out these two old men. Clearly, they were wrong. Roy Whittaker was the most honest person I'd ever known. Law and truth formed his life's unwavering roadmap. But attacking the commissioner and whoever the other bigwig was wouldn't do anything but complicate the situation. And end my law enforcement career.

Instead I nodded and took out my mobile to call Mrs Whittaker.

3

CHANNELLING MY INNER WHITTAKER

I stayed in Weatherford's office as I didn't know what else to do. Going home felt like I'd be abandoning the man who was more of a father figure than I'd like to admit. I'd called my foster kid, Jazzy, and told her I'd be late. She didn't care. There was no point telling her about the detective as I hoped it would all be sorted before I left the station. It had to. No way was Roy Whittaker involved in anything underhanded.

Hearing heavy footsteps in the hallway, I jumped to my feet. Weatherford walked into his office.

"Well?" I asked.

He shook his head. "He's been detained and they'll charge him in the morning."

"For what?" I asked.

"Possession and intent to distribute a Schedule 2 controlled substance. Found cash and cocaine in his SUV."

I hadn't seen whatever they'd found in the Range Rover, but the idea of Whittaker involved in a drug deal was unimaginable. It simply didn't fit.

"Someone is framing him."

Weatherford stood behind his desk and moved a few papers

around while he thought. "That's all I can think of," he finally said, looking up at me. "But it's being investigated by internal affairs. We've all been told, in no uncertain terms, to steer clear of the case."

"We have an internal affairs division?" I asked in surprise. I didn't think we were big enough to warrant a dedicated department.

"Not really a division," Weatherford replied. "Just one guy. Chief Inspector Leonard Monroe."

I'd heard that name mentioned before. Usually unaffectionately in a whispered tone. As I didn't care to gossip or waste time on pointless conversations, I hadn't paid much attention.

"Is he fair?" I asked.

Weatherford shrugged. "Probably. But he'll dig up everything, whether it pertains to the case or not. He's relentless."

"That's good," I responded.

The detective scoffed. "Tell that to Myers. He was investigated last year and cleared of all allegations of accepting bribes. Meanwhile, a one-time fling was brought to light as she was the one accusing him of taking money. Completely trumped up, but cost him his marriage."

"Then screwing around cost him his marriage," I pointed out.

"Fair point," Weatherford acknowledged. "I'm just saying Monroe digs like a bloody JCB. Turns your life inside out."

I didn't know what kind of animal a JCB was, and was in no mood to learn. It still seemed like a positive to me if this Monroe guy scrutinised Whittaker's life. He wouldn't find anything illegal or immoral. I was certain.

"What now?" I asked.

Weatherford shrugged again, and groaned as he ran a hand through his short, slightly curly hair.

"Looks like I'll be here half the night. The Commissioner has made me lead investigator, at least temporarily, so I have to get myself up to speed on every case currently in play, as well as continuing my own."

There wasn't anything I could think of to help him with that, and my mind was still spinning about Whittaker.

"Can you get with Williams and work up a plan for your diesel mechanic idea?" Weatherford asked. "That would help me out. Whittaker's right. If we don't have a way of getting physical support aboard with you, we can't let you go solo."

"Arm me," I replied. "I'll be a lot safer with a weapon."

"And where will you hide that in your…" he raised his eyebrows. "Evening attire."

It had been worth a try. But he was right. Even if I attempted to smuggle a gun aboard in my bag, they may well search my belongings. I walked to the doorway but paused as a female constable ran up the stairs and down the hall towards me.

"Detective!" she breathlessly called out before reaching the office. "Detective, we have a situation."

Weatherford looked up from his desk. "What now?"

"The Penningtons are here, sir," the constable blurted in a strong local accent.

"The Penningtons?" he asked, looking as confused as I felt.

"Yes, sir. About the missing girl, sir."

"What missing girl, Chantel?" Weatherford asked, then clicked away on his computer.

"Reported earlier today, sir," Constable Chantel panted. "But at the time, it was too soon for us to do anything. We sent a car by to take their statement."

"Okay," Weatherford replied. "I see it here in the reports log. It's still only been a few hours."

"Yes, sir," she said. "She was missing from school after lunch. But the Penningtons are here."

I'm not sure why I stayed, as I had my own problems to worry about, and the woman was waffling instead of getting to the point. But it felt like something significant was happening.

Weatherford raised both hands. "So have a car help them search the neighbourhood, and make sure they've contacted all the kid's school friends until they find her. You know the usual procedure after only an afternoon, Chantel. The kid's playing hooky."

"But they have a ransom demand, sir," the constable said.

Personally, I would have led with that part.

Weatherford shot up from his chair. "You're kidding? Of all the bloody days…" he muttered. "Penningtons?" he asked as he came around his desk.

"Yes, sir. *The* Penningtons."

That still didn't help me, but I saw the detective's expression change.

"This keeps getting better," he groaned, snatching his jacket from a rack. He stopped and looked me over by the doorway. "I need a second officer in the room. Do you have something else to wear?"

"Not here," I replied.

Weatherford turned to the constable. "Chantel, can you find her a uniform or something other than…" he waved a hand in my general direction. "That?"

"Yes, sir," she replied, and we all marched down the hall and descended the stairs.

Weatherford took them two at a time, leaving Chantel in his wake. When he reached the reception area, he glanced around. A distraught looking man stood with a woman seated next to him. She could have been his daughter, but I took a crazy guess that she wasn't. Their clothes and jewellery dripped money.

"Mr and Mrs Pennington?" Weatherford asked, moving towards them.

The man extended a hand impatiently, and they shook.

Chantel steered me through a door into the administrative offices.

"Not sure we got much that'll fit your skin…" she began, then checked herself. "Slender figure."

"Anything plain will do," I urged. "Doesn't have to be a uniform."

"How come you dressed like a hooker borrowed a T-shirt anyhow?" she asked.

"Undercover," I replied, and lifted the T-shirt to reveal the shiny red top underneath.

"Damn, girl. Can I get your undercover wardrobe when you done?" she laughed. "My husband get all up in my lady stuff over dat outfit."

I raised an eyebrow.

"I know, I can't fit my fat ass in your size, but let a girl dream," Chantel said, then laughed.

She opened the door to a storage room and shook a pair of large cardboard boxes on a lower shelf.

"Lost and found. See if dere's anyting in here dat'll work," she said, then left me to rummage.

I guessed they'd thrown out the soiled garments and perhaps even washed whatever remained, as everything in the boxes seemed clean. I found a pair of well-worn white trainers that would fit if I found thicker socks, but all the shirts were way too big. After a few minutes, I gave up looking with just the trainers and two pairs of thin socks to show for my efforts. I say pairs, but the socks were actually one black pair and two brightly coloured odd ones. I put the red and yellow socks on first and then covered them with the black pair.

"I got you leggings," Chantel announced, appearing from another office. "Gena's da only one here your size and she had dese in her gym bag."

I took the leggings. "What about a shirt? An RCIPS tee will do."

"Put dem on," Chantel replied. "I'll find someting."

Stepping into the storage room, I pulled the door closed and slipped out of the miniskirt and pulled on the leggings. I wasn't sure if Gena was shorter than me or if the leggings were designed to hit mid calf, but that's where they came to on my legs. The door opened a crack, and a hand reached in with a dark blue police shirt. I switched it for the Mermaid Divers tee, leaving the red top on underneath to save time. Hopping from one foot to the other, I tugged the trainers on and pulled the laces tight. They were at least a size too big, but would do.

"Well, you don't look so much like a hooker," Chantel commented. "Best you hurry up and find Detective Weatherford."

"*Takk*," I said as I bolted across the offices, pausing before going through the door. "Who are the Penningtons?" I asked, looking back at Chantel.

"Da Penningtons?" she echoed. "You don't know who dey are?"

I frowned at her. I didn't make a habit of asking questions I already knew the answers to, but I guess she didn't know that.

"He a big developer. Built a bunch of dem new condos on Seven Mile Beach and West Bay. Gives money to various charities to make himself look good wit da locals, but he ain't buildin' nuttin' we all can afford."

I nodded and entered the lobby. Weatherford was still talking to the Penningtons, but led them towards another door once he saw me.

"Detective Sommer will join us," he said, taking me by surprise. No one had referred to me as a detective yet. I'd passed all the exams and tests, but a position hadn't been available so far. Officially, I was still a constable.

Mr Pennington ignored me and followed Weatherford. Mrs Pennington eyed me suspiciously before ignoring me. We entered a small conference room used for meetings with witnesses and victims rather than suspects. It was carpeted, with ten seats around a rectangular table. The parents quickly took a seat, with Weatherford starting a video and audio recording of the meeting before he sat down.

"As I explained in the lobby, Mr and Mrs Pennington, this conversation is being recorded in case we need to revisit any details we speak about. Saves us bothering you if it's something we already discussed."

"We understand," Mr Pennington replied.

"Thank you," Weatherford said. "Present in the room are Mr

Rupert Pennington, his wife Mrs Rebecca Pennington, Detective Nora Sommer, and myself, Detective Vincent Weatherford."

It was going to take a few more times hearing those words before they didn't make me feel uncomfortable.

"Earlier today, you reported your daughter, Chloe, was missing from school. Is that correct, sir?" Weatherford asked.

"The school called us to say she hadn't attended her first class after lunch," Rupert replied.

"They thought we may have picked her up," Rebecca added. "Obviously we hadn't, so I called the police right away."

I wondered if the wife was Chloe's mother or the younger replacement model. She looked to be mid-thirties, so either was possible. The woman was a beautiful brunette, with a Barbie doll figure, and a meticulously assembled outfit including matching accessories and jewellery. She spoke with a nondescript English accent.

"You or the school have talked to her friends, I assume?" Weatherford asked.

"Of course," Rupert replied impatiently, waving his mobile phone around. "I told you, we've received a message from the bloody kidnapper."

Weatherford politely nodded. "I understand, sir. Just trying to establish a timeline. Why don't you play us the message you received?"

The father was trim, with a hint of a belly beginning to take shape. His accent was slightly more posh than his wife's, and his suit was less flashy than her outfit. He played a texted audio recording which appeared to have come from an email.

"I have your daughter," a digitally altered male voice began. "She will die five days from now if you do not confess your sins. The clock has started."

I looked at Weatherford, who stared back and raised one eyebrow.

"That's all there is," Rupert said, shaking his head. "It was sent to both our mobiles at the same time, presumably to make sure we received it. I've no idea what he's talking about."

"Needless to say, Mr Pennington, we need a list of any and all people you think may hold a grudge against you," Weatherford said. "And I'll stop by the school first thing and speak to anyone who may have witnessed Chloe leaving."

"She wouldn't just leave with anyone she didn't know," Rebecca snapped. "She's a very bright girl."

"I'm not suggesting she would, ma'am," Weatherford replied. "But we need to find out exactly when and where this person may have taken your daughter."

"May have?" Rupert fumed. "I just played you the bloody recording!"

Rebecca took her husband's hand. "Where's Detective Whittaker?" she asked.

"He's currently unavailable, ma'am," Weatherford explained calmly. "I'm acting lead detective. I assure you we'll apply all resources available to find Chloe, ma'am."

"Has your daughter ever skipped school before?" I asked.

I knew I was supposed to sit there and be the silent witness in the room, but the question came to me and fell out of my mouth. Because it needed to be asked.

The parents both glared at me like I'd abducted their daughter.

"No!" Rebecca said.

Rupert rested a hand on her arm. "They're just questions, Becca. It's okay." He turned to Weatherford. "But I don't want you wasting time and resources thinking our little girl has run away, Detective. I guarantee you she would never do that."

Weatherford nodded. "I'll need to borrow your mobile so we can retrieve the message and see if it's traceable, sir. And do you have a current picture of Chloe we can use?"

Rebecca dug around in her large designer purse and pulled out a series of glossy 8x10s. She spread them across the table.

"Chloe is eleven?" Weatherford asked.

I picked up one of the professionally taken glamour shots of the daughter.

"Yes. Twelve in three months," Rebecca replied.

Fy faen, I thought to myself as I looked at a second photograph. Chloe may be eleven, but with makeup and dressed like a film star, she could pass for fourteen or fifteen. The window of sickos was much wider for gorgeous young prey. The voice had used the word sins. Too often, the people who shouted the loudest about sins were the ones who committed the worst forms.

"What are your first impressions, Detective?" Rupert asked.

I'd run across men like him before. Big-time businessmen who were used to being in charge and calling the shots. He would be a nightmare to deal with. Second-guessing everything and desperate to do anything he could to feel like he had control of some aspect of the situation. He didn't. If Chloe had been abducted and the voice we heard had her, then the kidnapper was in control. We were already too many steps behind, with only a short time to catch up.

"I think we need to post your daughter's picture across the news and use the public as our eyes," Weatherford replied. "And start from where she was taken. We'll canvass the area for witnesses and look for CCTV which may have captured her outside the school."

Rupert looked at me. "What about you? How are you going to help find our daughter?"

I resisted my immediate response and took a breath, thinking about how Whittaker would handle this moment.

"We need a better photograph to circulate," I replied, holding up one of the pictures. "This isn't how she looked at school this morning. We need a normal, casual photograph, preferably in what she typically wears to class."

Rebecca leaned my way with an angry look on her face, but Rupert rested his hand on her shoulder. Maybe Whittaker would have phrased that differently. People didn't usually react to him that way.

"Go on," Rupert said.

"This is about you," I continued. "The kidnapper has a personal issue with you." I looked from one parent to the other. The wife would be the most likely person to suspect her husband's wrong-doings, and now that her daughter's life was at stake, she'd be our best way to find the truth.

"We need that list of grudges."

"I don't know what the guy is talking about," Rupert said again. "I swear, I'll give the bastard anything he wants to get Chloe back, but I can't give him what I don't have. My company is completely above board, I'm faithful to my wife, and we donate a good deal of money to various charities here in the Cayman Islands. I can't think of anything I've done to deserve this."

"He believes you have," I said. "So I'd think a little harder about it."

I sat back and shut up. All three of them were now looking at me. I wasn't doing a good job of channelling my inner Whittaker.

4

TOOTHPASTE AND TEXTING

If anyone wanted to commit a crime in George Town, between six and seven o'clock would have been the time to do it. All police personnel on duty were recalled to Central Station for a briefing where Weatherford and Sergeant Hadley assigned tasks for the evening. Using a photo Rebecca had found on her phone, a widespread search began, and the hunt for witnesses would continue long into the night. I hung around for the briefing, then checked in with Weatherford before I left.

"I'll be here first thing in the morning," I said. "Unless you need me to do something tonight?"

"No, get some rest," he replied, already looking haggard after only a few hours in charge. "If you can get together with Williams tomorrow, that'll be one thing I don't have to worry about."

"*Ja*," I replied, although my thoughts were jumping around between the kidnapping, Whittaker, and the stripper yacht case. "Odd about the five days, don't you think, sir?"

"How do you mean?" Weatherford asked.

"Why five days?"

He rubbed his brow and thought for a moment. "Yeah, that struck me as strange. That's a long time to give us to find him, and for him to remain hidden with a young girl on a small island."

"He wants press," I suggested. "Five days is enough time to build international attention."

The detective nodded. "True, and I think you're right. The kidnapper has a personal connection to the Penningtons. He's making a point. Maybe not a close personal interaction, but he's dealt with them on some level."

"Anything jump out in their background checks, sir?"

He shrugged, shuffling through a handful of papers on his desk, then read from the one he was looking for.

"Married back in the UK fourteen years ago. Her first. Rupert's second marriage. Met the first in college. Married five years. No kids. His ex remarried and lives in Wales. Three kids. Nothing suggesting there was any animosity." He thumbed to another page. "Rebecca was a model and an actress. B-movies by the look of it. Rupert built up a development company over there. Bought his partner out in 2009."

"2009?" I questioned. "Wasn't that around the time of a big finance and property crash?"

Weatherford nodded. "Yeah, but looks like Pennington thrived and later sold the UK company for a stupid amount of money in 2015. Started the business here a year later. Now he's a permanent resident."

"Former partner had to have been pissed off," I ventured.

Weatherford tapped a few keys on his computer. "Looks like he died of cancer nine months later. I'd say he helped the guy out. Gave him some cash to finish out his days. There's a picture from a magazine article of Rupert sitting on the guy's hospital bed."

He was right, there didn't seem to be anything there, so I moved on. "Do either of the parents have form?"

He shook his head. "Nothing worth mentioning. Speeding tickets. Parking. He had a possession charge, which was dropped."

"When, sir?"

He studied the sheet. "2011."

"Before they married," I pondered aloud.

"The year before," Weatherford clarified, and I wondered if they were together at the time.

"I think the wife might be the best lead," I said, reliving the interview in my mind.

"I can't imagine she's involved in abducting her own daughter."

"*Nei*. I think the father has screwed someone over and if the wife figures out who it is, she'll tell you."

Weatherford frowned. "Surely he'd tell us if he knew who it might be."

I shrugged. "I didn't say he knows. Men like him tread on people without noticing."

The detective scoffed. "True enough." He turned and walked behind his desk, dropping heavily into his chair. "I'd sure like to have Roy here for this one."

I agreed but didn't want to say anything, as Weatherford had enough on his shoulders without me adding to his doubt. I couldn't think of anything useful to add, so I said goodbye and left the detective to what I imagined would be a late night.

By the time I arrived at Central Station the next morning, I was itching to get involved in the abduction case. Because I was on loan from West Bay for the stripper yacht business, my usual partner, Jacob, had been teamed up with someone else, which left me available for whatever was needed. It was a little after 6am and the sun was peeking over the island. I knew Sergeant Williams was an early riser, so I tracked him down at the station.

"I almost didn't recognise you in da uniform," he joked with a flirtatious grin.

Williams was lean and muscular, with a lot of confidence backed up by years of experience. He'd been tough on me when we'd first met, but I'd earned his respect after several cases together, and now he gave me *dritt* about anything he could think of. Which was fine with me. It's how he treated all his firearms team.

"I have an idea that'll get you killed along with me, so I don't have to die alone," I told him.

He laughed. "Can't wait to hear dat."

"The detectives won't let me go to the yacht unless we have backup aboard with me. So I'll disable the engines, then you'll come out as a mechanic to fix it."

Williams nodded, his expression switching into mission mode. "Do they have a tech or engineer with them?"

I shrugged. "No idea, and can't find out until we get out there. Figure I'll do the Friday night shift and report back."

"That'll leave you without backup the first night," Williams pointed out.

"Without backup aboard," I replied. "You'll be on the fishing boat close by."

"Will Whittaker go..." Williams checked himself. "I guess it's down to Weatherford now, right? Will he go for dat?"

"I'll take care of Weatherford," I replied. "You figure out how I can disable the boat so it requires a mechanic to come out. Then we have to make sure it's you they call."

"Tortuga Marine is the biggest repair service on the island and I know the owner," Williams said. "I'll talk to him and see what we can do."

I nodded and walked to the stairs.

"Hey," he called after me and I turned. "If I'm aboard, do I get to see your show?"

I flipped two fingers at him and carried on up to Weatherford's office.

I wasn't the most observant person with mundane stuff like people getting haircuts and what they wore, unless they were a suspect, but I was pretty sure Vincent Weatherford hadn't been home.

"Morning, sir."

"Hey, Nora," he greeted me with bags under his eyes.

"Williams is on the marine mechanic idea."

The detective looked up, initially confused. "Oh, right. Thank you." He stood and let out a long breath as he checked his watch. "I'm about to go to the school to meet with their IT person. She's been gathering CCTV for me."

"I'll drive you," I offered.

He nodded, then stopped as he came around the desk. "We can't risk you being seen, Nora. Not while you're undercover on a case."

"I don't look like a stripper at the moment. It's fine, sir."

He frowned. "I think a common outfit for those strippergrams you can hire is sexy copper."

"I don't think they wear RCIPS issue trousers and buttoned-up shirts, sir. No one wears these clothes to look sexy."

Weatherford walked to the door. "I suppose you're right."

I followed him. "Besides, sir, bad guys don't get up early. It's a perk of the job."

He grunted as we strode down the stairs. "Think you can find us a coffee shop on the way?"

"Probably. And a toothbrush, sir."

The detective breathed into his hand and took a sniff. He grunted again.

Fifteen minutes later, with a cup of hot coffee, a cleanly shaven face from the cordless razor he kept in his car, and fresh breath thanks to a newly purchased toothbrush, toothpaste, and mouthwash, Weatherford was ready to face other humans. I drove his Ford Bronco SUV to the private Island International School just south of the Camana Bay outdoor shopping centre. I'd briefly looked at their website when choosing where to send Jazzy to school and choked on the tuition fees. It seemed like a nice place, but I couldn't spend half my salary on her education.

Only a few cars were scattered about the car park this early, so I found a spot closest to the buildings.

A heavyset man came out to greet us. "Detective Weatherford?" he asked.

"Yes, sir," Weatherford replied. "And this is Detective Sommer."

"I'm the school director, Bill Hatfield," the man replied, shaking hands with us both. His gaze wandered over me for an extra moment.

Without any makeup, I already looked young for my age, and I was just over the minimum age to make detective. Combined with wearing a constable's uniform, I'm sure the director was wondering who they'd sent to his school.

"I had our IT tech come in early to put everything together for you," Hatfield continued as he led us into the administration building. "As you can imagine, we're all desperately worried about Chloe."

"Do you know when she was last seen on school grounds?" Weatherford asked.

Hatfield opened a door to an office and waved us inside. "I think we can narrow that down for you, Detective."

A woman stood from behind a bank of three computer monitors as we entered.

"Priya, this is Detective Weatherford and…" the director looked at me.

"Sommer."

"Sorry, yes, Detective Sommer," he said. "Priya handles all our IT needs, including our security cameras."

"Nice to meet you," Weatherford said, extending a hand. "What can you show us?"

Priya sat and pointed to the far-left screen. She had multiple windows open, each with a different CCTV camera cued up.

"Miss Pennington's last class before lunch was maths. Here the class lets out," she said with an Indian accent, and clicked the play button on the first video. "That's Miss Pennington," she added, indicating the girl using a pen as a pointer.

We watched the kids filter down the interior hallway towards the camera, most in pairs or small groups, all chatting or checking mobiles. Chloe walked on her own, face buried in her phone. Just before they passed under the camera, another girl spoke to Chloe.

"We switch to the outside camera," Priya said, as she stopped the first view and started the next one.

Kids poured out of the double doors into a covered outdoor walkway. Most of the students turned away from the camera. Chloe paused in conversation with the other girl for a moment before they walked in opposite directions.

"Who is the other kid?" I asked.

"That's Emma Schmidt," Hatfield replied.

"We spoke with her parents last night," Weatherford said. "Emma claims she didn't know where her friend went."

"Stop the tape, Priya," I asked. "Rewind to when they split up."

She did so, and as we watched again, I followed Emma more carefully.

"Stop," I said again. "We should talk to her directly and we need her mobile."

Weatherford leaned closer. "She's texting, isn't she?"

"*Ja*. Right after she turns around to look at Chloe leaving."

"We'll see who comes in today," Hatfield said. "I have a school-wide gathering first thing to ask if anyone knows anything, and to reassure the students that the campus is safe."

"Okay, where does Chloe go from there?" Weatherford asked.

"That's the strange part," Priya said, starting the video in the next window. "She disappears."

We watched the camera angle I presumed was back to back with the prior location, and Chloe was nowhere to be seen. After a moment, a couple of older kids walked into the car park, which was full of vehicles.

"Some of the older students leave campus for lunch," Hatfield explained, "but the younger children all eat in our cafeteria, or their parents sometimes pick them up. That has to be arranged through the school office."

"So how could she slip by the cameras?" I asked. "Are you sure the timestamps are correct?"

"They are accurate," Priya assured us. "You can see the other students in one camera and then the other, and the timing matches."

She was right. "So there must be a way to avoid the crossover."

Priya nodded. "I'm afraid so." She started another video in the next window. "We have corner cameras in the car park, which give a hundred percent overlap. But I've checked all four and can't see Miss Pennington anywhere."

"What about cars leaving?" Weatherford asked.

"I haven't had time to go through and verify every vehicle belongs to a student yet," Priya replied.

"Where are the two walkway cameras we were looking at?" I asked.

"The path we entered on," Hatfield replied. "Where we came into the admin building. The classrooms are in the opposite building."

"Go out there, Nora, and call me," Weatherford said, but I was already halfway out the door.

I called the detective's number as I walked past the classroom entrance on my left and stood underneath the walkway's roof support where both cameras were mounted.

"You're out of view," Weatherford said over the phone.

To my left, the building extended all the way to the edge of the car park. On the right, the admin building stopped short and a strip of grass extended from the structure to the asphalt. I walked along the grass, staying close to the wall.

"How about now?" I asked.

"Nothing," Weatherford replied.

"Check the south-east car park camera."

I waited while they looked.

"It captures the edges of the car park," Weatherford said after a few moments. "I can see a bit of the building which sticks out farther, but not the admin building."

I turned and walked back to the pathway. "What about now?"

"Right there," Weatherford blurted. "Caught some movement. Maybe your arm."

I heard him ask Priya to check the same camera from yesterday, so I walked back to her office. They were carefully watching again.

"Yup, there," Weatherford said as we all saw a brief blur of movement.

"I'm sorry I missed that," Priya said. "I should have caught it for you."

"Easy to miss," Weatherford reassured her. "Are there any other cameras in that direction? Out the back of the buildings?"

"No, I'm afraid not," she replied.

"We're requesting Chloe's phone records from the mobile company," Weatherford said to me. "They'll receive a judge's order this morning, but you know how long they can take."

"We need the Emma kid's mobile," I replied. "She knows something."

"Are there any leads on who might have taken Chloe?" Hatfield asked.

"Early days," Weatherford replied.

"And this evidence suggests she removed herself from your school," I added, then realised my Whittaker filter was still broken.

5

ACRONYMS AND EMOJIS

Emma looked down at the table in the conference room Hatfield had made available to us. Her parents fidgeted in their chairs on either side of their daughter.

"You told us you hadn't spoken to her," the mother urged. She had an English accent.

"I can play you the CCTV if it helps you remember," I said.

For some misguided reason, Detective Weatherford had decided I'd be more suited to speaking with the kid while he began interviewing teachers. Perhaps because he knew I fostered a teenager. If he'd witnessed my finely tuned attempts at acting parent-like, he wouldn't have come to that delusional conclusion. Currently, I was fighting the urge to grab the kid by the chin and lift her head up so she would finally make eye contact. That way she'd be able to see I was moments away from tasing the truth out of her.

"I just asked if she was coming to lunch," Emma mumbled.

"And what did Chloe say?" I asked, trying to hide my impatience.

The kid shrugged her shoulders. "She just said no."

"Bullshit," I responded, and everyone in the room jumped a little, including Hatfield.

"Detective, please," he said.

"The exchange is on the video, Emma," I continued, ignoring the director. "You say something, she responds, then you say something else. Tell me the whole conversation."

"She's trying to remember," the father said, speaking fluent English with a German accent.

"*Nei*," I replied, tapping the table with my finger. "Your daughter knows exactly what was said. Don't you, Emma?"

The girl sniffled.

"Chloe make you promise not to say anything?" I asked, attempting a softer tone.

Emma's head bobbed slightly.

"Okay, and now that a man has abducted her and is threatening to kill her, do you think she still wants you to keep that secret?"

"I don't want to get her in trouble," Emma sobbed.

"You should tell the lady whatever you know, Emma," her mother urged.

"Or you can help her avoid being grounded for a week by letting this maniac kill her," I snapped. "Your choice."

Emma burst into tears. I sat back in the chair and groaned while her parents fussed all over the brat.

"*Fy faen*," I muttered.

"I must ask you to be more sensitive with Emma. She's in shock over this terrible business," Hatfield said.

I turned his way, but managed to stop myself from snapping at him. One spoilt little shit being bothered didn't compare to another one being murdered, in my opinion, but he had his precious tuition fees to protect. And he was also right. No matter how I felt about this ridiculous dancing around the hotels, getting the information from the kid was the priority, and if it meant treating her more delicately, it was worth it. *Hotels?* That didn't sound right. The phrase talked about dancing around some kind of building.

"Emma," I said in the nicest tone I could muster, "the most important thing right now is to find Chloe and get her home safely. You may have been the last person outside of the kidnapper to have spoken with her. It doesn't matter how trivial your conversation may have been, or how you think it might get you both in trouble, I need to know what was said."

"Come on, Emma," the father urged firmly. "Tell the detective what you know."

The girl wiped her eyes, and the mother released her embrace, but continued soothingly rubbing her daughter's back.

"Chloe's been skipping school at lunchtimes," Emma said, and finally lifted her head. She backhanded the snot mixed with tears from under her nose and sniffled a few more times. "She wouldn't tell me where she was going, but she comes back with a hundred dollars each time."

"What?" the mother asked.

"How long has this been going on?" I asked.

Emma sighed. "A week, I guess."

"So, what was the conversation between the two of you?"

"I asked if she was coming to lunch," Emma replied. "She said no. I asked if she had a new BFF."

"That's best friends forever," Hatfield said, and I scowled at him.

I was the person least interested in stupid sayings and acronyms, but even I knew that one.

"And what did she reply?" I asked.

"She said no, this is different," Emma replied.

"And that was it?"

The girl nodded.

"Who did you text?"

"Chloe."

"What did you say?"

"I asked her what she meant, but she never replied."

"Can I see your mobile?" I asked.

Emma looked at me with renewed suspicion.

"You're doing great, sweetie," her mother whispered. "Show the police lady your phone."

Begrudgingly, Emma fished it from her pocket, unlocked it, and handed it to me. It was one of the fancy newer iPhones that could double as a small television. I bet it cost as much as I spent on my cell plan for the year. I opened the text feature and began scrolling through an insane number of messages sent between friends since yesterday lunchtime. They were all in coded abbreviations and stuffed with emojis. I finally found the text which Emma had referred to.

"Diff how?"

I scrolled through earlier messages, most of which were between Emma and Chloe. They were all innocent, childish banter about how boring class was, current bands, and how another girl was being a bitch. I scrolled the other way again to double-check there were none from Chloe's mobile. There weren't, which I already knew. The Penningtons had the phone tracking feature enabled for the family, and we'd seen from their apps that Chloe's phone had been turned off before she'd left the school grounds. Knowing she'd sneaked out willingly, I figured she'd shut her mobile off herself. I handed the phone back to Emma.

"How did you first know about Chloe skipping school?" I asked.

"She told me she had an errand to run last week."

"Which day?"

"Friday, I think. I thought she was being picked up by her parents for an appointment."

"Did they often pick her up for lunch?"

Emma shook her head. "We don't get enough time. I mean, if you drive through for fast food you can make it back, but not if you go somewhere nice."

"And Chloe's parents would only take her somewhere nice?" I asked.

She nodded.

"Okay, so last Friday, Chloe left at lunchtime. Did she talk about it when she came back?"

Emma shook her head.

"So, when did she leave next?"

"Monday."

"And did you talk about that?"

"I asked where she went, and she told me I wasn't to say anything about it because her mum and dad didn't know."

"You must have been curious."

Emma shrugged. "Yeah. Chloe showed me the hundred-dollar bill."

"Did you ask how she got it?"

The girl sighed and dropped her head.

"Emma?" I urged.

"I asked if I could get a hundred dollars too."

Her mother gasped and clutched her daughter again. The father put a hand to his brow and groaned. I could only imagine their mixture of relief and terror at their kid being so close to falling into the hands of a predator.

"I don't think Emma was in danger," I said. "We believe Chloe was specifically targeted."

It was unlike me to offer information they had no business knowing, and I surprised myself. I wondered why for a few moments. Perhaps because I had a kid under my watch? The lump in my throat at the thought of Jazzy being kidnapped suggested I'd found my reason.

"*Takk,*" I said as I rose from the table. "We may have more questions, but that's good for now."

I found Weatherford in an empty classroom, talking to a teacher. The woman looked suitably concerned. The detective thanked her, and we both walked outside and stood at the edge of the car park, which was now half full of vehicles.

"Anything from the girl?" Weatherford asked, and I gave him a quick rundown of what I'd learned.

"Seems whoever she was meeting groomed her over the past week," I added. "We can look at CCTV in the area from lunchtime on Friday, Monday, and yesterday. Maybe we can spot a vehicle consistently present."

"I'll get someone on it at the station," Weatherford replied as he stared at the walkway camera and the grassy patch Chloe had to have walked along. "So, where would be the obvious place to go from there?"

We walked along the grass and paused at the far corner of the building. A chain-link fence ran from the structure along the north edge of the car park. It was maybe a metre and a half high, so scalable, but not easy for an eleven-year-old. I looked up at the camera mounted on a tall light pole in the corner. It was at least five metres off the ground.

"She wouldn't be seen directly under the camera mount," I pointed out. "And the big pole would make it easier to jump the fence."

"Based on the angle I saw from the recordings," Weatherford replied, shading his eyes with a hand, "the camera would capture anyone on the car park side of the fence from roughly 20 yards away from the pole. I doubt it sees anything outside the fence."

I looked past the wire. A wide concrete pathway separated the buildings from the school's sports facilities. I could see tennis and basketball courts. The pathway ended at the road which ran by the front of the car park. The frontage road continued to condos and businesses to the west, some lining a channel which eventually led to the North Sound.

"We need to know what cameras are out here," I said, and dug out the business card Priya had given me.

She answered on the second ring. "This is Consta… um, Detective Sommer," I corrected myself. I still didn't think I was officially in a position yet, but if Weatherford was using the rank, then so would I. "Do you have a map or diagram of your CCTV locations?"

"I have a list of locations," the IT woman replied.

"Do you know the boundaries they all cover?"

"I'm pretty familiar with them, yes."

"Bring your list and join us outside," I said. "We're in the southeast corner of the car park."

Priya told me she'd be right out, and I hung up. Two minutes later she appeared, carrying her laptop.

"I brought this so we can see the views," she said as she walked up. "Which areas are you interested in?"

I liked her initiative and scolded myself for not thinking of it first.

"Is the walkway beyond the fence covered?" I asked.

"Not really," Priya replied, balancing her laptop awkwardly in one arm while typing with the other hand. "There's a camera at the other end of the admin building which aims at the swimming pool. It catches a section of the path, but not this end."

"We should check that in case Chloe doubled back on the walkway," Weatherford said. "What about the road out front?"

"Yes, we have a camera on the road because of several incidents with parents," Priya replied. "Some of them get rather *keen* to pick up and drop off their children."

"Can you bring up the road view for yesterday lunchtime?" I asked.

Priya clicked away for a few moments and then held the screen so we could all watch. She set it to three-times speed so the cars and people zipped around, but I couldn't see Chloe anywhere. The view was from the north-west corner of the car park, looking east.

"Go back and play at regular speed from the time Chloe left the buildings," I requested.

"She must have crossed this road at some point, surely?" Weatherford wondered aloud. "Unless she went all the way around the back of the sports fields where the condos are."

"Here," Priya said, and we watched the video again.

"No camera at the far end of the road?" I asked as the vehicles and humans now appeared sluggish.

"I'm afraid not," Priya replied. "I had a budget to meet, so some of my recommended locations had to be cut."

"What was that?" Weatherford blurted.

Priya rewound again, and we all peered at the screen as the video played once more.

"That's her," I said, seeing a speck in the distance cross the road.

"Hard to tell who it is," Weatherford said, and he was correct.

The figure was beyond the sports fields and far too small in the distance to be accurately identified, but I knew it was Chloe.

"But that's scrubland and storage for construction equipment over there," the detective muttered, staring into the distance.

"And the water," I pointed out. "He picked her up by boat."

"Shit," Weatherford groaned. "He could have taken her anywhere."

"*Ja*," I agreed. "But if we check the time between her being picked up and the time the demand was sent, we'd have some idea."

Weatherford groaned again. "That was over four hours. Hell, they could be in Cuba with a fast boat."

6

UFFY TYPES

The day dragged on with procedural rubbish, eating up time and getting us nowhere. It was all necessary, but the Cayman police had limited resources when it came to major cases alongside the everyday petty crime and reports. It was crazy to think that losing one detective could severely hamper an investigation, but it was true. In a force with only a handful of detectives, one missing was a large percentage of manpower. Not to mention Whittaker was the best investigator we had. I liked Vincent Weatherford, but he'd be the first to admit he didn't have the experience of our boss.

I stepped into Whittaker's office, closed the door, and called him. It rang until I was sure I'd get voicemail, but then he answered.

"Nora."

"Sir," I responded, and then had no clue what to say.

I'd been driven by an urge to speak with the man I considered my mentor, but I hadn't thought through any form of conversation. What do you say to a man who's suspended from duty?

"I should make it clear up front that I'm not allowed to discuss any open cases," he said after a few moments of silence.

"*Ja*, that's okay, sir. I just called to see if I can do anything."

"I'm not sure what anyone can do at the moment, but thank you," he replied. His voice carried his usual calm demeanour, but I could hear a weariness or perhaps just sadness in his tone too.

"The kidnapping is tying up all resources," he continued. "As it should be. But it means investigating my situation must wait."

"Who would have done this?" I asked.

"The kidnapping? As I said, I really shouldn't be talking about any cases, Nora."

"*Nei*. To you. Who did this to you?"

He sighed. "I have no idea. I'm sure there's more people than I can count who'd like to see me in jail. Everyone I've put there, for starters."

"But no threatening letters or outbursts lately?" I asked.

"Nothing that comes to mind. But Nora, you mustn't concern yourself with my situation. I believe in the system. It'll get worked out given time."

His optimistic view pissed me off. I didn't share his faith in any system, especially the criminal justice process. Our hands were half tied behind our backs before we started. Police had rules and laws to follow, which often hampered our progress. The people we were chasing had no such restrictions.

"I appreciate you checking in on me," he said after more silence. "And please be careful."

"*Ja*," I replied, and hung up.

I felt more helpless for the man than before I'd called him, but there wasn't much I could do for him at the moment, so I returned to Weatherford's office.

Chloe Pennington's photograph and/or story had been all over the island's television news, internet, and radio all day. The station's phone lines had been inundated with sightings of school-girls, none of which were the one we were looking for. Officers had poured over the CCTV from Esterly Tibbets Highway, which was the main road from which anyone going to or from the school had to use. There were plenty of vehicles seen every lunchtime, as nearby Camana Bay housed a bunch of businesses, as well as places to eat. Naturally, many workers went to and from the place around the same time each day when they took their lunch breaks. It was necessary work, but I was already convinced the kidnapper had used a boat.

"It takes a while to get across North Sound," I pointed out to Weatherford.

He looked up from his computer. "Sure, but in four hours at a comfortable cruising speed for most any boat, someone could reach anywhere on Grand Cayman. With a bigger, faster boat, they could reach the sister islands."

"Anything from the email that the video came from?" I asked.

"The Technical Support Unit got back to me earlier," Weatherford replied unenthusiastically. "The kidnapper bounced it through a bunch of something or others so we can't trace it. They rattled off IT jargon I didn't understand, but the bottom line is there's nothing useful for us."

"But he'd need a decent internet connection," I said as I thought it through. "There are satellite options for internet in open ocean, but that means accounts, with names and email addresses and credit cards. He's here on Grand. Makes more sense."

"Why not a larger vessel offshore?" Weatherford responded. "Like our other friends on the *Manannán*."

I considered his comment for a moment. "It's possible. Look on that website that tracks yachts and ships. See who's around the island, sir."

The detective looked at me blankly. "Here, you drive," he said, and rolled his chair aside.

I went behind his desk and opened a new web browser window, searching for 'tracking ships' as I couldn't remember the website name myself. Several options came up, and I chose the first one. I zoomed in and centred on Grand Cayman. About two dozen little coloured arrows and dots appeared.

"That's not all the boats on the island by a long shot," Weatherford said.

"No, but all ocean-crossing vessels have to have a transmitter so they don't get run over in the night by a cargo ship," I explained. "See, we have two cruise ships, there's the *Manannán*, and a cargo vessel passing by to the north."

"I'm surprised the Scotsmen are letting the world track their movements," Weatherford commented.

"They'd be stupid not to," I replied. "Our coast guard would have good reason to contact them if they didn't. We'd have an excuse."

"Of course. Okay, so it doesn't look like there are any other larger motor yachts off our coast at the moment," Weatherford concluded. "So unlikely, right?"

The screen showed a bunch more boats in marinas around the island, so in theory any one of them could be a viable location to hide the kid, but unlikely. Marinas were busy places, at least during the day, and she'd been taken in the middle of the day.

"I think he's working alone," I thought aloud. "It's personal."

Weatherford nodded. "Agreed. Hasn't asked for money. He's all about the confession, and bringing attention to whatever that confession is."

"Anything useful on Pennington's list of people he's pissed off?" I asked.

Weatherford scoffed. "Nothing obvious. Mostly people from years back in the UK. We're running checks on the names to see if any jump out. I asked him to get a list from the foreman he uses on his construction sites. Could be we're looking for an employee Pennington doesn't even know about."

"The kidnapper knew Chloe's schedule and how to reach her," I said. "Getting the kid's mobile number wouldn't be easy, but contacting her through social media would be."

"We have her laptop and TSU is going through it now," the detective replied. "I checked with them an hour ago, and nothing suspicious so far." He looked at his watch. "Make that two and a half hours ago. Damn, the day is flying by and we're getting nowhere."

"What about the teachers?" I asked, trying not to let Weatherford's stress affect my thinking.

"Hatfield told me no one was absent," he replied. "They'd have missed the afternoon classes if your boat theory is right. I don't see how anyone could make it back in time."

The detective's computer dinged as I chewed that over. The email was from the immigration department. I stepped aside so Weatherford could open it.

"We have IDs on your lochmen."

I read the email over his shoulder. My brain had to switch cases. Ewan MacLeod, his brother, Iain MacLeod, and Dougal Blair. Ewan and Dougal served together in the British army. Iain had a degree in computer technology.

"None of them have anything more than a speeding ticket," Weatherford commented.

"Ewan has to be Ness," I said, matching the names to the pictures in the file.

"Resides in Sint Maarten," Weatherford read aloud. "So he's the boss who set this whole thing up."

Beyond their real names, there was nothing that stood out to me. I'd already figured two of them were military types.

"Why are they using codenames when they have to know authorities could easily track them down?" the detective wondered.

"But the girls they hire don't have those means available," I responded. "And I bet the clients have to leave their mobile phones either behind, on the shuttle boat or with someone once they reach the yacht. They're hiding their identification from them."

"Makes sense," Weatherford acknowledged as he read the report over again.

A thought swirled in my mind and I tried to find a conclusion to share it with the detective, but I couldn't find an answer. My natural instinct was to keep it to myself, but Whittaker had been on my arse lately about voicing my ideas and theories, as even if they weren't right or fully developed, it might trigger a better notion from someone else. I could understand his reasoning, but it still felt like I'd just be sharing my confusion.

"Something doesn't make sense to me," I said, deciding to follow Whittaker's desires even if I didn't fully agree.

"What's that?" Weatherford asked.

"We think there's more going on than just a floating strip club, *ja*?"

He nodded. "My contact in Jamaica thinks so, and I don't see how the economics justify the risk. That yacht is expensive to run and maintain, and there's only so many clients they can host each evening. Maybe they're paying more than I imagine, but if a wealthy man wants a stripper, he could hire a pretty girl here on the island and rent a hotel room for less than I bet they're charging. There has to be more to it."

"So why do the strip joint front at all? Wouldn't it be better to move around unnoticed if they're trafficking drugs or girls?"

Weatherford sat back and thought about it for a while. We were both silent except for him tapping a finger on his desk.

"Extras!" I blurted.

"Add-on menu," he said at the same time. "Exactly. The girls are the lure. I bet the additional items available once they're safely away from home and in international waters are the real money-makers. We need photographs or video, but we can't risk any kind of surveillance or recording device on you."

"Bearing in mind the job, it would be hard to hide anything," I agreed.

He blushed and fiddled with his computer mouse.

"I can't get a mobile on the yacht," I continued. "But Williams should be able to."

"Get with Williams again," Weatherford said. "There has to be a way he'll need a mobile to connect with an analytics tool or some technical device."

"*Faen*," I muttered.

The detective looked at me with an air of confusion before his face registered the same conclusion I'd just come to.

"No cell service twelve miles out," he groaned. "He'll need a satellite connection."

"Or just a camera," I replied. "We won't be able to send out a live feed, but we can still take pictures or shoot a video."

"Okay," Weatherford agreed. "See what we have for a small camera. Try Eileen in TSU. She'll know what we have."

I'd dealt with Eileen in the past through Detective Whittaker, but she ran the TSU department and wasn't usually available for requests from lowly constables. And then I reminded myself I was now a detective. Sort of. Unofficially, it seemed.

"*Ja*," I acknowledged, and we both fell silent again.

My mind switched back to the Pennington case and returned to the teachers.

"Hatfield said no teachers were absent," I said. "So no one is on holiday or off sick?"

Weatherford went to reply and then paused and thought again for a moment.

"He said everyone was in their classes after lunch, which is different."

He reached for his mobile and pulled a business card from his pocket. He dialled the number and put the call on speaker.

"Principal Hatfield," the man answered.

"This is detectives Weatherford and Sommer, sir. I had a quick follow-up question."

"Of course. How can I help you?"

"You told me that all the teachers had returned to their classrooms after lunch break on Wednesday, correct?"

"That's right, Detective," Hatfield replied. "And all our staff are background checked and vetted. I assure you, no one employed by the school would be involved."

"Were any support staff out?" I asked before Weatherford could continue.

"Not to my knowledge," Hatfield replied. "But you're really barking up the wrong tree if you're looking at my staff, Detective."

"Can you check your knowledge?" I asked, ignoring his claims.

"I'm sorry?" he replied.

"Detective Sommer is asking if you could double-check all your staff were in during the afternoon, including support personnel," Weatherford clarified, so apparently my English wasn't up to muff. Or duff. Or some uffy-type word.

"Oh, I see. Yes, of course."

"Do you have anyone out sick or on holiday, Principal?" Weatherford asked.

"Obviously, as a school, our staff get holiday during school breaks, so no," Hatfield replied. "Oh, but we do have a teacher out sick at the moment. Mr Garner has the flu."

Weatherford and I looked at each other.

"What does Garner teach?" I asked.

"He's one of our sports coaches."

"Which sports in particular?" Weatherford asked.

"Why is this in any way relevant, Detective?" Hatfield questioned.

"Call it an odd curiosity, Mr Hatfield. Which sports?"

"Well, he's the head coach for girls' basketball, assistant coach for football, and all our sports staff handle general PE," he replied. "Oh, and he also coaches sailing."

That got both our attention.

"Does he own a boat?" I asked.

"Umm, I think he does, actually," Hatfield replied. "I recall him speaking about a small boat he owns. He goes fishing some weekends."

"We need Mr Garner's home address," Weatherford asked without hesitation.

7

____

STINKY WEED

Sports coach Joseph Garner lived in a yucky green-painted single-storey home on Fern Street, not far south of the airport. The location was a small, older community with newer developments quickly filling in the surrounding landscape.

"Maybe I should have been a teacher," Weatherford commented as he parked the car. "It must pay better than I thought."

The home wasn't flashy by any means, but in the current housing market, it was probably worth a ridiculous amount.

"He might have roommates," I commented, noticing multiple tyre tracks in the gravel to the right of the main concrete driveway.

"True. Doesn't mean he owns the place. Could be four of them splitting rent," the detective said as he got out and we walked to the front door.

If Garner shared the house, then the others were still at work, as the only car currently in the driveway was the teacher's white Toyota. I rang the doorbell, and we waited. After a few moments, we heard footsteps, then a pause. I presumed we were being analysed through the peephole. The door finally opened.

"Joseph Garner?" Weatherford asked.

The man in his mid-thirties was barefoot, wearing tracksuit

bottoms and a wrinkled T-shirt. From his ruffled hair, I guessed we may have woken him from a snooze on the sofa. He nodded, and we both showed our badges.

"Detectives Weatherford and Sommer."

"What's this about?" he asked, looking past us to see if there was something he'd missed while he was sleeping. He had an odd English accent. Birmingham area was my guess.

"May we come in for a minute?" Weatherford asked.

Garner stepped aside, and we walked into his living room. It was dim with the curtains drawn and the only light coming from a video game on an enormous big screen TV. The game controller lay on the sofa facing the screen.

"Sorry the place is a mess," Garner muttered. "I've been off work sick."

He didn't sound sick, but maybe he had a raging rash I didn't want to see or some stomach ailment which required close proximity to a bathroom. Or he could be taking time off to kidnap a young girl.

"When was the last time you were at the school?" Weatherford asked.

"Last week," Garner replied. "Is this about the Pennington kid?"

"What's been ailing you, Mr Garner?"

"Stomach bug," he replied, brushing a hand across his midsection. "Flu of some sort, I think. Hasn't been much fun."

He walked over and drew the curtains back, letting the late afternoon light into the room. It highlighted more mess. A few empty beer cans and an open bag of crisps didn't seem like dodgy stomach items, but I'm not a doctor.

"Do you own a boat?" Weatherford asked nonchalantly as he slowly paced a lap of the room, inspecting pictures and books as he went.

"Hole in the water in which to throw money, right?" the coach replied.

Weatherford smiled. "Where is it?"

"I keep it at a mate's place as he's near the water."

"We're on a small island. Nothing is far from the water," I pointed out.

I wasn't sure what Weatherford expected from me, as I was used to accompanying Whittaker, but he didn't seem to mind me speaking up. Throwing an occasional comment or question in was often a good way to keep a suspect off balance.

"Of course," Garner bumbled. "It's just more convenient."

"Where?" Weatherford persisted.

"At a marina."

Weatherford nodded. "So, you have a friend who owns a marina? Which one?"

"George Town Yacht Club."

"Your friend owns George Town Yacht Club?" Weatherford questioned.

"No, no," Garner spluttered. "My friend lets me use his boat storage there."

The detective looked at me and raised an eyebrow, which I took to be my cue.

"You have a friend who pays for boat storage so you can keep your boat there. That's a good friend."

Garner shook his head and sighed. We had him completely flustered.

"My mate has a slip he uses when he's here on the island. When he leaves, he pulls the boat on the hard, and I move mine in the water," Garner explained.

"You made that more difficult than it needed to be, Mr Garner," Weatherford said. "Where were you at midday yesterday?"

I was used to Whittaker cleverly sliding in key questions, but apparently Weatherford had learned the same tricks. No doubt from our boss.

"Here," Garner replied. "Off sick."

"When was the last time you took your boat out?" I asked to keep his head spinning. If he was lying about several things, he'd soon trip over himself. It was hard to keep lies straight in multiple timelines.

"Been weeks."

"Would you mind if we took a look at your boat?" Weatherford asked with an innocent tone.

Garner didn't immediately reply, chewing over his next words carefully.

"Look, I don't know how you've decided I could be involved in Chloe Pennington's disappearance, but you're barking up the wrong tree. I assure you I know nothing about it."

"Then you won't mind us looking at your boat," I responded.

"It's just a waste of your time when you could be focusing on who really took her," Garner pleaded.

"We'll worry about how we spend our time, Mr Garner," Weatherford replied sternly. "But you can waste more of our time insisting we get a warrant, or you can show us to your boat and be back home within an hour."

"And maybe we'll forget to tell Hatfield you seemed perfectly okay playing video games and drinking beer at home while he has someone covering your coaching," I added.

"Bloody hell," Garner groaned. "We have to be symptom free for 48 hours before we can go back. School rules, so we're not still contagious."

I looked at Weatherford, and his eyes flicked towards a hallway to the bedrooms.

"Where's your bathroom?" I asked.

Garner pointed. "Down there. Second door on the right."

I left the living room and heard Weatherford asking again about seeing the boat. As I ducked into the first bedroom on the left, Garner was relenting and saying he'd show us.

The room was sparse and appeared unused. So much for a house full of roommates. A neatly made double bed had a bedside table on the left, and mirrored sliding doors hid a built-in wardrobe to the right. I slid one of the doors open about 20 centimetres, cringing as it squeaked on its track. Rather than make more noise, I turned on the torch app on my phone and stuck my head through the opening. A bunch of sports jerseys hung from the rail, and mesh bags of footballs filled the bottom of the wardrobe.

Leaving the closet door ajar for fear of making more noise, I crossed the hallway and into what I guessed to be the master bedroom. The queen-sized bed was unmade and various clothes were scattered about. The doors to a similar wardrobe slid easily, to my relief, and revealed the usual array of hanging garments, with shoes on the floor. On the opposite side, a door opened into the en suite bathroom which smelt stale, like it needed a good cleaning. Or supported his bad stomach story.

I found one more bedroom down the hall to the left. It had a double bed which was made up but the room looked lived in. Personal items like photographs in frames and knick-knack rubbish people like to accumulate sat on the dresser. I looked at the pictures and presumed the young guy common in each photo was Garner's roommate. I heard Weatherford raise his voice from the living room and hurried across the hall to the bathroom I was supposed to be visiting. Quickly flushing the loo, I strode out as Garner was standing in front of his bedroom door.

"Who's your roommate?" I asked.

"Jean," he replied, looking at me suspiciously. "He's a nurse at the hospital."

I continued to the living room and shook my head at Weather-ford. He subtly nodded as Garner returned, tucking a wallet in his sweatpants pocket. Before we left, I checked out the window to the back garden. I didn't see any outbuildings, so apart from a feeling Garner wasn't being completely truthful with us, we'd found nothing to suspect him of taking Chloe. Our only reason for speaking to him in the first place was thin. If we'd had any other leads, we'd probably have sent a uniform to speak with him or skipped him altogether.

"I have to be honest," Weatherford said quietly as we followed the white Toyota towards George Town Yacht Club. "I could really use Whittaker to lean on about now. We've got nothing. No forensics, witnesses, CCTV more than the kid ditching school. Nothing. I guess I took for granted being able to stick my head in his office and chat about our cases."

"Have you spoken to him?" I asked.

He shook his head. "Texted him to say I was sorry and to let me know if there was anything I could do. I shouldn't have done that. Chief told us we were to have no contact with him while he was being investigated."

We rode in silence for a while.

"You?" Weatherford finally asked as we pulled into the marina.

"I called him."

"And?"

"He said he couldn't discuss any cases."

Weatherford scoffed. "Typical Roy. A hundred percent by the book. There's no way he was selling drugs. Not a chance."

"Then we'd better find this kid," I replied. "Then we can figure out who set him up."

The detective grunted his agreement as we climbed out of his car and walked over to where Garner waited by a 21-foot Bayliner cuddy cabin on a trailer between a row of far nicer vessels. The blue and white gel coat was badly sun faded and the weather cover was patched with duct tape and similarly faded to a grey with only a hint of its former blue. Many of the poppers holding it down were missing, but enough remained to keep the cover in place. The outdrive tilted up, and the propeller looked like it had also seen better days.

"Well, there it is," Garner said, waving a hand at his vessel. "As you can see, it's been sitting here for a while."

Weatherford sighed. "Alright, Mr Garner. We appreciate your cooperation."

He turned to leave, but something struck me as odd about the boat.

"Take the cover off," I ordered, and both men paused.

"What?" Garner questioned, clearly thinking he was free to go.

Weatherford gave me a questioning look.

"Pull the cover," I repeated and waited until he began tugging the fasteners free.

"Right-hand trailer wheel," I whispered to Weatherford when he came close to me.

"You don't need the whole cover off, do you?" Garner asked. "You just need to peek inside, yeah?"

"All the way," I ordered, which was met with another disgusted expression.

"Shit. Well spotted," Weatherford said quietly, having seen the small piece of seaweed draped over the rail of the trailer.

In the Cayman heat and sunshine, seaweed shrivelled into a crispy decaying biscuit once it was out of the water. The small leafy strand hanging on the rail hadn't been out of the ocean for more than a day or so. With the cover removed, we both looked over the gunwale. Water sat in the lowest corner.

"Haven't been out in weeks," Weatherford said. "Isn't that what you told us?"

Garner's expression tightened. "That old cover leaks. It's just rainwater or over-spray from someone washing their boat down."

I reached over, dipped my finger in the water, and touched it to my tongue. Then I turned and spat into the gravel.

"Salty rain, huh?" I said, trying to get the taste out of my mouth and the thought of the nasty little microorganisms I'd just licked.

Garner's head dropped. "I can explain."

I climbed on the trailer and into the Bayliner. The little door to the cuddy cabin wasn't locked, and I slid it open. Using my phone's torch, I looked around inside. It stank of mould and decay. Apart from a stack of old orange life vests and a plastic cooler, the area was empty.

"I'm listening," Weatherford said after I caught his eye and shook my head.

"I took the boat out yesterday," Garner reluctantly muttered. "I was feeling better, but I needed two days before I could go back to work. So I went out for a while."

"Alone?" I asked.

He nodded.

"When?" Weatherford asked.

"Mid-morning I'd say," Garner replied. "Just for an hour or two."

"An hour?" Weatherford asked. "Or two? There's a hundred percent difference."

The school coach threw up his hands. "I don't really remember. I went out into the middle of the sound, drank a beer or two, fished for a while, then motored back. Probably more like two hours."

I called the front desk at the station on my mobile. It rang three times before a voice I recognised answered.

"Chantel, this is Consta… Detective Sommer, with Detective Weatherford."

"Dey give you dat promotion, girl, you best start rememberin'. What you need?"

"Can you have someone call the George Town Yacht Club and get CCTV from the marina for yesterday? Eight in the morning until two in the afternoon."

"By get someone, you know dat means I gotta do dat, right? I don't have no little minions running round doin' all da tings I don't feel like doin'."

I wasn't sure what I was supposed to say. So I said, "*Takk,*" and hung up.

"Can I cover my boat back up?" Garner asked.

I stepped out.

"Sure," Weatherford said. "But you're coming with us to the station."

"Seriously? What the hell for?"

"For further questioning while our forensics team examines your boat," Weatherford replied.

"What about my car?"

"Leave it. Someone will bring you back if you're cleared to leave," Weatherford replied, and I frowned at him.

"This is bloody ridiculous," Garner complained as he buttoned the cover back down.

"What?" Weatherford asked me off to the side.

"We don't want him in the car with us, sir. We might catch his stupid stomach bug," I replied. "Tell him to follow us."

Weatherford frowned. "And what if he takes off?"

"Then we'll chase him down and taser the *dritt* out of him, sir."

Weatherford cracked a smile. "Is that the procedure they're pushing in training these days?"

"It's a variation," I replied.

"We've been in his house, Nora. I think we've already risked being exposed."

Weatherford's phone rang before I could further campaign for a germ-free ride. He stepped to the side. In less than a minute, he was back with a concerned look on his face.

"Penningtons are at the station. They received another text recording."

"What about him?" I asked, nodding at Garner.

"Follow us to the station in your car, Mr Garner," Weatherford ordered.

I ticked one small victory. I hated getting sick.

8

STRIPPER TOOLS

Rupert Pennington touched play, and we all listened to the new message.

"Is your daughter's life worth keeping your secret?" the distorted voice said. "Four days. Confess or Chloe dies."

Rupert's hand shook and Becca gasped with tears running down from her already red and puffy eyes. No doubt they'd listened to the recording multiple times before coming to the station, but the words still took her breath away.

"Have you traced the first call?" Rupert demanded.

"Our Technical Support Unit is still trying, Mr Pennington," Weatherford replied. "But these messages are sent via an encrypted system. I doubt we'll find her that way."

"I've tried replying," Pennington said, holding the phone up as though it was broken. "And it gives me an invalid number message." He sat back, pressed his hands to either side of his head, and groaned. "So, how are we going to find her?"

"We have every available officer working on this case, sir, I assure you."

"We'll pay whatever it takes to get her back," Becca said, wiping her face. "Why isn't he asking for money?"

"Because he doesn't care about your money," I replied, and Weatherford gave me a stern look.

"Everybody cares about money," Becca shot back, glaring at me.

"Perhaps," Weatherford intervened before I could respond. "But in this case, it appears the kidnapper is more passionate about a confession."

"A confession of what?" Rupert replied, thumping the table with his fist. "I'll gladly admit to anything I've done. But I've nothing to hide, Detective."

"Did your foreman or a manager suggest an upset employee or vendor who felt wronged, Mr Pennington?" Weatherford asked.

He shook his head. "I sent another list to you before driving here, but they're all a stretch. No one could think of anyone who'd be angry enough at me to take Chloe."

"Don't think of it that way," I said.

"What fucking way?" Pennington snapped. "She's been taken. Kidnapped. Abducted. How am I supposed to think about it?"

Becca rested a hand on his arm. He started to shake her off, but then settled down.

I waited for him to take a breath and calm himself. "I was saying, don't think about people who *you* think might be angry."

"Oh," he muttered, rubbing his forehead. "Right. I'm sorry."

"You don't know what someone else is thinking," I continued. "Give us names of any person or business who had a problem or got a shitty deal from you."

"Could even be a friend or long-term partner who may have said it didn't matter," Weatherford added, picking up on my point. "Situations can fester without us knowing sometimes."

"Shit," Becca blurted. "He wouldn't..." Her eyes darted to her husband. "Would he?"

"Who?" Rupert asked impatiently. "Who are you talking about?"

"Patrick."

"That's ridiculous," Rupert replied, but his face slowly tensed into deep thought as he considered whatever seed Becca had planted.

"Who's Patrick?" Weatherford asked.

"My brother," Rupert replied in a long exhalation. "He's many things, my brother, but a kidnapper of his own niece? That's insane. He loves Chloe."

"He doesn't give a shit about her," Becca scoffed.

Rupert shook his head. "Patrick would never do anything like this."

Becca raised her eyebrows at us. "I wouldn't put anything past that prick. He'd never get his own hands dirty. He doesn't have the balls for that, but he might hire someone to do it."

Rupert got to his feet and paced the room, shaking his head some more.

"Where does your brother live?" Weatherford asked.

"A condo Rupert gave him in one of his West Bay projects," Becca replied. "Ungrateful prick's never worked for anything in his life."

It was Rupert's turn to calm his wife down. He put a firm hand on her shoulder.

"He's not as bad as you make him out to be. Besides, why would he demand a ridiculous secret be revealed?"

Rebecca shrugged. "He's probably building up to the ransom part."

"From what you're saying, I'm unsure why your brother would want to harm your family," Weatherford said. "What would he hold a grudge about?"

"He wouldn't," Rupert snapped.

Rebecca scoffed. "Because my husband finally started telling him no, and he's broke. That's why."

"Okay, it does sound like we should have a word with him," Weatherford said, holding up a calming hand. "Can you give us his phone number?"

Pennington hesitated, but after a few moments wrote a number down on Weatherford's notepad.

"Does he own a boat?" I asked.

Becca scoffed. "Patrick doesn't own shit. He uses other people's things the same way he uses people."

Rupert threw his hands in the air. "I know you hate the guy, but for Christ's sake, Rebecca, he's my brother." He turned to Weatherford. "Call him. Do it, so she'll stop bitching about him, but you'll never convince me he'd get involved in anything like this."

"Has he even called you since Chloe went missing?" Becca asked, standing herself and poking a finger in her husband's chest. "Have you heard from dear Patrick?"

"Yes!" Rupert replied. "Of course he reached out."

"He called you?" she persisted.

Rupert gritted his teeth. "He texted me."

Becca scoffed. "He texted you? There's that brotherly love. A concerned fucking uncle."

Weatherford stood, so I did too. Everyone was now on their feet.

"Please, let's calm down, Mr and Mrs Pennington," Weatherford said, unable to hide his exhausted tone. "We'll speak with Patrick so we can rule him out."

My mobile buzzed, and I checked the time before the message. I didn't have long before I needed to get ready. The text was from Chantel.

I turned to Weatherford. "We have the CCTV we requested, sir."

"You have a lead?" Rupert asked, leaning across the table. "What is it?"

Weatherford held up a hand. "Please, sir. Nothing as yet. We're doing everything we can to track your daughter's movements when she left the school."

"When someone *snatched her* from school," Becca seethed.

I looked at Weatherford, knowing my explanation of the events would not be as well received as his wording.

"The evidence we have suggests Chloe deliberately evaded the school's cameras and left of her own volition," the detective said.

I was right. That was much softer than my version. Although I wasn't sure what volition meant, and would have to look it up later.

"We believe she voluntarily met with someone outside of school property," Weatherford continued. "Who likely took her from there."

"What? That's ridiculous," Rupert began, but the detective spoke up before the father could continue.

"We have reason to believe she met with this person several times over the prior week. We're still waiting for her phone records to confirm the text exchanges and hopefully they'll provide us with more clues."

"I don't understand," Becca whispered, looking from us to her husband.

"How did we miss this?" he muttered in reply.

"How did the bloody school miss this?" Becca said, her voice finding its feet again.

"We have to step out to follow up on something," Weatherford said before she could wind herself up into a tirade. "Best thing is to go home and let us do everything we can. I promise we're using all our resources to find Chloe."

The parents were too stunned to complain, and we managed to herd them from the room and head upstairs to Weatherford's office. He glanced at his watch.

"Nora, you need to go," he urged as he dropped into his chair and woke up his computer.

"Ja. Let's see the video first. I won't be late."

He jumped up and pointed to the screen. "Here. Start looking. I'm going to try calling the brother."

I slipped into his seat while Weatherford stepped back and dialled the number he'd been given. By the time I'd opened the video file and began fast-forwarding until I saw Garner's shitty little Bayliner being backed down the Barcadere boat ramp at the marina, Weatherford was leaving a message for Patrick Pennington.

Pausing the video, I opened our background software and

entered the brother's name. It wasn't hard to guess which Patrick Pennington was the man in question. He was the only one by that name on the island, and Becca may well have been right about him.

"He won't call back," I said as Weatherford rejoined me.

He leaned over my shoulder and read aloud. "Speeding, DUI, possession. Shit, this guy's a train wreck."

Clicking back to the CCTV footage, I sped ahead until Garner was idling out of the marina, and checked the timestamp.

"He's leaving at 9:56am," I said, jotting it down before continuing the recording at four-times speed.

We watched for a few seconds until Garner went out of frame, then I sped it up to twice that speed and vessels of various shapes and sizes zipped in and out of view. I slowed the frame-rate back down when the Bayliner returned and noted the time when it reached the boat ramp.

"One forty-seven," I said as I wrote the time down.

We both returned our attention to the screen and watched Garner at the helm, waiting, while a rusty older model pickup truck backed his trailer down the ramp into the water.

"Does that truck belong to the marina?" Weatherford asked.

"*Ja,*" I replied. "He would have called them. Same truck put him in."

"Certainly don't see anyone else in the boat with him," Weatherford said.

"Easy to hide in the cuddy cabin," I pointed out. "We need a camera in the boat storage area."

We watched the pickup truck pull the Bayliner up the ramp with water running off the boat and the trailer. Once it disappeared from view, Weatherford stood up straight.

"So Garner lied about the timing, which makes it possible he could have come from the channel near the school."

"*Ja,* and he told us he was in the middle of the sound, but the boat comes into camera view from the north, closer to the shoreline."

He rested a hand on my shoulder. "You need to get going. I'll ask someone to work on other camera angles from the marina and send someone by Patrick Pennington's place to invite him in to see us."

I stood up and moved to the doorway.

"I have to press on with the Pennington case, but Williams will watch out for you at George Town Harbour. He'll be there before four," Weatherford added. "And Nora…"

"*Ja,*" I said, turning to look at him.

"Be careful. You can call this at any time, right?"

"Sure," I replied, and hurried down the hall.

The truth was I could call it off before I left the harbour with the lochmen, but after that, I was on my own. I'd have no way of contacting anyone unless I could reach a marine radio or satellite phone. Skipping a breath, I realised I was actually nervous about what lay ahead. I'd spent a long year amongst predators similar to these men and had worked hard to make sure everyone I'd been able to find had paid a price for what they'd done. Yet here I was, voluntarily throwing myself to the wolves again. Which meant I needed to make sure it was worth it.

There wasn't time to drive home and change, so I grabbed the two duffel bags I'd left in the Jeep and disappeared into the women's locker room at the station. Stripping down, I set my work clothes aside and took a quick shower. I tied my hair up in a big knot on my head to keep it dry and scrubbed the day from my body. They wanted me without makeup, so that made things a lot faster, and I put on leggings, sports bra, and a sweatshirt for the ride out. Shoving my work clothes into one bag, I double-checked the contents of the other. Makeup kit, a variety of skimpy under-wear, two button-up blouses, a miniskirt, and two pairs of high heels. *Faen,* I hated wearing high heels. They'd be the first things I'd ditch on stage. Putting on a pair of trainers to wear in the mean-time, I made sure I had my fake ID, zippered clutch for cash, and of course, the wig. I was waiting until I was in the car to put that on.

Tossing the bag I didn't need into the Jeep, I put my mobile and real credentials into the lockbox. The old clunker car I'd used before was parked around back, and it hesitantly started on the second try. I made sure to drive around George Town so I approached the harbour from the north in keeping with my fake ID address. Parking, as usual near the waterfront in George Town, was almost non-existent, but I finally found a spot on Goring Ave.

When I reached the harbour on foot, I spotted Lomond, the man I now knew to be Dougal Blair from Sheffield, standing on the dock beside a 33-foot rigid inflatable boat, or RIB, with twin outboards. The boat was kitted out with multiple seats for taxiing people and a long Bimini to keep the sun off the passengers. It wasn't the most luxurious tender for the *Manannán,* but a fast and efficient way of getting bodies back and forth to shore.

Lomond took my bag from me and offered a steadying hand to get on the boat. I didn't need any assistance, but I took his hand anyway to play the part. There was a woman aboard who I hadn't seen before. She was in her thirties, with short black hair and a tanned complexion.

"This is Morar," Lomond said. "She handles the talent."

"*Hei,*" I said, using Finnish.

I remembered a Morar from the list of Scottish lochs and made mental notes about her features to track down her ID when I was back at the station.

"Got everything you need?" she asked sternly while looking me over. She had a Hispanic accent.

"*Juu,*" I replied, wondering what exactly a stripper might leave behind that they couldn't get by without. The end result would be the same even if I arrived stark naked.

"You speak English?"

"Of course," I replied.

"Where's your mobile phone?" she asked.

"Left it behind," I replied, and she eyed me suspiciously.

"Put your arms up," she ordered, and I did so.

She patted me down. Lomond searched my bag while Morar took her time checking all my hard-to-reach places.

"You should buy me dinner first," I said, but she ignored me.

Hearing footsteps, we all turned and saw Violet Blaze trotting towards the boat. She was already dressed like a hooker, but I guessed they were the only outfits she owned. She also had a full-sized wheeled suitcase in tow. So maybe I was underestimating the tools of the trade needed for professional stripping.

9

———

WASTE DISPOSAL DANCER

The moment we cleared the harbour, Lomond opened up the twin outboards, and the RIB took off across the light afternoon chop. Violet clung to her seat and nervously looked over at me. I couldn't tell whether she feared the boat ride or what lay ahead. She leaned closer, and I made sure Morar wasn't watching us, before I eased towards the girl so she could talk to me without shouting over the wind and engine noise.

"Is it happening tonight?" Violet asked.

I carefully observed Morar for a few moments before risking a reply. Lomond was focused on driving the RIB, but his compatriot stood next to him, leaning against the bench seat, and I wanted to be sure she wasn't trying to listen. Most likely our voices were lost to the wind whistling over the boat as it made impressive speed across the ocean.

"*Nei*," I finally replied.

"Good. I need to make some money."

I sat back, but she wasn't done and clung to my arm, pulling me closer.

"We're cool, right?"

I nodded.

She frowned.

"I need to hear you say it."

"You'll be okay," I said, more to shut her up than knowing I could make that guarantee. Ultimately, it wasn't even close to being my call, but she could blow this for us before we got started if she freaked out.

Morar turned and looked at us.

"I have four full outfits. I hope that's enough," I said loudly to Violet, whose face was a picture of confusion.

"What about you?" I asked, pointing to the enormous bag it had taken Lomond five minutes to go through, during which time he'd confiscated her mobile phone from her.

"Oh, right. Yeah, I brought everything I have. I even emptied the laundry basket."

Morar turned to face the front, leaving us to our trivial banter and me cringing at the notion of Violet's used underwear. I reached into the small ice chest they'd pointed out to us and swallowed down half a bottle of water to wash away the unpleasant taste that had formed in my mouth.

As we neared, I got my first look at the *Manannán*. It was a beautiful boat. We'd had a hard time finding many details about it online, outside of it being a 92-foot twin-engine catamaran, originally built in 2004 as a luxury motor yacht. Now, seeing it in person, the yacht didn't show its age, either in design or condition. At least from the outside.

We climbed aboard via small swim platforms at the stern of each of the twin hulls, then up moulded-in steps to the main level. The aft deck served as an outdoor cocktail area with several tall, round tables. Morar led us through tinted sliding glass doors into the salon, which was brightly lit by recessed fixtures, but I noticed the side windows had all been covered. The lighting would undoubtedly be dimmed once the sun went down and the customers arrived. To the starboard side was a long, curved bar with swivelling stools. To the port side, plush loveseats were arranged to form three sides around brass poles. There were three sets, all with carefully placed end tables with drinks holders.

"Bugger me," Violet muttered. "This is a bit flash, innit?"

I ignored her and did a quick mental count. The loveseats were intended for one customer each, so the girls could sit next to them. That put three customers for each dance pole equalling nine. Plus the six bar stools made 15 customers total. If each paid a grand and spent another $300 on drinks and whatever else was on offer, that made $19,500 a night. If they operated seven nights a week while in any location and stayed for two weeks, that added up to serious money. Over a quarter of a million every two weeks. But I couldn't see how they'd find 210 different customers from a place like Grand Cayman. Even if every customer spent two evenings, that was still over a hundred people willing to drop several grand on their entertainment.

Maybe the guarantee that the boat's antics were completely legal was enough, but I knew from experience that wealthy men on the island could find pretty girls willing to spend a weekend with them for a few thousand dollars. I was certain Violet would jump at the chance. It still didn't completely add up in my mind.

"I'll go over the evening's schedule later," Morar said, continuing through the salon to the hallway beyond.

We followed, passing curved stairs to the pilothouse deck on the right and a galley on the left with a serving window into the salon. The hallway beyond had several doors on each side, and Morar opened the last one on the port side. The berth had two chairs in front of wall-mounted mirrors where beds would usually be, a wardrobe on each side, and an en suite head including a shower.

"Drop your stuff in here and meet me in the salon in fifteen minutes," the woman instructed. "You can leave clothes in the berth for the three days, but take everything with you when you leave Sunday. There are laundry bags in the wardrobes for anything you need cleaned before the next day."

Morar closed the door behind her, leaving Violet and me to look around the cramped space.

"I could bloody well live here," Violet enthused. "Do you think it's just us?"

"*Nei.* They have other girls here."

"Who live on the boat, you reckon?"

"I think so," I replied, edging around her stupid great big suitcase to look in the bathroom.

Like everything on the boat, it was clean, modern, and sparse but efficient. They even supplied soap and shampoo. I took my meagre bag, and either hung the clothes in the little wardrobe or placed them in the drawers below. Violet followed suit, and began unpacking her clothes, promptly strewing them around the berth under the guise of sorting. I reminded myself that I needed her on my side, and strangling her within five minutes of arrival on *Manannán* probably wouldn't help our objective.

When we returned to the salon, two other girls lounged in a pair of the loveseats. They looked us over distastefully as we approached.

"Hey, I'm Violet," she said, giving them a little wave.

Morar stepped over from the bar. "Shandy and Raven, meet Violet and Viivi," she said, and turned to us. "You'll be working together for the weekend. We operate in shifts. Three dancing while the fourth floats."

"Where you from?" the one with the jet black hair asked. I guessed she was Raven. Everything about her was the opposite of me. She was short with a curvy figure and a beautiful dark skin tone. She had full lips and long eyelashes, but not the really stupidly long ones that girls had to build muscle in their eyelids to open.

"Finland," I remembered to say.

"You smokin' hot, babe. You gonna make cash."

She spoke English with an island accent, but it wasn't Caymanian. Violet looked put out that I'd been singled out.

I shrugged. "We'll see. You girls have the curves men like."

Shandy was slimmer with a slightly lighter skin tone, but was almost as busty as her friend. From the way her full chest seemed to perch closer to her chin than I'd expect, I guessed she'd had surgical assistance with her shape.

"What about you?" Shandy asked Violet in a similar accent.

"I'm English, but I live in Grand Cayman," Violet replied, perking up once she was involved in the conversation.

"Ground rules," Morar said, clearly having had enough of the chitchat. "I'm in charge, and what I say goes. Don't do what I say, and you're not coming back. Cause a fuss, insult a guest, fight with the other girls, or steal from us, and you're swimming home. That understood?"

Violet's expression froze. I was confident she couldn't swim the length of the boat, let alone twelve miles to shore.

"*Juu*," I said.

Violet just nodded.

"If the clients get too touchy, tell me. Understand? I'll handle it."

We both nodded.

"If the clients proposition you, you remind them it's against the house rules. Understand?"

"It is?" Violet said, sounding disappointed.

"Yes," Morar replied firmly. "And arranging to meet back on the island will earn you a long swim. Am I clear?"

Violet flinched. "Yeah. Got it."

My companion was disappointed because she wanted to make more money. I was disappointed as it was another point on which the lochmen were steering clear of something that'd get them nicked. Although, again, prostitution was legal in Sint Maarten, I doubted they had the proper permits and certainly weren't available for the inspections required to maintain one. I began wondering if they were, in fact, running nothing more than a floating strip club with suitable security and precautions in place. In which case I was wasting my time, and more to the point, I didn't give a shit. Everyone involved was doing so of their own free will.

"You may imbibe with the clients, but you'll be served watered-down drinks and under no circumstances will we tolerate you getting drunk. No one is paying money to watch you trip over yourself."

Raven laughed. "Don't forget da boat rock, too. Sometime you gotta do balancin' tricks."

"Yes," Morar agreed. "Which reminds me. If you get seasick, take it outside to the stern. That's the back of the boat."

The last part staved off Violet's next question.

"What about VIP rooms?" I asked.

"Yeah. You got VIP rooms?" Violet echoed excitedly, smelling more money.

"We do. But remember, all client requests go through me. If they ask for a VIP dance, signal me. Understood?"

"Signal, how?" Violet asked.

Now Shandy laughed. "Just look her way. Dis woman see everyting on dis boat. Ain't nuttin' she don't catch."

Raven laughed too. Morar didn't, but I caught the glint of pride in her eyes. She rambled on more about routines, dos, don'ts, and emphasised the part about handing over tip money multiple times. Which made me wonder if anyone had ever actually been thrown overboard for breaking the rules.

"Relax for the next 45 minutes," she said to finish. "We'll meet on the sundeck for dinner at seven. That's the top deck. Clients arrive at eight, so you'll be waiting to greet them fifteen minutes before that."

Morar left, going up the steps to where I presumed the main staterooms and pilothouse must be. The boat was a cat, so we were standing on the lowest full deck. The only thing below us were the twin hulls housing the engines, fuel tanks, generators, and other ancillary equipment.

"The VIP rooms are back there?" I asked Raven, pointing in the direction of the hallway where we'd been given a berth at the end.

She nodded. "Dere's two on each side. Last two doors are da dressing rooms."

"You two live on the boat all the time?" Violet asked.

Shandy nodded.

"That's so bloody cool," Violet enthused. "How do I get that gig?"

"You don't," Raven snapped, getting to her feet and poking a finger in Violet's chest. "So don't be tryin' to step on our toes, you hear?"

Violet took a step back. "Shit. Fine. I was just asking. Don't freak out."

I looked around the salon. I didn't see anything resembling a written menu of services, and Morar hadn't said anything about it either. She had repeatedly told us to direct all requests to her. That was smart. Nothing in writing. All they needed was a client sneaking a souvenir off the boat to gloat with his mates. Shown to the wrong person, or even worse, show up online, and they'd be done.

This was going to be harder than I thought. All I could do was play along and wait for an opportunity to cause a problem with the boat so Williams could join me. Maybe then we'd film something incriminating. So my next task was finding how to access the twin hulls which housed all the mechanicals. Not exactly a question I could slide into conversation, and I hadn't even seen a crew member yet.

Raven and Shandy walked towards the hallway, heading for what I guessed to be their berth opposite ours. I presumed theirs still had beds crammed into the little room.

"Are we allowed upstairs?" I asked before they left.

Raven shrugged. "Sure. Ain't nuttin' but da helm and da crew berths."

"Where are the crew?" I asked.

"Up dere," she replied. "Katrine tends bar in da evenin' and does da meals and cleanin'. We don't see Rannoch or Harray much. Dey da Captain and First Mate."

"Okay, *kiitos*."

Raven laughed. "I wanna learn some Finnish 'fore you go, girl."

"Okay," I replied.

"What was it you just said?" Violet asked.

"Tank you," Raven answered. "Right?"

"*Juu. Kiitos* means thank you."

"*Kiitos*," Raven repeated in her sing-song accent. "I like it."

Over the next hour and a half, I learned that Violet was a waste disposal machine when it came to food. She was skinny as a rail but could make every morsel put in front of her disappear. I was concerned about sharing a bathroom with her.

Other than that, Morar ate with us, but the crew stayed separate. I got a brief glance at the captain, but I presumed the first mate was sleeping, as there were only the two of them. Someone had to be at the helm at all times. Katrine brought our food, and later was preparing her bar when we came out ready to greet the clients. She looked to be in her twenties, had metal pierced through every available piece of flesh, and tattoos on her arms and up her neck. At first glance, she could have been mistaken for the lead singer of a death metal band. On closer inspection, I noticed her tattoos were of cupcakes, cartoon characters, and a unicorn. She also had a warm smile, and Shandy and Raven seemed to be relaxed around her.

The RIB pulled up to the stern and the three lochmen handled tying it up and helping the guests aboard. We waited inside the salon. Fortunately, the lights were now dimmed and soft music played as I felt goofy and awkward standing there in my hooker outfit.

"*Fy faen*," I muttered to myself as the first few men came through the sliding salon door.

I instantly recognised one of them from the pictures I'd seen earlier in the day. It was Rupert Pennington's brother.

Chloe's Uncle Patrick.

10

SWEDES, TIPS, AND ADDICTS

My first reaction was to turn away and avoid Patrick Pennington seeing me. But that was stupid. He didn't know me, and I couldn't hide from the man all evening without being fired on day one. They weren't paying us to lock ourselves in the bathroom. I got lucky. Patrick's eyes shot straight to Raven. If he liked girls with curves, then I wouldn't be on his radar.

"Back for more?" Raven asked as he approached her.

"Couldn't resist," Patrick replied, letting her lead him to the first semicircle of loveseats.

I thought this was opening night for the Cayman Islands, but I realised I was wrong. They must have hosted clients already with just the two girls. Made sense. Get a handful of customers aboard and let them sell the idea to their rich friends.

"What's your name?" a man in a well-tailored business suit asked me. He was late forties or early fifties, slender with the hint of bulge appearing around his middle, brown hair too perfect not to be coloured, and a very expensive-looking watch. And no wedding band or untanned ring on his finger.

"Viivi," I replied, remembering my undercover name just in time.

"Perhaps you can tell me how this works," he said with a mischievous grin.

Surely they'd been told everything on the way out, or before that, as at some point they'd all received a sales pitch before they'd agreed to hand over their money.

"You pay money and I get naked," I replied. "It's not complicated."

He laughed. "Swedish?"

Faen. Why do they always think Swedish?

"Finnish," I replied. "What's your name?"

I was a Norwegian pretending to be Finnish while he thought I was Swedish. If we could roll Denmark into the mix somehow, we'd complete a Scandinavian soup of confusion.

"David," he replied, extending a hand, which I firmly shook. He spoke with an indistinct English accent.

I glanced up to see how many customers had arrived. Eleven, I counted quickly before returning my attention to David. His eyes were just arriving back on my face.

"I brought money, if you don't mind supplying the naked part?" he said.

I laughed, because I thought that was funny. "Sure."

The rest of the evening went fine. I took skimpy clothes off, then put them back on just to take them off again a bunch of times. Five men and one woman with her husband had me dance for them, and both David and the married couple paid for private dances in a VIP room. The couple spent most of that time groping each other to the point where I felt like I should leave. But they insisted I stay and paid a hundred dollars extra for my troubles.

It seemed all the clients had been well instructed after all. Everything I was asked about was related to the dancing, songs, and VIP room. Having seen the headcount was less than I'd figured would be their maximum, I was more convinced another service was being offered, but I didn't see any evidence. Morar hung by the bar, and Shandy had been right. The woman didn't miss a thing. The lochmen stayed out of the way, probably so as not to intimidate the clients, and only Lomond circulated occasionally to make sure everything was going well.

At the end of the evening, the clients loaded into the tender to be ferried back. We had to wait. Once the RIB returned, then Violet and I, along with the three lochmen, were transported ashore. I guessed it was some form of security measure to keep the girls away from the clients. Although it was late at night, it wouldn't be good for a suspicious wife to see her husband arriving back at the island with a pair of strippers sitting next to them.

"You made a shit-ton in tips, huh?" Violet said, huddling close to me with the wind rushing over the boat.

It was still 28°C outside, but the night air had a chill to it when it hit you at 20 knots.

I shrugged. It seemed I had done well when all the tips were added up and our share handed out. Morar had kept everyone's money separate as we'd subtly handed it off to her throughout the evening. It was hard finding places to stash banknotes when you weren't wearing much. Raven had made the most, then me, Shandy, and Violet had been last. Even so, she'd at least doubled the daily rate we'd been promised. We were told we'd get that part on the last night. Presumably to make sure we turned up for the other two. I worried Violet would blow the cash she now had and be too stoned to make the boat the next day.

"I'll pick you up tomorrow," I said. "Save us both finding a place to park."

"That would be great," she replied sleepily. "I don't have a car at the moment, so I had to take the bus."

She'd left her oversized suitcase on the *Manannán* and brought a plastic bag of things to wear before her return. She hadn't been lying. Violet had brought along not just every stitch of stripper clothing she owned, but every item of any clothing she owned.

"Do you have somewhere to stay?" I asked before I'd really thought it through.

"Probably," she replied, checking her cheap watch to see the time.

It was somewhere around two in the morning.

"I'll knock on a door or two. Someone will still be up."

I couldn't imagine how she'd been getting by before picking up this dancing gig. Probably trading services for a bed to sleep in and a shower. I doubted those taking her in were the steady job types, either. We sat in silence while I argued with myself about what to do. The last thing I needed was a drug-addicted hooker spending the day in my little shack, especially on a weekend when Jazzy would be home much of the time. Maybe we'd be better throwing her in jail at the station. She'd have a place to sleep and meals provided, but then no money to dig herself out of the mess she was in.

I shook my head and groaned. It was very doubtful Violet would use the cash she was making to add security to her life. There was a far greater chance she'd drink and snort her way through it. *But what did that say about me if I assumed the worst and didn't help?* It meant I was smart enough to know better.

The RIB slowed, and we eased up to the dock in the dim lights from the remaining street lamps along George Town waterfront.

"Six tomorrow afternoon," Ness instructed as he helped us to the dock. "Don't be late."

I nodded and walked away, with Violet trudging along beside me.

"Could I get a ride to a friend's house?" she asked as we neared the road.

"I have a couch. It's pretty comfortable," I replied, cursing myself inside.

"Seriously?" she said, her voice perking up. "That would be mega. Thanks."

We walked to the piece of *dritt* car I was using and wished I could trade it for my Jeep, but it wasn't worth the extra time. Besides, Violet would probably freak out if I drove by the central police station.

"I have a kid," I said as we got in and cranked the engine over.

It took a few tries, but it finally started.

"Shit. You're young to have a kid."

"She's a teenager," I replied, trying to think how I should tell Violet not to be a crackhead whore around Jazzy. Tricky for someone who doesn't usually bother filtering what I say.

She gasped. "You have a teenager? What, were you like ten when you got yourself up the junction?"

I wasn't sure what up the junction meant, but it didn't sound like somewhere I wanted to go.

"No, I sort of inherited her."

"Like from a sister or something?" Violet said. "I had a cousin who got preggers when she was thirteen and tried raising the thing but ended up in juvie, so they took the baby away. Ended up with another cousin to raise. Like that?"

"No, not like that," I replied, already regretting this decision. "I found her living on the streets and we sort of adopted each other."

"Huh," Violet breathed. "That's pretty cool."

Now I hoped she didn't think I was a candidate for adopting *her*.

"I won't do anything crazy around her, if that's what you're worried about?"

Then I felt bad for thinking the worst. It was easy to forget that people usually have a good idea of how they appear to others. Especially someone like Violet, who'd spent her life being told she was useless by just about everyone.

She'd been right, though. It was exactly what I was thinking, so I stayed quiet and didn't respond. I didn't want to lie to her.

Both tired and ready to sleep, we rode in silence until I pulled over by the side of Conch Point Road in West Bay. With no street lamps or homes in sight, it was pitch black once I turned the head-lights off.

"Where are we?" Violet asked nervously as I got out.

"Home," I replied.

The breeze whistled through the trees on either side of the road, and bugs chirped and croaked.

"Did they give you your phone back?" I asked.

Violet turned on the torch feature and shone it in my face. "Yeah."

I looked away. "Hand it to me."

"I don't see any homes," she said, without passing me her mobile.

"It's through the woods. Now give me the phone unless you know the way?"

"I've seen this movie," Violet muttered, but gave me her device.

I lit the way around the side of the chain-link fence and found the hole I'd made.

"Bloody hell. Is this a squat, or what?"

"No. The legal access to my shack is a path half a kilometre down the road, then along the beach. This is much faster."

The sound of the waves gently meeting the ironshore coastline became louder and my little house appeared as we stepped from the cover of the trees.

"Shit. You're oceanfront? This must have cost a fortune," Violet exclaimed.

"Shhh," I hushed. "The kid's asleep."

"Oh, shit. Sorry," Violet whispered. "How did you afford this on a copper's pay? You gotta have a side hustle."

I didn't really know what a side hustle was, but I was pretty sure I would have noticed if I had one.

The truth was, I couldn't afford an oceanfront property, even if it was a one-bedroom shack with no direct access. A cool old man had given it to me after I helped him a few years back. That was before I joined the police force. Which was good, because he stole some diamonds from a *drittsekk* who deserved to lose some of his diamonds. They were now in an urn on the reef out front of the shack. The diamonds, not the *drittsekk*. But Violet didn't need to know any of that.

"I look after it for a friend," I said, which was close to the truth.

If Archie Winters ever returned, I'd give him his home back.

I tiptoed up the creaky wooden steps, handed Violet her mobile back, and put my key in the lock. Something stirred in one of the chairs on the deck and the light beam swung around.

"Aaaaah!" Violet screamed and then the torch shone all over the place as she clattered back down the steps.

"Will you be quiet!" I hissed. "What's wrong?"

"Come away, quick!" she shouted. "There's a bloody great big lizard on your chair."

The torch beam settled on the chair where a very large blue iguana turned away from the bright light and looked up at me, ready to leap away from danger.

"*Din fjols*. That's Edvard. You scared him."

"What? He's a bloody pet?"

"No. He adopted us, too. He hangs out."

Violet carefully walked up the steps, staying as far away as possible from the native endangered lizard.

"Does he come inside?"

"No. He usually spends the night in the woods."

The door opened without me touching it.

"You're making a lot of noise," Jazzy mumbled sleepily.

"Jazzy, this is Violet. She met Edvard."

"I fed him greens earlier, and he passed out on the chair," Jazzy replied, squinting past me to get a look at our visitor.

I pushed the door open enough to walk inside and Violet followed with her mobile in one hand and her bag of clothes in the other.

"Hey," she said, and Jazzy said hello in return.

I closed the door and turned the light on, seeing as everyone in the place was awake. Violet gazed around the inside of the shack.

"This is pretty cool."

"I know you," Jazzy said, looking at Violet.

Our guest's brow creased. "I don't think we've met."

"You probably don't remember," Jazzy said. "I don't think you were very well at the time."

Violet looked at me, then back at Jazzy. I could see the concern in her eyes.

"Shit. At the school?"

Jazzy nodded.

"Yeah," Violet groaned. "Not my finest moment."

"There's the sofa," I said, pointing out the obvious. "I'll get you a blanket. Bathroom is back there on the right. Let's get some sleep."

The three of us milled around in the small space until everyone had washed, cleaned their teeth, and settled down to sleep. Jazzy and I shared the queen-sized bed as there wasn't enough room for two separate beds in the sleeping area, which was open to the living room and kitchen. I'd thought about getting bunks, but had never done anything more than think about it. I was just about to drop off to sleep when Jazzy nudged me.

"You awake?" she whispered.

"I am now."

"They found her asleep around the back of our main building."

I didn't say anything. I dreaded to hear any more details, but of course the teenager couldn't resist.

"She was stoned or drunk and covered in her own puke. She really stank."

"That's lovely. Go to sleep."

"I'm just saying. I think she's an addict or something."

"I know, Jazzy. And we're helping her."

"Then don't be surprised if our shit's gone along with her in the morning."

I groaned. Jazzy's words sounded like something I'd say, or at least think. And the same thought had crossed my mind during the drive home.

"We both needed a little help once, remember?" I whispered.

There was silence, but I knew the kid was chewing over the situation. I began to drift off to sleep again before Jazzy responded.

"Okay," she said. "If she hasn't nicked all our shit in the morning, I'll do what I can to help her."

11

INSPECTOR INSPECTING

I was up earlier than I'd hoped. Sleeping in wasn't possible with Chloe Pennington missing, Whittaker suspended, and the lochmen case stalling out. I got up to pee at seven and my mind began whirring. After that, it wouldn't let me go back to bed. Jazzy had finally settled into the sleeping habits of a teenager after shaking the overly cautious, light sleeping patterns from her past. In the living room, Violet was a softly purring snore beneath a cocoon of blanket, so our shit appeared to be safe for now.

Not that we had anything much worth stealing. One old laptop, one newer, cheap laptop. A pair of incredibly basic mobile phones. One, actually, as mine was locked in the Jeep at the station. The coffee maker was probably the nicest thing we had. Which I skipped brewing in favour of slipping out the door quietly.

I picked up coffee from Cafe Del Sol, one of my friend AJ's favourite coffee shops, and treated myself to a pastry for breakfast. The streets were quiet on Saturday morning, with a few workers commuting and a couple of tour operators in minibuses on their way to pick up customers. Arriving at Central Station, I retrieved my stuff from the Jeep after parking the crappy car around the back. Weatherford was in his office, and I handed him a coffee and a pastry.

"I shouldn't," he said, patting his prominent stomach. "But thanks. I missed breakfast on the way in."

I sat in the chair opposite and sipped my coffee while he devoured the food.

"How did it go?" he asked, still chewing.

"Fine. I still don't know what they're up to, but it must have to do with extra items for the clients."

"Do they have a menu of some sort?"

"*Nei*. Too smart for that. And it's not a brothel either," I said.

"Legal in Sint Maarten, so not much we could do about it if it was."

"Everything goes through a woman they call Morar. I saw a couple of clients talking to her, but never saw drugs exchange hands or people taken away to another part of the boat."

"Morar? Do you think that could be her real name?" Weatherford asked.

"*Nei*. It's another loch. They have a captain, first mate, and a bartender who also cleans the rooms. They all have loch names. There are two dancers who live on the yacht and they're the only ones without codenames. Although Raven and Shandy probably aren't on their birth certificates, either."

"We have the captain's real name somewhere," the detective replied. "His name and licence have to be on record."

"Doesn't matter," I replied. "I doubt he's involved more than being overpaid for his role and turning the other nose. He may well believe everything's legal."

"Cheek," Weatherford said.

I had no clue what he meant.

"Turn the other cheek, Nora."

"Oh."

I guess that made more sense. It was hard to turn the other of something you only had one of.

"Anyway," Weatherford continued. "From what you're saying, it might be true about the captain."

"*Ja*. It's possible. But let's see what more I can find out tonight."

He nodded. "Okay. What about crippling the boat to get Williams aboard?"

"That's going to be harder than I thought. There are service hatches somewhere to access the engines and mechanicals, but I didn't see them from the areas I was able to move about. The boat is big, but not so big that I can sneak away without someone noticing me."

Weatherford sighed. "I need to pull the plug if we can't have backup in place for you, Nora. Especially based on what you've seen so far. We should focus all our efforts on the Pennington kidnapping. We're still no closer to finding her."

"I can help there," I replied, determined to bring the detective good news so he wouldn't pull me from the boat. We'd managed to get me undercover, so it was worth seeing it through for at least the weekend. "Patrick Pennington is a client. Send uniforms to his place this morning. He'll be crashed out asleep."

"Seriously? The uncle was on *Manannán* last night?"

"*Ja*."

"Did he see you?" Weatherford asked as he picked up his desk phone and dialled an extension.

"Probably, but he wasn't interested in me."

Weatherford raised an eyebrow. "Really? I mean, we work together, so I don't want this to sound weird, but I can't imagine any man not noticing you."

"He likes his women darker and more rounded," I replied, holding my hands well away from my chest for emphasis.

"Oh," Weatherford stammered and blushed.

"Yeah, sorry," he said into the phone. "Sergeant, can you get a couple of West Bay uniforms to drop by and bring Patrick Pennington in for questioning? It's the address someone checked yesterday. He should be there now."

He thanked the sergeant and hung up.

"What about Garner?" I asked.

"Rasha's group in forensics is looking at everything they pulled from the boat yesterday, but nothing so far," Weatherford replied. "I released him last night and had someone tail him. He went home and stayed there."

"Maybe he has Chloe hidden away in the attic," I said.

Garner had lied to us, which was nothing new. Everyone lies to the police. People think we give a shit about their internet browser porn history, or the fact that they smoked a joint at the weekend, and start adjusting the truth to steer us away. But Garner was different. There was something more sleazy about him.

"We searched the house while we held him here. She's not in his attic." Weatherford replied, and must have seen the sceptical look on my face. "Don't worry, he's still on our suspect list."

I nodded. "I have something I need to do."

"On which case?" he asked casually. He seemed curious rather than prying.

"Looking at CCTV. See who put that shit in Whittaker's Range Rover."

Weatherford frowned at me and tilted his head to one side. "You can't be touching Whittaker's case, Nora. You know that."

"Then I'm going to look at CCTV related to the lochmen case, sir."

He shook his head. "Don't get us both in trouble, okay?"

"Never, sir," I replied. "Let me know when you have the uncle here. I'd like to observe."

"I will," he replied and returned to his computer.

As I still wasn't officially a detective, I didn't have a dedicated office, workstation, or even a laptop. I had to use the community computers downstairs, which were open to any officer with a login. It was also a common room with a lot of foot traffic between departments, with no privacy. But it was all I had available, so I settled in and began attempting to retrace the movements of Whittaker's SUV.

The first part was simple. The vehicle had sat in the car park at the station on Thursday from when he arrived until he'd been nabbed in the afternoon. I ran through the station's car park footage but knew it would be a waste of time. It would take someone more stupid than daring to plant anything right out front of the station. Obviously, we'd have cameras, not to mention personnel coming in and out of the building all day.

I watched backwards at high speed until the point when Whittaker arrived, and I noted the time in the morning. He took his bag from the back seat, but didn't access the tailgate. From the direction he drove in and parked, I knew he'd arrived from the west on Elgin. From there, it was a matter of backtracking the route I figured Whittaker had taken from his house. He usually brought a travel mug of coffee from home and ate breakfast with his wife before he left, but I hoped the timing would tell me whether or not that had been his routine on Thursday. It would be a lot easier to ask him, but that option was off the table.

We didn't have government CCTV all over the place on the island, but enough that most major routes passed one or two, and I found the Range Rover on several at the times and places predictable for his drive to work. Of course, I didn't have access to any cameras he had set up at home, if any, and outside his house may well have been the easiest spot for someone to break in. Wherever they did it, the person had to be pretty slick, as the Range Rover had an alarm.

I fast-forwarded through the next camera I found, already growing tired of the monotonous search. Not seeing the SUV, I double-checked the timestamp and reran the footage. No Whittaker. I pulled up the map I'd been using as a guide. He'd passed by the camera on West Bay Road at Lawrence Boulevard but wasn't on the Gecko Link roundabout camera a few minutes before that. I backed up the footage and still nothing for twenty minutes. West Bay Road ran parallel with Esterly Tibbetts Highway along that section of Seven Mile Beach. Gecko and Lawrence were the only two connectors. I hit rewind again. Twenty-seven minutes earlier,

Whittaker turned south from the roundabout. He'd stopped some-where along West Bay Road for over twenty minutes.

"Constable Sommer, isn't it?" a posh English voice came from behind me.

I swung around to see a man I didn't recognise wearing a beige suit. He was older, probably fifties or early sixties, with greying hair and moustache. He looked like a mid-level businessman who'd been looked over a zillion times during his career and would retire having never made manager.

"*Ja,*" I replied, closing the browser window.

"What are you doing?" he asked.

"Why is it your concern?" I replied, but I already had a good idea who I was talking to, so I should probably tread more carefully.

He produced a badge from his pocket. Chief Inspector Leonard Monroe. "My concerns are not your concerns, Constable. What are you doing?"

"I was searching CCTV for a case I'm working on," I said, figuring being evasive was a waste of time, but I'd play the game anyway.

He must have had TSU flag certain files to alert him if someone accessed them. Apparently, I'd set off an alarm.

"Did Detective Weatherford tell you not to work on Detective Whittaker's situation?"

Situation? That struck me as odd phrasing. *Was he gunning for Weatherford now?*

"*Ja.*"

"Then why are you looking through CCTV of Whittaker's route to work?"

"Because he's been set up," I replied, when, of course, I should have kept my mouth shut.

"That's your unbiased evaluation, Constable?"

"Biased doesn't mean I'm wrong. Sir."

I figured it was time to throw in a 'sir' and see if I could start climbing out of this hole I'd dug for myself.

"It is my job to determine what Detective Whittaker was or was not involved in. Not yours, Constable," he said in the flat tone of a schoolteacher, bored after years of delivering the same lessons to a bunch of kids who didn't care. "If I find you misdirecting your time on cases which do not concern you again, then you'll face disciplinary action. Is that completely clear, Constable?"

I sighed. "*Ja.*"

"Are you sure, Constable Sommer? Your words say yes, albeit in Norwegian, but your expression doesn't convince me."

"My face has a mind of its own, sir. But my brain heard you."

His mouth twitched as though he might smile, but he didn't smile. He turned to leave.

"Sir," I said, making myself cringe.

He paused and looked back. "Yes?"

"Have you found out where he was for the missing twenty minutes?"

He drew in a long breath before replying. "Focus on your assigned cases, Constable. No more warnings."

With that, he left, and I closed the windows I had open and logged off the computer.

As I sat there thinking, I couldn't decide whether Monroe had been legitimately protecting the integrity of his investigation or trying to keep certain information buried. In theory, he was doing his job, but why take the time and effort to walk down from wherever he hung from the rafters like a vampire bat to berate me in person? He could have emailed Weatherford, saved himself time, and put his warning on record.

My mobile buzzed, and I checked the message. "Patrick Pennington in interview room now. Make sure he doesn't see you."

Weatherford didn't need to add the last part, but I guess everyone was covering their bases today. I made my way to the viewing room and looked through the one-way glass at Chloe's uncle. I immediately texted Weatherford back.

"Drug test."

I watched the detective look down at his mobile hidden below the table. He typed a reply which popped up on my phone a few moments later.

"Already on it."

I returned my attention to the room, where a bedraggled and very red-eyed man took long gulps of coffee from the paper cup he'd been given.

12

CRASHING THE BLOOD-SUCKING COKE TRAIN

Uncle Patrick looked like daylight was causing thunder claps in his head.

"When did you last speak to your brother?" Weatherford asked.

The man peered over the now empty coffee cup. "Rupert? Yesterday. I think. Why?"

His voice sounded like a gravelly, sleep-deprived version of his brother's.

"Are you sure you spoke with him?"

Patrick shook his head, but quickly stopped. In his state, it had to feel like his brain was slopping around like a poop in a punch bowl. I'd heard that phrase once, or something like it. I'd wondered why anyone would choose to poop in a punch bowl, but Uncle Patrick looked like he'd been smashed enough last night to do it.

"I spoke to him, or texted, maybe."

"And how do you get along with your brother?"

"What?"

Pennington squinted at Weatherford as though he were glowing like a thousand light bulbs.

"Simple question, sir," Weatherford patiently repeated. "How do you and Rupert get along?"

"He's my brother. We get along great. Why am I here, Detective?"

"I'm not sure if you're aware, Mr Pennington," Weatherford continued. "But your niece, Chloe, Rupert's daughter, has been abducted."

"Of course I know," Patrick blathered.

"Yet, unless I'm mistaken, you chose to get blind drunk last night instead of spending time with your family and supporting them."

Ouch. I was impressed Weatherford hit him with a gut punch so soon. A good one, too.

The man finally relinquished the empty cup, misjudging exactly where the table was, so the paper cup fell over and rolled awkwardly back and forth in an arc. Remnants of coffee dribbled onto the surface, while Pennington stared, transfixed by the movement.

"We all handle grief differently, Detective."

"I dare say we do," Weatherford remarked. "Can you describe your relationship with your niece, Chloe?"

Patrick gasped and rubbed his forehead. "Is that what this is about? Chloe? You think I had something to do with Chloe being taken? You're insane."

"Are you close?" Weatherford asked, ignoring the tirade.

"She's my niece, for fuck's sake. Of course we're close!"

The detective remained perfectly calm. "When was the last time you saw Chloe?"

"Whenever I was last over to my brother's house, Detective," Patrick replied in a quieter tone.

I couldn't tell whether his rant had been too painful with his hangover, or he'd realised he wasn't helping himself by getting mad. Probably a bit of both. I'd been surprised he'd arrived without a solicitor in tow, but some people figured they'd seem guilty right away if they lawyered up before a conversation had even started. Uncle Patrick struck me as the misguided type to believe he could handle it himself. I doubted he felt that way now, and it was only a matter of time before he clammed up and spewed the L-word.

"Within the past week, Mr Pennington? Month? Christmas?"

"Who put you up to this?" Patrick asked, leaning forward and tapping the table with a finger. A thought had clearly fallen into his head. "It was her, wasn't it? Rebecca."

Weatherford said nothing.

"That bitch! My brother married a blood-sucking whore who's had it in for me from the beginning."

"Between a week and a month?" Weatherford asked, ignoring Patrick's accusations. "Please answer the question."

Pennington looked off to the side while he gathered his wits. "Something like that. Rupert had a cocktail party three or four weeks ago. I stopped by."

"And Chloe was there?"

Patrick shrugged. "Probably."

"Where were you Thursday lunchtime, Mr Pennington?"

"Here we go again," the man muttered. "I was not taking Chloe from school. I can tell you that."

"Fair enough," Weatherford replied, sounding like he was going to take Patrick's word for it. "If you tell me where you *were*, then we can eliminate you from our inquiries and you'll be free to go."

"Thursday?" he questioned, buying himself time to think it over.

"Yes, sir. Thursday between noon and one."

"I was home. I made lunch for myself at home."

"Anyone else with you to corroborate that, sir?"

He shook his head. "I live alone."

Big surprise. I was sure he attracted plenty of fortune-hunting women, but it wouldn't take them long to figure out he's only as wealthy as his brother allows him to be.

"What is it you do for a living, Mr Pennington?" Weatherford asked.

"Real estate development. Investments. I have many irons in the fires, as they say."

"Do you operate from an office?"

"Don't need the overhead. I can do everything from my condo."

"Any staff?"

"Nope. Waste of money. I handle everything myself."

"Quite the entrepreneur, sir," Weatherford said in the perfect tone, so Pennington couldn't quite tell if he was being condescending or complimentary.

I knew which.

"You're a boat owner, aren't you?" the detective asked.

"I have been. I often buy and sell boats. Nothing in stock right now, but I'm always on the lookout," Patrick replied. "I can get you a great deal on anything you're looking for. Discount for our island's finest."

I groaned. The sleazy salesman side of the idiot couldn't even stay hidden in a police interview.

"One more question before you go about your day, sir. Where were you last night?" Weatherford asked, and I quickly realised we could have a problem.

I texted the detective as fast as my fingers could type. "He can't know we know about the boat."

"Hmm, with a friend on his yacht," Pennington tentatively replied.

"Your friend can attest to that?" Weatherford asked before he glanced down at his mobile.

"Sure."

Weatherford paused but didn't reply to my message. For a moment I wondered if he'd try to pressure Pennington into helping our case. Instead, he stood.

"Thank you for coming in to see us, Mr Pennington."

"I didn't have much choice," he muttered in return as he rose from his seat.

"You're free to go once you've provided us with a blood test for alcohol and narcotics, sir."

Patrick froze. "What? You never said anything about a blood test."

"I'm telling you now, sir. It'll only take a minute. Wait here and I'll have a nurse with you shortly."

"No, no, no," Pennington responded. "I'm calling my solicitor."

Weatherford shrugged his shoulders. "You're welcome to do so. But he'll tell you we have the right to demand a blood test if we suspect illegal narcotics."

Patrick slumped back into the chair.

"I wasn't going to compromise the lochmen operation," Weatherford said as we walked to his car a while later. We'd both been busy with paperwork since leaving the interview. "I wanted to keep the heat on him, and he was clearly hungover from more than booze."

"*Ja,*" I replied, feeling bad for not trusting the detective's judgement.

"It'll be interesting to see the results of his blood test," Weatherford continued once we'd pulled out of the car park. "Sandbar okay for lunch?"

"*Ja,*" I replied to his statement and question. "It'll be cocaine."

"Probably," he agreed and gripped the steering wheel tightly. "We're still nowhere on finding this poor kid and no closer to figuring out what it is the kidnapper wants from Rupert Pennington."

"Patrick might have motive," I pointed out. "Although it's weird he hasn't asked for money. He doesn't have a confirmable alibi either. But he'd need an accomplice."

Weatherford drove to the waterfront and searched for a place to park. It was Saturday morning with two cruise ships in port.

"This was a dumb idea to come this way," he muttered, but finally found a spot.

"What makes you say he'd have to have an accomplice?" he asked as we walked across the street to the casual restaurant overlooking the water.

The ocean looked calm and inviting. I'd rather be diving the reef by my shack than searching for an abducted eleven-year-old. But I'm sure the kid would rather be doing just about anything than what she had going on. I was trying to keep the ticking clock out of my mind, but it was hard not to feel the pressure. Weatherford also had the weight of the new position to deal with. Whittaker usually filtered and deflected the burdens piled on from above in difficult and very public cases. All the responsibility now fell on Vincent's shoulders.

"Luring and planning this took patience," I replied. "Uncle Patrick doesn't have any. And he can say what he wants, but I'm sure Chloe wouldn't hold him in high regard, so why secretly meet with him? Doesn't fit. She was keeping it secret from her best friend. Kids that age share everything with their best friend. This had to be a secret so strange or unique that she wouldn't talk about it."

Weatherford stopped short of the entrance to the restaurant. "I suppose we can't rule out this being sexually motivated," he groaned quietly. "Although I can't bear the thought."

"I don't think it is," I replied, chewing the idea over in my mind. "Chloe could pass for a fourteen or even fifteen-year-old in some of the pictures we've seen, so who knows, but why would the kidnapper make demands?"

Weatherford nodded. "He wouldn't if it was about sex. He'd hide her away and do… whatever it is those freaks do to poor kids."

"*Ja,*" I said, and pushed through the front door.

We ordered quickly and found a seat away from the crowd around the bar. The detective's mobile constantly chirped and beeped as texts and emails piled in and he tried his best to keep up with each one. More bogus sightings, Rupert Pennington asking for updates, and then the one we'd been expecting.

"That's the fastest result I've ever seen from a blood test," he said, reading a text. "Not the full report, but they confirmed his blood alcohol level is still over the legal limit and cocaine in his system."

I nodded. It was good to have the confirmation, but now we had a new problem.

"Patrick Pennington has dropped himself into both cases," I said.

"Yeah. That's a conundrum for us," Weatherford replied.

I wasn't sure what a conun-drum was, but if it meant screwed up, he was right.

"If we bust him for the coke, it might scare off the lochmen," Weatherford continued, echoing my thoughts. "But if there's a chance he's involved in Chloe's kidnapping, then we need to keep squeezing him."

"We could try making a deal with him to help us with the lochmen," I suggested.

"Would you trust him?"

"*Nei.*"

"Me neither," Weatherford said, and we both stopped talking as our food arrived.

My fish tacos looked good, and I realised I was quite hungry. And tired. I didn't need to be showing up on *Manannán* with bags under my eyes.

"Do you think he'll be back on the boat tonight if we release him?" Weatherford asked.

I shrugged as I chewed a bite of taco. "He'll want to."

The detective's mobile rang, and he quickly gulped down a mouthful of sandwich before answering.

"Weatherford."

I couldn't hear the other side of the conversation, but I watched Vincent's eyebrows rise as he listened.

"Okay. Thanks for letting me know. Call me back if you find anything else."

He ended the call and looked at me.

"Half a kilo of cocaine in Patrick's condo."

"That takes a possession up to a distribution charge," I responded.

Weatherford nodded. "We can't release him now."

We ate in silence for a few minutes with a cool breeze off the ocean making the hot, humid summer day bearable. I kept running the situation over in my mind. Nothing quite added up, but new possibilities seemed to be emerging.

"From what Rupert and Rebecca said, Patrick doesn't have money, right?" I said.

"We can get a warrant to pull his bank records now," Weatherford replied, pushing his empty plate away. "But yeah, they made it sound like he was skint. Mind you, people like him fall into money here and there, then blow it and scramble to scrounge up more. I bet his account balance is like a saw blade."

"What if his drugs came from the *Manannán*?" I suggested. "He's raising money from distributing here on the island. Could be his evenings on the boat are rolled into the deal."

"It's possible," Weatherford agreed. "Are you still thinking we turn him in trade for leniency?"

"*Nei*. You're right. We can't trust him not to screw it up. Besides, if he's collecting the drugs in international waters, we still have an issue nicking them."

"Cocaine distribution is illegal in Sint Maarten," Weatherford said.

"Of course, but it'll be a plane wreck nicking them out there."

"Train wreck."

"What?" I asked.

"It'll be a train wreck is the phrase," Weatherford said with a laugh.

"Why? A plane crash is a big mess."

"I didn't invent the phrase, Nora. But it's train wreck. They make a big mess too."

"Fine. It'll be a big mess with trains, planes, and even a boat."

"Yup. But then all we can do is arrest Patrick when he returns with coke on him. We can do that now," Weatherford said.

"The lochmen don't overnight on the yacht. They come back and forth and stay on the island. All three will be on the tender bringing Uncle Patrick home."

"It would be his word against theirs," the detective said thoughtfully. "They'd claim he must have brought it with him."

"Yeah. Which is why I need to witness the exchange."

"Hmm. From what you said, that won't be easy."

"I'll try harder tonight."

Weatherford looked at me, and I could see he was concerned. No shit. He had plenty to be worried about. But we might have stumbled across our best way of catching the lochmen, and we couldn't miss the opportunity.

The detective picked up his mobile and made a call.

"Sergeant. Was the coke well hidden in the condo?"

I waited, unable to hear the response.

"Okay. Get pictures of everything, then put it back. And make sure it appears you never found it."

13

FOLLOW HIS ARSE

"Why are we driving back this way?" Weatherford asked for the third time.

Probably because he knew I'd given him a BS answer twice already.

"We have too much to do back at the station to be running around town on a wild goose chase."

"Pull over here," I said as we passed the junction with Lawrence Boulevard.

He growled and mumbled something under his breath, but pulled to the left and turned his hazard lights on.

"The CCTV picks Whittaker up again here, sir," I explained. "Somewhere beyond the tunnel ahead and before the next camera at Gecko Link, he stops for over 20 minutes."

Weatherford thought for a moment, but I could see by his brow creasing and his shoulders relaxing that his focus had shifted to what I'd just told him.

"And you know this how?"

"I looked at the CCTV."

"You're supposed to stay completely away from Whittaker's case, Nora."

"That's what Monroe said."

Weatherford's head whipped around, and he stared at me. "Monroe talked to you?"

"He caught me searching the CCTV."

The detective blew out his cheeks. "Shit. And yet here we are investigating Whittaker's missing twenty minutes. Thanks, Nora. I appreciate you tanking my career along with yours."

His tone was dead serious, but he rolled his eyes.

"Most things I prefer doing alone, sir, but sometimes it's nice to have someone with you."

He laughed. "You're a piece of work, young lady," he said, and pulled out onto West Bay Road again, continuing north.

We passed under the tunnel. Or bridge. I could never decide what it was except a mass of concrete along an otherwise pleasant stretch of road behind Seven Mile Beach. A big-time developer had talked the government into letting him construct the monstrosity as a means for people to walk from Camana Bay on the North Sound to Seven Mile Beach, crossing over the top. A similar tunnel/bridge thing covered the bypass in front of Camana Bay, although the land in between was yet to be meaningfully developed.

In the 200 metres before the Gecko Link roundabout, we had multi-million dollar oceanfront condo complexes on our left, and businesses on our right. A fast-food restaurant, petrol station, and a U-shaped shopping plaza. Weatherford slowed to a stop again.

"Whittaker doesn't eat fast food," he said. "Could have filled up with petrol?"

"For 23 minutes?"

"Unlikely, but possible. Could have got a phone call while he was there," Weatherford suggested.

"We're looking for someone's opportunity to slip the drugs and money in the back of his Range Rover," I replied. "Pretty ballsy to do that in the courtyard of a petrol station."

A horn honked from behind us and Weatherford glanced in the rear-view mirror. It would be an impatient tourist. Locals only honked to say hello or thank you. He pulled to the centre turn lane and the white hire car Jeep sped past with an arm hanging out the window, gesturing their frustration.

"Hasn't settled into the island way just yet," Weatherford said, accentuating his Caymanian lilt.

He turned into the Galleria Shopping Plaza and drove slowly between the parking spots. It was like a square, with the main road forming one side, and shops and businesses the other three. A building filled the centre like a hole in a doughnut. Restaurants, real estate companies, a bookshop, hair salon, a discount shop, and several other retailers filled the spaces. None of the restaurants were open in the mornings for breakfast. They all began serving at lunchtime.

"Meeting an estate agent?" Weatherford wondered.

"Not at seven in the morning, sir. I don't think estate agents get out of bed that early."

"I wish we could just ask him," the detective muttered. "Be a lot easier."

"He won't discuss it with us," I replied. "He's relying completely on Monroe to figure it out."

"And hopefully he will," Weatherford said, driving back to West Bay Road. "If he hadn't looked at the CCTV you found, then at least he has it now. He'll be asking Roy why he stopped."

I looked back over my shoulder as we rejoined the traffic flowing south. "That car park would be empty at seven in the morning," I thought aloud. "But unless Whittaker went inside somewhere, there'd be no opportunity to plant the stuff in the Range Rover."

Weatherford tapped on the driver's side window. "What if he met someone on the beach side?"

Both options, The Sovereign and the Cayman Club, were private beachfront condo buildings. The Sovereign was gated and the Cayman Club had a guard shack.

"You know they have CCTV we could ask to see," I groaned. "If it wasn't for Chief Inspector Leonard Monroe breathing down my face."

Weatherford looked over at me and laughed. "Neck, Nora. Breathing down your neck."

"He was breathing down my face when I saw him."

The detective's mobile dinged once more, and he unlocked it and handed me the device.

"See who emailed."

"You have three new ones," I said, opening his police-issued email. "The first one is from the chief, telling you to give me a raise."

Weatherford laughed. "More likely, Monroe telling me to suspend your ass."

That was far closer to being a possibility.

"We have Chloe's phone records," I said, seeing the newest email.

"Finally," the detective enthused. "We need a break in this damn case."

I had a pretty good idea that the mobile phone records wouldn't give us anything, but I scrolled through the call and text list anyway. TSU had identified the numbers and noted names beside the logs.

"Parents and best friend on the call list," I read aloud. "Texts are mainly to her friend, a few other friends they've identified as classmates, and her mum. Nothing suspicious in the past two weeks."

Weatherford slapped the steering wheel. "Damn."

"WhatsApp," I said, scrolling back through the list beyond the two weeks, because I had the time to do it.

"WhatsApp?" he echoed. "Oh, right. She used WhatsApp instead of texting."

"Probably. So without being able to look at her actual mobile phone, we can't see who she chatted with or what they said. WhatsApp encryption even keeps the company from seeing them."

Weatherford shook his head and ran his hand through his hair. "Which leaves us nowhere. Still."

Shortly after arriving back at the station, Weatherford got a call from the officers searching Patrick's condo, saying they were done. I was careful to stay out of the way while Uncle Patrick was released, watching from behind the reception counter in the lobby.

"You need more clothes, girl?" Chantel asked, looking me over. "You look respectable today, like you a policewoman or someting."

She laughed heartily.

"I'll bring the leggings and shirt back tomorrow," I replied. "Haven't washed them yet."

"Dat's fine," she said, trying to see what I was looking at. "What da hell you up to? Fancy someone out dere or someting?"

I couldn't understand why she'd think that. If I fancied someone, I wouldn't sneak around spying on them like a schoolgirl with a crush.

"No. Be quiet. We're releasing a suspect, and he can't see me."

"Why? You gonna follow dis guy?" she asked, lowering her volume by less than I'd hoped.

"No. But he'll see me later and he can't know I'm a copper."

I watched Weatherford walk Patrick Pennington to the middle of the lobby. I couldn't hear exactly what they were saying, but their body language gave the gist away. Patrick had his hands on his hips and his cheeks glowed with anger. The detective was calm and repeatedly thanked the man for his cooperation.

"He fine, dat one," Chantel said. "I wouldn't mind me a piece o' him."

"He's a suspect in a kidnapping and probably a drug dealer," I pointed out.

I suppose Patrick was decent looking, but I certainly couldn't see him that way.

"You investigatin' Weatherford now?" Chantel squawked. "First it Whittaker, and now my man Vincent? No way. Dey both fine men."

"Will you shut up?" I growled. "Not Weatherford. The other guy's our suspect."

"Oh. Den why you lettin' him go, sister?"

Patrick stomped towards the front door, and Weatherford shook his head as he watched him leave. I hurried to the office window. Patrick stood outside and looked at the time on his mobile before shoving it back in his pocket then looking around.

"He da one take da girl?" Chantel asked, arriving right beside me.

"Maybe."

"Den why you not following his ass?"

"I don't need to follow his arse. I know where he'll be later."

That was a stretch. I didn't *know*. I had a theory and was betting on the man's addictive nature. He'd want more of Raven and her bountiful assets to make himself feel better.

"Dat when you put your hoochie-mama outfit back on?"

"*Ja*," I muttered. "Then I take it off," I added.

"You do what?" Chantel began, then pressed her nose to the glass. "Who dat now?" she asked as we watched a Jaguar SUV pull up and stop next to Patrick.

"His brother," I said, spotting Rupert behind the wheel.

Patrick climbed in the passenger side and immediately the two men launched into an animated argument. We couldn't hear anything, but arms waved, and both men were clearly shouting at each other. After a few moments, Rupert must have remembered he was still sitting in front of a police station and sharply drove away, taking their disagreement out of our sight.

I rushed to the lobby and caught Weatherford before he went upstairs. I passed on what I'd seen with the Penningtons and we both agreed we had no idea what it meant, but it was worth filing away. After going over a plan for that evening on the *Manannán*, with Patrick and the lochmen, I left to go home. I had just over four hours before I needed to be at the dock with Violet, who I'd not heard a word from all day. I chose to take that as a good sign. But it could mean Jazzy was tied up in the shack and all our shit was gone.

Driving the pile-of-bolts car instead of my Jeep to save time, I sweated and bounced my way home. The AC didn't work and at least one of the tyres was more square than round from being locked up. Or more likely dragged when the car had been towed to our yard.

I discovered Jazzy was not tied up when I reached the shack. She was sitting on the deck with Violet, listening to some awful rap music playing from our guest's mobile. Edvard was nowhere to be seen. He had better taste in music.

"Hey," I greeted them.

"Hey," Jazzy replied, and Violet turned the music down before speaking.

"You left early."

"*Ja*. Work."

"I keep forgetting you're a copper," Violet laughed. "Bloody weird, to be honest. I've spent most of my life avoiding the likes of you."

I decided not to return the sentiment, although it would mostly be true.

"I need to get some sleep before we leave," I said, and started towards the front door.

"I was thinking of diving," Jazzy said, and I stopped.

She had taken an interest in both scuba diving and freediving lately, which were passions of mine, so it made me happy. My friend AJ was certifying her for the scuba diving, and Jazzy had come out freediving with me several times. I was a terrible teacher, but I hadn't scared her off yet.

I weighed up the benefits of sleep versus a therapeutic dive on the reef, and came to an easy decision.

"I'll get changed." I looked at Violet. "Are you coming?"

"I don't have a bathing suit."

"I have one you can wear," I replied and continued inside.

We weren't the same size, but close enough. I was much taller, but our hips were about the same. She'd stretch my top out a little, but the Lycra would survive.

Twenty minutes later, we swam out from the tiny old marina

left over from the Spanish Bay Reef Resort, which had been demolished years before.

"How far are we going?" Violet asked nervously. "I've only been snorkelling once before and we didn't go this far out."

"To the reef," Jazzy replied, swimming on her back.

"But I could see tons of fish back there," Violet complained. "It's getting pretty deep."

"That's the point," Jazzy replied with a laugh. "The cool stuff's out there."

"Define cool stuff?" she replied, dipping her mask in the calm, warm water to see what was below us. "Aren't there sharks and shit out there?"

"Hopefully," Jazzy teased.

The sandy sea floor gave way to the coral reef, shaped like fingers pointing towards the deep water. I continued until I recognised a big orange sponge below us. This section of reef was usually teeming with life and from what I could see through the gin-clear water, today was no different. I'd been working air in and out of my lungs on the swim out, and now held a deep breath before dipping below the surface.

The weight belt around my waist offset the buoyant air in my lungs and I gently kicked my fins to descend, pinching my nose to clear the pressure from my sinuses as I went. Ten metres down, I stopped just above the sand in the ravine between two fingers of coral. A thousand colourful little fish zipped around the reef formations and sea fans swayed in the barely perceptible surge.

Closing my eyes, I let the silence of the underwater world pull the anxiety and stress from my day. I opened them again as I felt Jazzy brush my arm as she arrived at my side. She grinned, but I could see she wasn't able to relax during her dives yet. That came with experience and the confidence that the air in your lungs would allow you to stay down for several minutes at a time.

We both looked up, and Violet waved down at us from the surface. Her eyes were wide and amazed at the world she could see. A part of our planet most people could only visit through a television or computer screen.

Maybe this would be a step towards Violet finding a way to break the cycle of self-destruction she'd become hopelessly caught up in. Knowing there was more to this world than drink, drugs, poverty, and strangers' beds. For a moment, I was consumed by an uncharacteristic feeling of optimism. If people like Jazzy and me could find our way to a better life, perhaps Violet could too. Regardless, it felt like we were doing the right thing by at least trying to help. And maybe she wouldn't screw up my undercover operation. Or steal all our shit.

14

SEA GODS AND UNHAPPY FISH

Violet nattered on while we rode out to *Manannán*. My mind bounced between my task ahead, Whittaker, and Chloe Pennington. My concern over the kid was beginning to cause an anxiety which would do nothing to help find her. Usually, I could separate myself from the cases and remain objective, but the missing kid was different. I had no reason to care so much about a rich girl who would probably annoy the *dritt* out of me – beyond basic empathy, of course. So maybe it was her age, or perhaps that I'd never had a case like this before.

The kidnapper had sent a new recording shortly before I'd left the shack. Weatherford had forwarded it to me.

"Chloe is going to die in three days unless you publicly confess, Pennington. You know what I'm talking about. Reveal your secret or watch your daughter die."

We'd not had time to discuss it before I'd left home, and I didn't want to talk about the case in front of Violet, so it would have to wait until morning. But the message felt different to me. Not that it came from a different person. More urgency, which was to be expected, I supposed. Everyone was feeling the clock ticking as we continued to make no progress.

Which brought my thoughts around in a circle to Detective Whittaker. Apart from being a mentor and father figure to me, he was also the policeman I'd learned the most from. He'd always been there with a plan or a method, or at least an idea of what to do next. Vincent Weatherford was a fine detective, and I trusted him. But we both knew we were working with one leg tied behind our backs.

Or an arm? Maybe a hand.

It didn't feel like there was enough time left in Chloe's case to clear Whittaker's name and have him officially reinstated. So I needed to find a way to get my boss involved in a way he felt comfortable doing. Given he'd made it clear he was playing strictly by the rules, I had no idea how to cross that line.

"What does mananananana, or whatever it is, mean?" Violet asked as the tender eased to the stern of the yacht.

"Manannán is a mythological Scottish sea god," I replied.

She looked at me as though I'd sprouted horns.

"How the bloody hell do you know that?"

"I Googled it," I replied, stepping to the platform where Morar waited to greet us with her seemingly permanently stern expression. She struck me as being quite Nordic for a Hispanic.

"Hey," I said, carrying my bag past her.

Morar acknowledged me with a nod, but was more interested in Violet. I went up the steps to the aft deck and paused, looking back down. Morar gave Violet a similar nod, but I figured she was checking to make sure the girl wasn't wrecked.

I continued through the salon to where Shandy and Raven lounged in a pair of the loveseats.

"What's my Finnish word of da day?" Raven asked with a grin.

I thought for a moment. My Finnish vocabulary pool wasn't very deep and my philosophy of no one else speaking Finn was potentially backfiring on me.

"*Perkele.*"

"Perky what?" Raven repeated with her island accent, then laughed. "What does that mean?"

"It says you're frustrated," I said. "But more rude."

"Perky lee," she said again.

"*Perkele*," I responded.

"*Perkele*," Raven echoed more closely. "And it means damn it, or someting like dat?"

"Something like that." It was a little harsher, but close enough.

Raven laughed again and lowered her voice, looking over at Shandy. "I'm gonna use dat next time dat creep Maree tries puttin' his pudgy little hands on me."

"Hi," Violet said as she joined us.

"You lookin' all happy today, princess," Shandy said in a careful tone, making it hard to determine if she was being nice or condescending.

"I went snorkelling," Violet replied proudly. "We had fun."

Raven shook her head. "You seen what down dere, girl? You ain't getting my tasty ass bobbin' on top for some damn shark to come nibblin' pieces off dese curves."

I smiled and made my way down the passageway towards the berth we'd been assigned the night before. Dinner would be served shortly, and I had a little over an hour to figure out how to access the engines before the clients showed up. I paused by the galley, where Katrine was preparing the meal. They certainly got their money's worth out of her. She cooked, cleaned, and bartended, all of which could be considered full-time jobs on their own.

"Smells good," I said, because it did, and I wanted to get to know her better.

Something told me Katrine was somewhat oblivious to all that went on in the background, but maybe I was being naïve, as I liked her in the little we'd interacted so far.

"Thanks," she replied in what I took to be an Irish accent. "Fresh snapper the captain caught today."

"I hope they pay you well," I said. "You're always busy."

She shrugged her shoulders. "I used to work on a liveaboard dive boat, so I'm used to the hours. I make money for three or four months, sometimes six, then travel for myself."

"If you get time off, let's go diving. I know a few good places."

"You dive? Very cool," she replied, wiping her forehead as she worked. "I'd like that. Usually Mondays, but then sometimes we move on that day too. I never know the schedule until it happens."

"Makes it fun stocking the galley," I said.

She laughed. "They get frozen pizzas when they surprise me with a move day before I've restocked."

"We'll shoot for Monday," I said, and continued down the hall. I wasn't sure how I'd pull off a rendezvous on the island, but I hoped to have this case wrapped by then, anyway. More importantly, I might need Katrine on my side before this was over with.

Our berth was just as we'd left it except it had been cleaned, judging by the smell of flowery disinfectant, and whatever clothes we'd left to be cleaned were folded and left on the chairs. I unpacked my bag and put the laundry away, which took only a few minutes, then left the berth in search of engine room access.

The yacht was a catamaran, with all the major machinery housed in the two hulls resting in the water. The *Manannán*'s beam was around eight and a half metres, with a little over two metres' width in each hull, leaving four metres between them. Standing in the passageway of the lower deck meant there was only air between the floor and the Caribbean Sea. Somewhere along either side of the yacht was an access large enough for a mechanic to climb through.

I walked to the salon. Katrine had vacated the galley, and by the looks of the food preparation, all she had left to finish the meal was grilling the fish. She wouldn't be long. I could see Raven and Shandy on the aft deck beyond the sliding doors, smoking cigarettes. Which was exactly where I'd planned to start searching. I'd spotted multiple hatches and compartments when we'd walked in, all neatly nestled flush with the decking, their handles recessed. There was no point going out there now, so I looked around the salon.

Next to the bar, at the base of the stairs leading up to the second level, a door with rounded corners caught my eye. On the port side was a similar door, which appeared to open to a cupboard. Except I could see both doors had far beefier handles than required for a cupboard. At first I thought they might be mechanical panels or chutes for air conditioning ducts or wiring, but as I stepped closer, I saw the watertight seal.

Moving to the door on the port side, the farthest away from the stairs and least visible by the girls at the stern, I tried the handle. The moment the door opened, the sound of the diesel engine idling hit me and I smelled oil and the faint whiff of exhaust. It was dark inside, but the light from the salon was enough for me to see the large hole in the floor leading down to the hull.

"What do you think you're doing?" came Morar's voice from behind me.

I startled inside, but managed to softly close and latch the door before turning around.

"I thought it might be a loo," I replied with a laugh. "But it's not a loo."

"No, it's not, and you shouldn't be snooping around the boat," she snapped. "You have a head in your berth."

"Yeah, Violet has turned it into Chernobyl, so I was looking for somewhere else to pee," I said, coming up with the best excuse I could think of.

Morar wrinkled her nose. "By the stairs, opposite the galley, is the salon head for the guests."

"*Kiitos*," I said, and walked to the loo, although I didn't need to use it.

Fortunately, when I came out a few minutes later, having flushed and washed my hands for no reason, Katrine was back.

"Dinner in five minutes," she told Morar, so I offered to make sure Violet was ready to eat.

My roommate was still sorting through her clothes, so I told her we needed to be upstairs in a few minutes, then sat in my chair and thought about my discovery. I couldn't imagine how it would be possible for me to sneak into one of the engine rooms during the time they allowed me while aboard. There was always someone in the salon or too close to risk being caught. Not to mention I'd return stinking of diesel fumes. Hardly the stripper's perfume of choice. And I still had no idea exactly how to disable the vessel in a way they wouldn't realise was sabotage and required outside help. *Faen*, I muttered to myself. I needed a better plan.

"What's that?" Violet asked, so I guess I'd cursed louder than I'd intended.

"Dinner time," I replied, rising from the chair. "Let's go."

We walked down the passageway into the salon and looked out the sliding doors at the beautiful sky on the horizon, bathed in the orange hues of sunset.

"Can we snorkel out here?" Violet asked as we ascended the stairs.

I laughed. "Sure. You won't see anything unless a few fish swim by."

"There's no reef out here?"

"No. The sea floor is 6,000 feet below us," I said, using the imperial number she'd understand more than metric.

"No shit," she exclaimed. "That's creepy."

But I didn't hear her reply. I was too busy trying to picture nautical charts in my head.

Dinner was nice. Grilled fish again. I think everyone enjoyed it. Except the fish. I never saw the captain or first mate, but whoever was on duty took their food in the bridge, as I noticed Katrine carrying a plate in that direction. I needed to talk to the captain, or to Ness.

At 8:00pm the RIB arrived, and I looked to see who was aboard. Eleven men and two women filed through the sliding doors. The head count was up. And Patrick was back. So was David, who made a wasp-line for me. Wasp-line didn't sound right. Some flying bug line. Regardless, he was standing in front of me, so I had to talk to him instead of analysing the crowd.

"Good evening, Viivi."

"Hey, David," I replied.

His eyebrows raised slightly in surprise as I'd remembered his name. It was an old trick, but usually worked.

"Would you mind if I spent time with you again this evening?" he asked, like I had a choice in the matter.

"You don't have bad breath, so I'd like that," I replied.

He laughed and pulled a small tin of breath mints from his pocket. "I try to be respectful."

I ran on autopilot. If I allowed thoughts of my prior life in the private gentleman's club to seep into my mind, I knew I'd freak out, so I stayed focused on the case. I'd never been good at pretending to be sexy, so I was lucky several of the clients were happy looking at me performing like a robot. At least I felt that way.

After dancing in the first two rotations, I finally had the opportunity to take a break. The lochmen were absent, as they had been the night before, but Morar was watching everything and everyone like a buzzard. Or eagle. *Dritt*, I needed to give up on these stupid English phrases.

I used the loo, then moved to the bar and had Katrine hand me a bottle of water.

"You're good at this," the Irishwoman said.

"*Kiitos*," I replied. "I think. Not really something to put on my CV."

Katrine laughed. "Unless you're applying for more jobs like this."

I smiled. "True."

Movement on the aft deck caught my eye, and I spotted Patrick beyond the sliding doors. It was dark outside, but the accent lights were enough for me to see that he was talking with Ness. Actually, from his body language, I'd say he was arguing with the man. After a few moments, Ness shook his head, prodded a finger in Patrick's chest, then slid the door open and came inside. Pennington stayed on the aft deck and swigged the remainder of whatever was in the tumbler in his hand.

"I have a question," I said as Ness walked past me on his way to the stairs.

He stopped and leaned on the bar.

"Drink?" Katrine asked.

He sighed. "Sure."

Katrine must have known his preferred alcohol as she stepped away to pour him his drink, and he turned to me.

"What's your question?"

"Why do you motor around out here, running the engines all the time?"

He scoffed. "Do you know how deep the sea is here?"

"I do. I know you can't anchor here," I replied. "So why don't you go somewhere you can anchor?"

Katrine handed him a scotch over ice, and he took a sip before responding.

"Because we need to remain in international waters, which I'm sure you've realised," he said, eyeing me cautiously. "You're a smart one. You knew that, right?"

"That I'm smart, or that the boat has to stay beyond twelve miles?"

He laughed. "Both, I suppose."

"*Juu*," I replied. "But you can anchor more than twelve miles offshore."

"Where?" he asked. "It's this deep or more all around Grand Cayman."

"Twelve Mile Bank."

"It's in international waters?" he asked, taking more of an interest.

"*Juu*."

"How deep is it?"

"Thirty-five to forty metres."

"Shit. We could anchor there."

I raised an eyebrow to emphasise that this was the point I was making.

"Okay. I'll have the captain check the charts," he said before downing the rest of his scotch.

He started up the stairs, but I heard him muttering under his breath. "And he better have a good reason why a stripper is telling me this instead of him."

I grinned to myself. Internal conflict in the group was good. It could lead to mistakes. And I knew something I hoped they wouldn't realise about Twelve Mile Bank. If they got caught up in how much money they'd save on diesel, then my new plan might have a chance.

15

CRACK WHORES AND HOODIES

The rest of the evening dragged by slowly. Shandy called Morar over when a guy got too handy after one too many drinks, and she had Lomond come down to have a word with the man. Reasoning with drunk people was like having a conversation with a foreign person who doesn't speak your language. There are lots of words endlessly repeated and vigorous gesticulations, but nothing gets accomplished. Saying things more slowly or with goofy accents doesn't help. In the end, the man was invited upstairs, where he remained for the rest of the evening, only to reappear when the RIB left for shore.

I wasn't certain where Patrick went after his heated discussion with Ness, but he too turned up when it was time to be shuttled home. The touchy-feely guy had sobered since he'd disappeared. Pennington had not. Wherever he'd been, they'd kept him lubricated.

We took showers and helped Katrine clean up the salon while Violet and I waited for the RIB to return. It was another inefficiency on their part that the lochmen hadn't bought a more suitable tender or modified the one they had. If the vessel had even a small cabin of any kind, the girls could be taken ashore without interacting with the clients and saved Lomond and company 24 miles of wasted time and petrol. But I wasn't here to fix their business model.

Before the tender returned, Morar got us together and distributed our tip money. Somehow, I came out on top, probably thanks to David, who'd been generous. And because Patrick had been removed from stuffing cash in any place he could manage on Raven. She looked surprised she'd come in second, but I didn't get the sense she was mad about it. Morar, on the other hand, was not happy with Violet.

"Someone always has to come in last for tips," she said, not making any effort to sound sympathetic. "But you're well below the others."

"I'm sorry," Violet stuttered, looking mortified to be singled out. "I'll do better, I promise."

"Do better how?" Morar asked. "Are you saying you haven't been trying to be nice to the customers? Or you can improve your dancing?"

"Dat ain't da problem," Raven said flatly. "Viivi colder dan penguin poop and she makin' cash like Taylor Swift."

"What do I need to do, then?" Violet asked.

"You gotta not look like a crack whore," Shandy said. "Dat's what."

I cringed. Violet's mouth fell open, but nothing came out. She turned to Morar, but she just shrugged.

"I can't help the way I look," Violet finally whimpered.

"Some you can, girl," Raven said. "You pasty like a damn snowball. You livin' in da Caribbean. Get your lily-white ass in the sun sometime."

"Not just your face," Shandy added, bringing attention to Violet's slightly sunburnt cheeks from our snorkelling.

Tears fell down her bright red face, made worse by her embarrassment.

"If you can't improve tomorrow night's earnings," Morar said with an air of finality, "then it'll be your last day."

I wondered whether 'last day' meant not invited back or not provided transport home like they'd threatened at the beginning. The lochmen couldn't risk having disgruntled former employees making noises while they were still working the island. Or if they planned on returning. Presumably their business plan meant circling various islands, which they'd repeat after a while.

"I'll help her," I said. "She'll be okay."

Violet clutched my arm as though I were the only thing between the world and a precipice to hell. She wiped away the tears with her other hand, and I was glad to hear the RIB pull up outside.

The ride back was solemn, and I noticed the wind was stronger tonight, which picked the seas up a little. Not rough, but a change. Violet huddled next to me, shivering the entire way despite being wrapped in a sweatshirt.

"You need a windbreaker," I told her. "The chill air goes straight through what you're wearing."

"I feel so stupid," she groaned into my shoulder.

"You don't know these things if you haven't spent time on boats."

"I don't mean the bloody jacket," she sniffled. "I screwed up again."

"It'll be okay," I said, although I wasn't sure how it would be.

"I finally have a gig which earns good money without having to be screwed, and I'm blowing it." She laughed. "Without that too."

Maybe she was forgetting I was an undercover copper whose sole aim was to nick these people and make the stripper yacht go away, but it probably wouldn't help to point that out.

"We'll get some of that fake tan *dritt* tomorrow and do something different with your hair. You'll make more than anyone."

"Maybe a wig? Like you," she said, which reminded me I couldn't wait to get the damn thing off.

"Sure. Good idea," I replied, and she seemed to settle down for the remainder of the ride.

"Hey," Ness said as I was about to climb out when we tied up to the dock.

"*Juu?*"

"I talked to the captain. You were right about Twelve Mile Bank."

I nodded. "Good. The yacht will ride smoother anchored with the current."

"How did you know about it?" he asked.

"I dive. We go out there sometimes."

He stared at me for a few moments. "How come you're doing this?"

"Because it'll be better for everyone," I replied.

"Not the moving the boat thing," he replied. "This gig."

I shrugged. "Money."

"Sure, but you're smart. You know you could land one of these rich guys and have him paying for you to live the life." He nodded towards Seven Mile Beach. "Shit, you could be hooked up in one of these multi-million dollar condos along the water. But I've seen that piece of shit car you show up in. So why are you doing this?"

"Because it's on my terms. Nobody else's," I replied, coming up with the best answer I could conjure in the moment. "I work something like this for a while, tend bar and make decent cash, then dive Twelve Mile Bank without some middle-aged wanker grabbing my arse."

Ness laughed. "Fair enough." He leaned closer. "If you'd like to do a run on the yacht for a while, I reckon I can see to it."

My eyes inadvertently flicked towards Violet, waiting on the dock.

Ness scoffed. "Think about it. But don't say a fucking word to her."

"Okay," I said, and forced a brief smile.

I needed him to think I was flattered and considering his offer, as opposed to how I really felt. Thoughts of where to stick my Taser were flashing through my mind. Violet was a major screw-up, but she was still a human being with feelings that people had obviously stomped on throughout her life. People had to stand up and help themselves at some point, but I was witnessing how difficult that could be once you'd been knocked down enough times.

"Six tomorrow evening," Ness said as I stepped to the dock.

"*Juu*," I called back before Violet looped an arm through mine as we walked away.

I paused, gripping the door handle and contemplating what I was about to do. I was tired with too many things spinning in my mind, and if I screwed this stupid plan up, I'd be kicked off the force at a minimum. It was four in the morning. I'd slept for two hours before sneaking out of the shack without waking the other two. That wasn't hard. Jazzy was used to my weird hours from changing shifts, and Violet had the ability to sleep soundly whenever the opportunity arose.

Already sweating from the layers of clothes I was wearing, I slipped the dark baseball cap on and covered it with the hood of the black sweatshirt. Making sure my ponytail was completely hidden, I pulled the stretchy bandana up to cover everything except my eyes, which would remain shadowed by the hood and cap. Black neoprene dive gloves finished off my stealth outfit.

I'd parked half a kilometre north in a car park off West Bay Road and now hurried through the public access path to the beach, then turned south. The beach was deserted and only occasionally lit by accent lights from the various beachfront condo complexes. Reaching the Cayman Club, I stayed close to the trees lining the north side of the property and moved inland alongside the buildings in the dark. Nearing the corner, I was looking ahead at the lights on the circular driveway when I tripped over something hidden in the grass. Barely staying on my feet, I stumbled forward, and a cat screeched as it took off ahead of me. I stopped and caught my breath. I hadn't tripped over the cat, but I must have startled it, which in turn had scared us both to death.

Once again, I questioned whether this was the smartest thing to be doing, but I convinced myself I was committed, and it was too late to turn back. Which was bullshit, as I could have returned to the car the way I'd come and no one would be the wiser. But I didn't do that. Instead, I eased around the corner and ran across the courtyard of the main entrance to where cars were parked nose in around the island in the middle of the driveway. Palm trees lined the central island and neatly trimmed shrubs completed the land-scaping. The security hut was hidden on the far side, closer to the road. Facing the main entrance was a small building which appeared to be the gym.

Ducking behind a palm tree, I weighed my options. Break into a car, or the gym. Of the three cars nearest to me, two were hire cars, and one was an older compact of some sort with fading silver paint. Probably the security guard's vehicle. The hire cars would belong to visitors renting units for a week or two. I didn't want to cause the guard any trouble, and it would probably be a big hassle for the tourists to deal with the insurance, so I turned to the gym.

Pulling out my lock-picking kit, I moved to the door and crouched down. Fumbling in the dark, it took a little longer than I'd like, but after a few minutes, the lock clicked open and I slipped inside. *Now what?* It wasn't like I could steal a dozen dumbbells, or walk out with a treadmill. I realised for the umpteenth time what a half-arsed shitty plan I'd come up with and looked outside at the hire cars again. The closest one was an SUV and I could see a base-ball hat on the dashboard. It had 'Shut Up and Do Me' embroidered on the front. What kind of douchebag wears a hat like that? The hat alone should ensure, what I presumed to be a guy, didn't get screwed, so I decided to oblige him. The bloke deserved the hassle of dealing with an insurance company.

Taking a small dumbbell, I stepped outside and smashed the passenger side window. I knew it wouldn't be alarmed, as none of the hire cars were. Unused to the systems, people would be setting them off themselves all over the island, so the hire care companies didn't waste money on them. Opening the door from the handle inside, I checked the glovebox. I found the usual paperwork and a map, along with a few tour pamphlets. Taking the stupid hat, I stomped on it a few times, grinding it along the pavement with my heel, then threw it back inside. I'd accomplished all I needed to, so leaving the door open, I ran across the courtyard to the side of the buildings and jogged back to the beach. One down, one to go.

The Sovereign had a different layout with no guard shack, but a gate from the road opened by a remote. Each owner had one. I was arriving from the beach side, so I didn't need to worry about the gate, but it meant their security guard might roam instead of snoozing in a hut. Time was also an issue. I had no idea when the Cayman Club security would notice the SUV and call the police. When that happened, I'd prefer to be home in bed.

Paving stones made it easier to hurry along the edge of the buildings, and I was glad to see the parking extended all the way to the edge of the property. I didn't have time to search for an obvious douchebag vehicle, so I picked up a rock and broke the window of the first one I came to. It happened to be a small twelve passenger van owned by The Sovereign. Probably their courtesy airport shuttle. The shattering glass made more noise than I'd hoped for, so I opened the driver's door and tugged on the wires underneath the dash. Hopefully, it would look like someone had tried to steal the van before being scared off.

"Hey!" came a voice from across the car park, and a flashlight beam swung across the van.

I ducked down behind the vehicle and looked for alternative escape routes. The way I'd come looked like the best bet, but only if the guard didn't come around that side of the van. His footfalls slowed as he dropped from a run to a more cautious approach. I didn't blame him. His crappy salary wasn't worth the guy putting himself in harm's way.

"I've called da police," the guard shouted in a local accent.

I could have stood up and told him we'd got here really quickly, but it would be hard to explain why I was dressed like a stereotypical thug.

He was still moving, creeping around the van, which would cut me off from the building. His light flicked back and forth as he hunted for the intruder. If he was smart, he'd be taking a wide arc around the van to avoid being jumped, but he couldn't be far as there was only one empty parking space before the building. I ducked down and looked underneath the van. A pair of tennis shoes moved carefully along the passenger side. If he continued in that direction, he'd have to turn around the front of the vehicle. I looked around for anything I could use. I certainly didn't want to hurt the guy, but I couldn't afford to be caught either.

"Stand up and show yourself!" he shouted. "I'm armed."

I wanted to ask him what he considered being armed meant. It was possible he had a truncheon of some description, but he certainly wouldn't have a firearm or a Taser. Still, I didn't fancy getting clubbed with a nightstick. Stitches in my head might hamper my stripper career and be a detriment to my run of good tips.

When he reached the left front corner of the van, I sprung from the driver's side and hit the poor fellow in the chest with my forearm as I bashed him aside. From the ease with which he tumbled, I guessed he didn't weigh much more than me, so I hoped he wasn't keen enough to risk chasing a burglar down the dark walkway. I sprinted and didn't slow when I hit the beach. The sand felt like running through treacle, but after a hundred difficult metres, I checked back over my shoulder and didn't see a torch beam. Slowing to a walk, I stayed under the shadows of the trees and buildings, fighting to catch my breath. In the distance I heard sirens wailing in the night, and once more I reminded myself what a dumb idea this had been.

16

FAVOURS AND LONG SHOTS

I managed a couple more hours of restless sleep, but by 6:30 I was up again. I'd set the alarm on my mobile, but left it on vibrate only, then clutched it in my hand when I fell asleep. The buzzing scared the hell out of me, and in my sleepy haze I wondered if we were having an earthquake until I realised what was going on. I quietly moved outside and called my partner, Jacob. Well, he was my partner when I was still a West Bay constable. Which, officially, I still was.

"Is dis dat big shot undercover detective callin' da lowly likes of me?" he laughed when he answered.

"Have to make sure you're not screwing up without me to keep you in line," I replied, and listened to him laugh even more.

From the road noise in the background, I guessed I'd timed it right and caught him on his way into the station.

"Jacob, I need you to do something for me."

"Okay," he said, his tone turning serious. "Is dis gonna get me in trouble like most of da tings you have me do?"

"Not if you do exactly what I say."

The line went silent.

"This is for Detective Whittaker," I added.

"He's askin' for dis? I thought he were suspended."

"He's not asking, but it's to help him. He's been framed, and I need to prove it."

"Jeez, Nora. Dat's dangerous ground you're treadin' on, right dere. And now you want me helpin' you?"

"*Ja.*"

More silence.

"Let me tell you what it is, then you decide if you'll help or not."

"Okay," he replied without enthusiasm.

"We need CCTV from the entrance to The Sovereign and Cayman Club condos from Thursday between 6:20am and 6:45am."

"So go ask dem for it," Jacob said.

"I can't be seen doing that. But I think you'll find there'll be reports of break-ins at both places earlier this morning. So you can go by as a follow-up, and while you're there and looking at CCTV from today, grab the footage from Thursday in case someone was casing the joint that day."

The road noise had stopped, so I presumed Jacob was now sitting outside the station trying to decide how to tell me he wouldn't do it.

"All you're doing is being thorough by following up," I added.

"And you know about dese break-ins how?" he asked knowingly.

"I heard the calls over the radio."

He scoffed. Or some weird snorting sound which said he didn't believe me. That was okay. I wouldn't believe me either. But that didn't matter. We had to do this to clear Whittaker's name. Something must have happened during those twenty minutes.

"No promises," Jacob finally said. "I'll see what da sergeant says 'bout me droppin' by dere."

"Okay. *Takk.* Give it ten minutes before you ask Sarge, okay?"

"You gonna call him first?"

"*Ja.*"

"Dat'll give away what you doin'. And what I'll be doin'."

"*Nei*. Sarge knows when not to ask questions he doesn't want to know the answers to."

My tone expressed more confidence than I actually possessed in Sergeant Redburn's keenness to play along. He certainly wouldn't if he suspected who was behind the break-ins. But he'd known Whittaker for decades, and they respected each other. I was willing to bet he'd read between the lines and let Jacob go by the condos.

"Okay. Ten minutes," Jacob said, and hung up.

I took a deep breath and called Redburn's mobile.

"Constable Sommer. Or is it Detective now?"

"Hard to know, sir."

He laughed. "What's up?"

"I heard there were a couple of break-ins along Seven Mile Beach early this morning, sir."

"Yeah. Sounds like some punk kid who didn't know what da hell he doin'"

"Probably," I agreed. "So, those two condos happen to be of interest in what's going on with Detective Whittaker, sir. Would it be okay if Jacob dropped by there as a follow-up and took a look at their CCTV?"

"You think this dumbass has something to do with Roy's... situation?"

"*Nei*. I don't give a shit about the break-ins. I think there might be footage on their CCTV from Thursday, which could help prove Detective Whittaker is being set up, sir."

"Then get down dere yourself and..." he said before stopping himself. "Of course, you can't be seen investigating anyting to do wit Whittaker, can you?"

"*Nei*."

"You really think it might help Roy?"

"*Ja.*"

He must have held the phone away from his mouth as his voice went faint, but I could hear him call to Jacob.

"Tibbetts. Drop by The Sovereign and Cayman Club first ting. Follow-up for me on a couple of related break-ins dere dis mornin'."

He put the phone back to his ear. "He know what to look for?"

"*Ja.*"

"Done."

"*Takk.*"

"What are you doing here?" Weatherford asked as I entered his office at 7:45am.

"Girl's still missing, isn't she?" I replied and sat down across from him.

He nodded. "Still, you're trying to do too much, Nora. You need to sleep more than a few hours."

I wasn't interested in having this conversation and I certainly didn't get up after only sleeping for a few hours to waste time talking about my lack of sleep.

"Can you play the kidnapper's message to me?"

Weatherford grunted and clicked a couple of times with his mouse until the kidnapper's latest message played.

"Chloe is going to die in three days unless you publicly confess, Pennington. You know what I'm talking about. Reveal your secret or watch your daughter die."

I noticed the kidnapper altered the voice distortion each time. It was an ominous, digitised male voice, but that didn't guarantee the person holding Chloe was a man. Although statistically, it probably was.

"He's insistent Pennington knows what this is about," I said.

The detective nodded. "I'm having the parents brought in this morning to interview them again."

"Patrick was back on the boat last night," I said, while we were discussing the family. "I saw him have an argument with Ness. After that, he disappeared until the tender left."

"Any idea what the argument was about?"

"*Nei*. But Ness was the calm one. Patrick was upset."

"Do you think he went missing afterwards because they kicked him out of the..." Weatherford trailed off. "What do we call it? Club?"

I shrugged. "The salon. That's where we dance and the customers stay the whole time, apart from the VIP rooms, which are nearby. I'm guessing he was told he couldn't play anymore."

"See anything else?" he asked. "Oh, and did you find a way to disable the yacht?"

"*Nei*, and *nei*. But I have a better plan."

"We can't keep sending you out there with no backup, Nora. Not to mention, we still have zero evidence they're doing anything we could arrest them for."

"We can if they're running a strip club within Cayman waters, sir."

"Right, but they're smarter than that, aren't they? They're staying more than twelve miles out. Pretty easy these days with GPS."

"Search for a nautical chart of Grand Cayman," I said, then got up and walked around behind the detective.

He performed an image search in his internet browser and I pointed to the chart we could look at.

"See Twelve Mile Bank. It's directly west of Seven Mile Beach."

He zoomed in on the map. "Okay."

"I told Ness they should anchor there instead of burning diesel in the open ocean."

"Good thinking," Weatherford acknowledged. "But they can still make sure they're in international waters."

"The bank begins a little under twelve miles off Seven Mile Beach," I said, pointing to the chart. "But North West Point in West Bay protrudes enough that although it's north of the bank, it's still closer. If I can get them to anchor in the right spot with enough rode, the *Manannán* will end up in Cayman waters. We can bust them for the strip club, then search for whatever else they're up to."

"How are you going to determine where they anchor?" Weatherford asked.

"Because the top of the bank is mostly flat sand with coral bommies scattered about. When they anchor there today, there's a good chance the anchor will drag in the sand as the currents are strong over the bank. The wind picked up last night, which will help us. It's out of the north-west instead of the east."

"What if the anchor catches one of the bommies?" he asked.

"Then my plan might be a pile of *dritt*."

"They could also realise North West Point is closer," Weatherford added.

"Which will be *dritt* too."

He sighed. "Sounds like a long shot."

"It is, but currently it's our only shot unless we seize the tender for a routine search and get lucky. If they are trafficking drugs, they have to bring them ashore somehow."

Weatherford leaned back in his chair. "Okay. Get with Williams again. Have him coordinate with Ben in the Joint Marine Unit and be on standby tonight. If we can prove they're in our waters, we'll board the yacht. If that doesn't work, we'll grab the tender when it brings the customers back."

"Or we could wait on grabbing the tender until next weekend," I urged. "I'm pretty sure they're staying at least another week."

"They said so?" he asked.

"Morar told Violet Blaze to make more money or she wouldn't be back. No reason to say that if they weren't staying."

Weatherford blew out his cheeks and made a groaning sound. "Fine. Have the team on alert watching the distance from shore. We'll wait on searching the tender."

I checked my watch and wondered if Jacob had managed to obtain any of the CCTV footage yet. To view it, I'd probably need to drop by West Bay station, which would have to wait until after the interviews with the Penningtons. Violet's makeover had to fit into the day somewhere, too. I'd suggested a spray-on tan, but beyond knowing they existed, I had no clue where you could get one or how they worked. I pictured a manicurist with a spray can.

Weatherford's desk phone rang.

He listened for a moment. "Okay, thanks, Chantel," he responded and hung up. Getting up from his chair, he added, "The parents are here."

"How do you want to handle this?" I asked as we walked out of his office.

"I've been thinking about that," he replied as we started down the stairs. "They won't like it, but I'd like us to speak with each of them separately, which means they have to wait around a while. The alternative is we take one each."

"Make them wait," I said as we reached the lobby. "It'll be our best chance of getting them to admit to what the kidnapper wants."

"Agreed," Weatherford said before striding towards the Penningtons and extending a hand. "Thanks for coming in again. We appreciate you taking the time."

"Do you have any progress?" Rebecca asked without a greeting. "Have you spoken with Patrick?"

"I'll gladly update you with everything we know so far, Mrs Pennington," Weatherford said patiently. "But if you wouldn't mind waiting, we'd like to chat with Rupert first."

By the look on her face, she minded. "Just tell us together. Why waste time?"

"We won't be long, ma'am. Please, I'll ask Chantel to get you a coffee while you wait."

I glanced over at the reception desk, where Chantel raised an eyebrow at me. I decided it was best to let Weatherford ask her to pander to Mrs Pennington.

"This way, sir," I said to Rupert, who had been quiet, letting his wife blather on.

"Please tell me you're making progress," he said as I led him to an interview room.

I didn't know what to say. We were basically nowhere. We'd

had two potential suspects and not a stitch of evidence to suggest either had actually taken Chloe.

"Have a seat, sir," I said instead. "Detective Weatherford will join us in a moment."

Impatiently pacing, I didn't sit down, wishing Vincent would hurry up. I checked my mobile to make sure I hadn't missed a text from Jacob. I hadn't.

"Can you tell me something, at least?" Rupert urged. "All this waiting is tearing me apart."

I really needed to wait for Weatherford and could only guess that maybe Rebecca was bending his ear in the lobby. Or he had to use the loo before joining us. Whatever was delaying him was a pain in my arse.

"The kidnapper is very convinced you know what he's talking about," I said, tired of waiting.

Rupert threw his hands up. "But I don't! I honestly have no idea what the bastard's referring to."

The door opened, and relieved, I turned around. But Weatherford didn't come in. Instead, he beckoned me to join him.

"Apologies, but please give us just a minute, Mr Pennington," he said, while I stepped to the hallway.

Weatherford made sure the door was closed all the way before he spoke. "We just got a call from West Bay."

My heart stopped beating. My stupid plan had backfired and landed me in deep *dritt*, but even worse, I'd screwed Jacob. I felt my life crumble before me.

"A body washed up on the beach near Bonnie's Arch," Weatherford was saying.

"What?" I asked, unsure how a body related to me being caught doing a bunch of things I should never have done.

"They think it's Patrick Pennington."

"*Fy faen*," I muttered, realising it wasn't about me or the break-ins after all. *But what did this mean?* "How?"

"The officer at the scene said he has a wound around his neck."

"Strangled?"

"Sounds more like garrotted," the detective replied. "We need to go look for ourselves."

And then it hit me. I'd talked Detective Weatherford into releasing Patrick instead of nicking him for the drug possession. And now he'd been murdered. He was a worthless *drittsekk*, but I still couldn't help feeling slightly responsible.

17

___

BLOODY FINGERS. OR TOES

Patrick's body looked pale and beaten from hitting the ironshore, but at least the crabs and other sea critters hadn't got to him yet. The report from the scene had been correct. Garrotted was an accurate term. From the thin, deep wound around his neck, it appeared he'd been killed with a piece of wire.

"Feels like someone's sending a message," I said.

"A message to whom?" Weatherford asked. "Pennington certainly would have got the point while he slowly choked and bled out. Look at the defensive cuts on his fingers. This was not a friendly way to leave this life."

"He was also dumped for us to find him," I said, looking out across what I knew to be a lovely dive site. "The only reason he was thrown into the water was to mask any trace evidence."

"Agreed," Weatherford replied. "They could have left him here on the rocks. Or anywhere. It doesn't look like he was killed here."

I looked around the jagged ironshore. "*Nei.* There should be blood everywhere. He was brought here to be dumped." My eyes flicked to the sea once more. "Or thrown from a boat."

Weatherford rubbed his brow and shaded his eyes against the morning sun glinting off the water. "My bet's on a boat."

"There'd be a ton of blood on that boat," I ventured.

"Yeah. Hard to clean it all up. Maybe we should grab the *Manannán*'s RIB right now."

I thought that over for a minute while I watched the medical examiner carefully check for more injuries and then go through Pennington's pockets.

"Wallet," he said flatly, holding it up.

"Rules out a mugging," Weatherford commented.

There was little we could do at the scene, as I was sure we weren't actually at the scene of anything except the spot the body had bumped into the island. As we walked back to Weatherford's Bronco, I tried to imagine Pennington's movements after being dropped at the dock. Then I heard Whittaker's voice in my head.

"Discuss your thoughts."

"Time of death is going to be a wide window from the medical examiner," was the first point which seemed important to mention.

"Yeah. Immersed in the water will skew things," Weatherford replied.

"We're thinking this has to be the lochmen, right?" I asked, pausing when we reached the car park for the Bonnie's Arch condos.

Weatherford nodded. "That's my best guess. You saw them arguing on the boat and we think Patrick was involved in distributing drugs for them. If the lochmen are even distributing, of course."

"Then why drop the body near the shore where we'd find it?" I asked. "If they killed him on the boat, then why not tie a weight to his ankle, puncture his internal organs so he doesn't float, and dump him a mile out? He'd disappear without a trace."

Weatherford winced. "You know you're quite terrifying sometimes, Nora?"

I stared back at him. "Why?"

He laughed. "You just described a brutal and efficient method of body disposal without blinking an eye."

I didn't realise I hadn't been blinking like normal, and fluttered my eyelids a few times to make sure they were working. They seemed to be fine.

"But I get your point," he continued. "Why send a message, right?"

"Or who to?" I considered the bigger question.

We climbed into the Bronco and the detective started the engine, blasting the air conditioning to combat the rising heat and humidity.

"We should check for any boats stolen overnight," I said as he turned around and pulled to North West Point Road.

"I was thinking the same thing," Weatherford replied. "I don't see these guys being stupid enough to murder someone on their own boat. They have to know that it would be impossible to thoroughly clean a RIB and remove every drop of evidence."

He hit a saved number on his mobile and the call rang through the vehicle's speakers.

"Sergeant Hadley," answered the duty sergeant at Central Station.

"Hi Sarge, it's Vincent, and Nora's with me. Have you seen any reports of missing boats in the last twelve hours?"

"Boats?" he replied. "Why? You find one?"

"No. Chasing a theory tied to the body in West Bay this morning," Weatherford explained.

"Murder?" he asked.

"Looks that way."

"Dat's what I heard. Nothing has come across my desk about a boat, but I'll check with da udder stations and let you know if anyting turn up."

"Thanks," the detective replied and hung up.

We drove in silence for a while and I wondered if I was supposed to be sharing all my thoughts with my current partner. Whittaker hadn't made it clear where to draw the line. I was happy to lean on the side of silence to let us think things over for ourselves, and besides, I was having thoughts I couldn't share. Like why Jacob hadn't contacted me yet.

Weatherford's mobile rang, and he checked the caller ID before answering.

"That was quick," he said.

"Hadn't made it to me yet, but a small dive op in George Town reported their boat missing dis mornin'."

"Where from?" Weatherford asked.

"Off da public pier by Lobster Pot," the sergeant replied. "Moored 'bout hundred yards out. Didn't have mornin' clients, but arrived to teach a class and noticed it were gone."

"Lobster Pot building has CCTV," I said. "Catch anything?"

"We're checking," Hadley replied. "But I dare say da boat too far out to see in da dark, but maybe catch dem swimmin' out from da pier."

"*Nei.* You're looking for another boat arriving and taking it," I said. "It would have been running without lights, but look for signs of a wake."

"Will do. Any chance dis guy gettin' his boat back?" the sergeant asked.

"None," I replied.

"None?" Hadley echoed.

"I wouldn't be optimistic," Weatherford confirmed. "Thanks for getting back to us."

They hung up, and Weatherford looked over at me. "Mile out with a big hole in the bottom?"

"*Ja,*" I replied. "Our best chance is tracking where Patrick Pennington went from when he arrived at the dock from the *Manannán*. They had to pick him back up somewhere."

"The harbour has CCTV," Weatherford said. "He had to show back up there, or they left to pick him up elsewhere. Get someone on that when we get back, okay?"

"*Ja,*" I replied. "And the Penningtons?"

Weatherford shook his head. "I'll have to inform Rupert that his brother is dead. By the time you join us, maybe we can still ask him a few questions about the kidnapper's message."

It took me 20 minutes to set the harbour CCTV project in motion with Hadley and use the bathroom. Plus, I stopped for coffee. Honestly, I was taking my time, hoping Rupert Pennington would be over the initial shock of his brother's murder. I wasn't good around grief. Some people were great at saying the right things and comforting those who were suffering a loss, but I was shit at all of it. Carefully avoiding the reception area, so I didn't run into Rebecca, I killed time until I hoped the tears were mopped up and we could move on to figuring out how to find Chloe.

"Do you think this is connected to my daughter in some way?" Rupert was asking as I entered the room.

The man looked even more tired and haggard than when we'd left this morning, and his eyes were red. But his voice sounded solid, so maybe I'd timed my entrance well.

"We believe that's unlikely, but we can't rule anything out at this stage," Weatherford replied.

I sat down and placed my coffee on the table. Vincent glanced at the cup and then at me, so apparently he would have liked one too. I slid the cup his way.

"Can we discuss last night's message from the kidnapper?" the detective asked, and then took a sip of my coffee.

I'd really expected him to push it back to me.

Pennington nodded. "Of course. Anything we need to do."

"The person is insistent that you know what they're talking about," Weatherford said. "Have you come up with any other names you think might be useful?"

Rupert now shook his head. "I swear, I've no idea what this nutjob is referring to. Have you followed up on the names I gave you?"

"We did," Weatherford acknowledged. "Of the three you gave us, none of them are in the Cayman Islands, and only one has been here within the past year. We couldn't find a connection."

"How did this bastard communicate with Chloe?" Rupert

asked. "You said they'd been in contact for a week. Isn't there a trail of emails or texts?"

"WhatsApp," I replied. "Encrypted on the devices, so without Chloe's mobile, we can't see what was exchanged."

"And you released the teacher?"

"We could find no direct evidence that Mr Garner has been involved beyond having been out on his boat at the time she was taken," Weatherford replied. "But we have CCTV of him arriving back alone on his boat."

I was about to pressure the man further about people he may have pissed off, when my own words made me stop and think. But not about Chloe Pennington. I took out my mobile and looked through the handful of numbers I had stored in the cheap device. Opening WhatsApp, I typed a message.

"Need help on kidnapping case. He plays by rules, but young girl's life at stake. Please help. Kidnapper says Pennington sinned. Must admit to it. Pennington can't think what he's done. Figure pissed off employee or bad business deal. Shortlist from father gave zero. Need ideas. This is secure. Only me. Help."

I hit send, and the message was on its way to Rosie, Whittaker's wife. I knew I was risking angering my mentor by involving her, but these were desperate times.

As I was about to ask Rupert a question, my mobile buzzed and I couldn't believe Rosie had replied so quickly. Except it wasn't her. I had a text from Jacob.

"Have it," was all the message said.

Now I needed to get to West Bay station as soon as possible. Weatherford had been asking several questions about Chloe's other activities, but he was now sipping my coffee again, so I dived in.

"How do you get the contracts to build the developments you're involved with?" I asked.

Rupert frowned. "How do you mean?"

"What I asked. You have a development and construction company. How do you get the jobs? Do you buy the land and plan what you build? Or do other companies hire you to build their projects? Do you bid on jobs?"

"It varies," he replied, sounding reluctant to answer. "I try to stick with my own developments where I control everything, but we often partner with investors. Sometimes, they may already own the land and we handle the build for them. I don't usually end up in a bidding situation, as I only work with people I know and trust."

"So, no chance you've trodden on someone's fingers? Taking a project away from another developer?" I asked.

Pennington looked at me like I was crazy.

"Have you trodden on anyone's toes?" Weatherford said, apparently correcting me.

Stupid language.

"Like I said, most of the projects I'm involved with are mine or alongside long-term partners. I'm telling you, I really don't have a clue who this arsehole could be. Maybe they're a crackpot I accidentally annoyed on the road, or a waiter who thought they deserved a bigger tip."

"Anything is possible at this stage, Mr Pennington," Weatherford said. "But it would be highly unlikely for an aggrieved motorist to plan such an elaborate abduction and then expect you to know what they're talking about."

The detective was right. It didn't feel like a trivial incident blown up, although people with mental disorders could be irrational and unpredictable. Their interpretations of situations could become vastly separated from reality.

My mobile buzzed again. This time it was Rosie.

"I'll try," was all she said. And that's everything I could ask for.

The device buzzed again. Now Jazzy was texting me.

"Violet with you?"

"No," I replied, and held my breath while I waited.

Jazzy's reply sent shivers through me. "She's gone."

18

TATS AND TASERS

I really wanted to be there when Weatherford interviewed Rebecca. I figured she'd be primed and ready to spill anything she knew about her husband's business dealings or skeletons in his larder. She'd been aggressively volunteering Patrick as a suspect, so I doubted she'd be pining his loss, but I was interested to hear what she had to say now. Weatherford would have to get me up to speed later. *Larder?* That might not be right.

I needed to find Violet, although I wasn't sure why it was so important. It wouldn't affect me if she no-showed at the tender tonight. They'd be short a dancer, but that was their problem. In some ways, it simplified my life. She was one more unpredictable moving piece to the puzzle I hoped to solve tonight. But the clenching in the pit of my stomach urged me to find the girl.

On the drive to West Bay I called Jazzy, and she confirmed Violet had been gone when the kid got up around 8:30am. Jazzy had waited for a while to text me, thinking Violet had wandered down the coastline on a walk. She hadn't stolen Jazzy's bicycle, which suggested she'd called someone to pick her up. I'd been thinking about running a wire out to the fence by the road from the shack and rigging up a camera. Mainly in case someone nicked my

Jeep during the night when it was parked there. Now I wished I'd done less thinking and more buying and installing. I had precisely nothing to go on. She could be anywhere.

I called Jacob.

"Hey," he answered.

"Where are you?" I asked.

"We're headin' west on Batabano. Need to meet at da station?"

It was weird hearing my partner talk about 'we' when I wasn't the 'we' he was referring to.

"*Nei.* Not yet. I have another problem."

I heard him groan. "Am I in trouble too?"

"Nobody's in trouble," I replied. "Well, Violet Blaze might be."

"Who's Violet Blaze?"

"She's involved in this undercover thing I'm doing. But now she's missing."

"Okay. We need to put out a BOLO?" Jacob offered. "Just call Sarge."

"*Nei*, I need to find her myself."

"Where she likely to go?"

I'd turned off West Bay Road while we'd been talking and was driving east on West Church Street, which would become Batabano. Up ahead, I saw a patrol car approaching.

"Pull over," I said over the phone.

"Dat you?" Jacob answered, as I watched the patrol car slow and park in front of a convenience store.

I hung up and parked next to them. Jumping out, I met Jacob around the front of the vehicles. The partner he'd been assigned got out too. It was Constable Dexley. I considered him to be a good man who'd watch Jacob's back.

"Hey," I acknowledged, and he nodded in return.

"So where dis girl gone you tink?" Jacob asked.

"Probably the local drug dealer," I replied.

"Oh dear," Jacob muttered. "Dat's not good."

"Who's active right now?" I asked. "We nicked the Bush brothers."

Jacob shook his head and turned to Dexley. "You tink of anyone?"

"Been quiet in West Bay lately," Dexley replied. "Any chance she make it to George Town?"

It was possible. Hardly a long drive, but Jazzy had told me she'd walked out by the road once she'd seen Violet had left, and she wasn't there. It didn't rule out someone coming all the way from George Town, but between me leaving and Jazzy checking, there wasn't that much time.

"*Faen*," I muttered and searched my phone for another one of the few contacts I had saved.

I was annoyed I hadn't thought of him before. I put the call on speaker as it rang.

"Let me guess, you realised dere ain't no way you can live witout me?" came Jumbo Flower's booming voice.

I laughed, picturing the enormous young man grinning from ear to ear.

"I need your help."

"Dat always why you callin', sister," he replied. "But it usually someting fun, so what you need?"

"If I wanted a cheap, quick high in West Bay, who do I see?"

"Oh Lord above, dat ain't what I expected outta your mouth, girl."

"*Dritt*," I muttered, realising what I'd said. "Not for me, *fjols*. I'm searching for a girl who is probably looking for a fix."

"Shit," he said, with a long, drawn-out groan. "You know I ain't no snitch."

"I'm trying to save this kid, Jumbo."

I waited while he thought it over.

"She's worked the streets before, if that helps," I added.

"Who is dis girl?" he asked.

"Violet Blaze."

"Shit, why didn't you say dat up front? I know Violet. I like dat girl, but da kid messed up, man," he said. "Just dis once I'll give you a name. Dis guy's a piece of shit. I don't mind grassin' on his ass. He were small time till you put away da Bush Bros. Now he tinks he da man. He used to pimp her till she moved on. Friend o' mine one of her regulars till den. Honest, I thought he'd whacked da girl. Ain't seen her in months."

"I think she moved into George Town," I replied. "Who's the guy?"

"Don't know his real name. Puerto Rican goes by Chico. Hangs out in a repair garage off Fountain Road on Joseph's Drive. Don't go walkin' in dere alone, girl. I guarantee he packin'."

"Thanks, Jumbo."

"Sure. Call me sometime when you just wanna hang out," he replied.

"*Ja*," I said and hung up.

Jumbo was a petty criminal. But he was also a great guy who'd helped me out several times in the past, and I felt bad I hadn't ever called him just to see how he and his sister were doing. I could have explained that I never called anyone socially, but I doubt it would help.

"We need backup, Nora," Jacob pointed out, and he was right.

It was tempting to go in solo and stealthy to see if I could pluck Violet out of there, but we didn't even know if she was there. And if Chico was home, he sounded like the type who'd have a few buddies with him. I called Williams.

"We need to talk about tonight," I said. "We have a new plan."

"Good mornin' to you too," he responded. "I'm just goin' to lunch. Pick a time dis afternoon."

"How about twenty minutes from now in West Bay, and bring a couple of your unit with you?"

"What?"

"I need guns, but as you won't give me them, I need you and your boyfriends with guns," I said.

"I thought you wanted to talk 'bout tonight's op?"

"We'll do that after."

"Shit."

"Meet us at West Bay station," I said, and hung up.

"Okay, I'll go and make sure Chico's there. You get to the station and wait for Williams," I told Jacob.

"You sure he's coming?" he questioned.

My mobile buzzed. It was a text. I read it to myself.

"You're a pain in the ass."

"Yeah," I said to Jacob. "He's coming."

Parking behind a house under construction, I walked across Fountain Road to a duplex. The repair garage was a large warehouse-like building which looked like it had remained standing for its last hurricane. One more and it would come down in a pile of patched-up steel siding. From where I stood, a hundred metres away across open scrub land, I could see the office entrance. The service bay doors had to be on the far side. And that was when I realised it was Sunday, so why would anyone be there? Sure, there were cars all over the place around the building, but there would be. It was a repair garage.

"*Dritt*," I muttered, and was about to walk back to my Jeep when I noticed the front door swing open.

A man stepped outside and lit a cigarette. He was dark skinned, with a dozen gold chains around his neck and a mobile phone pinned between his shoulder and his ear. I couldn't make out what he was saying, but the accent sounded Jamaican. A plume of thick smoke emanated from his lips. It wasn't a cigarette he was smoking. I had my probable cause and retreated rather than risk spooking Chico if he was inside. I'd rather face Williams and his verbal abuse for raiding an empty warehouse than send Chico running when he saw a skinny white girl circling his crib.

Hurrying to the station, I hoped I'd have time to look at Jacob's CCTV footage from the condos, but Williams showed up just after me. He was a stocky, muscular man with buzzed hair, and looked every part the former soldier that he was. He'd only brought one of his men with him, but they carried assault rifles and sidearms to go with their black uniforms and tactical vests. I wouldn't admit it to Williams, but I was a little jealous of their outfits. They didn't look like people to mess with.

"What da hell you got goin' on in my town?" Sergeant Redburn growled, meeting us in the reception area. "Folks just gettin' outta church."

I wondered if Redburn ever took a day off. Or even a shift. It seemed like he was always at the station, no matter what time of day it was.

"We have a situation with a young female being held by a suspected drug dealer at a location we're about to raid, sir. No churches will be involved."

"What location?" he demanded.

"Car repair garage on Joseph's Drive, sir," I replied.

"I left a date waitin' on me for lunch," Williams grunted. "Can we get dis done?"

"Just hold up a minute," Redburn said. "I had my wife's car fixed at dat place. Weren't no drug dealers dere."

"I just witnessed a bloke smoking a joint out front," I replied. "We'll be in and out in time for Sergeant William's lunch date to realise what a jerk he is, sir."

Williams laughed. "Friendly fire. Dat's all I gotta say to you, beanpole."

I grinned at him. "There's a front office entrance and roll-up doors facing the lane. I couldn't see it, but I'm sure there'll be a door on the backside of the building."

I showed them the satellite view from the maps app on my phone. Williams took out his own mobile, which was a much newer, far more expensive TV-sized device.

"Okay, let's get a better look," he joked and found the same view.

It was much easier to see on his screen.

"Jacob, you're with me," Williams ordered. "We'll go in through the office. Dexley with Barrett. Cover the roll-ups. Sommer, cover the back door. We have comms, you two turn your radios down," he indicated to the two constables. "Turn them up if we're separated." He looked at Redburn. "Got a radio blondie can use, sir?"

They were both sergeants, but Williams deferred to Redburn, so I guessed he was a more important sergeant. Maybe because he was in charge of West Bay Station. I didn't pay much attention to that rank shit.

Redburn shook his head, resigned to the fact we were raiding the place despite his misgivings.

"I have one in the Jeep," I said. "And my Taser. And you never know whose arse that thing might land in."

"You idiots scare me to death," Redburn muttered. "You need more bodies? I can send two other patrols your way."

"Have them close by, but only show up after we go in, sir," Williams said. "And thank you."

Redburn supplied the rest of us with tactical vests and we split up into three vehicles to arrive at our designated spots faster. I led as I was driving around the back, and the Jeep was less likely to raise suspicions, buying us a few seconds.

Turning off Fountain onto Joseph's, I accelerated along the narrow lane and could now see one of the roll-up doors was partially open. The Jamaican I'd seen earlier stood outside with a Hispanic-looking man who had tattoos all over and wore a basketball jersey and baggy shorts. They both whistled at me as I drove by. I waved as I cut hard to the right and bounced across the scrub land, heading for the back of the building. Last I saw of them, they were diving inside, having seen who was following me.

I was right, there was a regular door near the far corner of the back wall. I pulled the Jeep around the corner and jumped out, radio on my belt and Taser in my hand. Shouts came from inside and I heard Barrett announce himself at the roll-up door. I wondered how many people could be in the garage and realised my Taser would only handle the first one through the door and then require reloading. I looked around for another weapon, but I was too late. The back door flung open and the man I guessed to be Chico aimed a handgun outside.

Fortunately, he chose the opening side to scan first, and I'd positioned myself to use the door as a shield. I fired the Taser, hitting him in the biceps, and the man jolted like he'd been run into by a truck before crumpling to the ground. Ejecting the cartridge, I pulled the spare from my pocket and clicked it in place. Inside the garage was complete chaos, with men yelling in a collection of languages and accents. The radio was squawking, but it was hard to make out what was being said. Pounding footsteps on concrete told me I had another customer approaching, but they pulled up when they saw Chico's body on the ground. The Puerto Rican wheezed and moaned.

I stayed behind the door and waited. After a moment, the barrel of a gun appeared, the man's arm extended. I reached forward and hit him point blank in the back of his tanned and tattooed hand with the second cartridge.

"Clear. Two suspects subdued," came Williams' voice over the radio.

"Roger. Clear. I got one here," Barrett responded. "Don't see any more."

"Back door is clear," I said into the radio. "Got a couple here."

I hit the second guy with another burst from the Taser before I ejected the cartridge and stepped over the two bodies. Inside, they'd gathered the suspects in the middle by one of the car lifts.

"Any sign of Violet?" I asked.

"In da room behind the office," Williams replied. "You'd best go help her, Nora. She don't look good."

"I got dem," Jacob assured me, coming over to the door, so I hurried to the front of the building.

The office looked clean and surprisingly tidy, so I could see why Redburn had mistakenly thought the place was above board. But down a hallway, past another office and the bathrooms, was a door slightly ajar. I noticed the heavy locks and deadbolts which would normally secure the room. I pushed the door open. Inside was dimly lit by a lamp. There were no windows, but a mammoth-sized big-screen TV hung on the wall beside the door. Three large couches sat against the walls. None of them matched. Violet was curled up on one, moaning. I rushed over and knelt on the grubby beige carpet beside her.

"Violet. It's me."

She peeked from behind her hands, and her bleary eyes tried to focus. After a moment, she blinked a few times, and I could see she'd recognised me before lurching my way, flinging her arms around my neck. She sobbed like a child with her face buried against my cheek.

"It's okay now," I said, the words falling from my lips.

Nothing felt like it was going to be okay. All she had on was a T-shirt, which she'd pulled down to cover herself as best she could. I dreaded to think what she'd been through for the past few hours. A nightmare she'd chosen to leave my house and willingly walk into.

"I came in last," she moaned.

"That doesn't matter," I said, rubbing her back.

"It matters to me," she cried. "And now I've screwed up. Again."

"*Ja,*" I said. "But we'll figure it out."

19

———

EARTHQUAKE IN A POTS AND PANS
FACTORY

Williams didn't mind me leaving him to take care of booking Chico and his friends. We found a significant amount of pills and weed hidden behind a panel in the back room. Williams was missing his lunch date, but he'd get the credit for the bust, which was perfect for me. The last thing I needed was my picture in the newspapers.

I picked up Jazzy from home and drove Violet into George Town. The only medical facility open on Sunday was the main hospital, so I had no choice but to take her there. Needless to say, she didn't have any kind of medical insurance, so I presented her as a detainee of the RCIPS. They admitted her and soon had her hooked up to an IV. Violet was asleep in no time. I left Jazzy in charge of her and drove to Central Station.

Sitting in the car park, it hit me how exhausted I was. I glanced in the rear-view mirror. The bags under my eyes supported the feeling. My afternoon plan had been to help Violet look less crack-whore-like and get some sleep before meeting the lochmen at the dock. But now Patrick was dead, Violet was in the hospital, I still hadn't had a chance to look at the condo CCTV, and we'd made no progress on finding Chloe. Time was running out. We were three days into the kidnapper's five-day window.

I checked my mobile to see if I'd missed anything important. No texts or voicemails. Several emails had hit my work inbox, and I scrolled through to see if any were important. One from Sergeant Hadley caught my attention. He'd provided a link to the server where he'd filed the CCTV from the harbour. But I didn't need to look at it once I'd read his message.

"Harbour CCTV attached from last night. Tender never moves."

"*Fy faen,*" I growled out loud. That punched a hole in my theory. I'd been sure the lochmen had stolen the dive boat using the RIB, then killed Patrick and dumped his body near Bonnie's Arch before scuttling the dive boat in deep water and returning in the RIB. It didn't rule them out, but it meant they'd adopted a more complicated plan if they'd indeed been responsible. *Stolen two boats? Returned one?* Their risk went up significantly each time they broke the law, but I'm sure they were smart enough to know there were cameras in the harbour, too. I still couldn't wrap my head around why they'd leave the body to be found instead of sending it down in the dive boat.

Shaking my head, I jumped from the Jeep and headed inside the station. Weatherford was just returning to his office as I arrived upstairs.

"Heard you nabbed a drug dealer in West Bay," he said when he saw me. "That have anything to do with Violet Blaze?"

"*Ja,*" I replied. "She relapsed. In the hospital now."

"She gonna be alright?"

I nodded. "Ja. I'll see how she's doing later. Not sure she should go back out to the *Manannán.*"

"Too risky," Weatherford responded. "Girl's unpredictable."

It was hard to argue with that.

"We'll see. The lochmen will be on edge after Patrick's murder. I don't want to give them more to worry about, and I'm scared they'll go after her if they think she's a loose end."

Weatherford shrugged his shoulders. "Your call. Is Williams up to speed on the new plan?"

"*Ja*," I replied. "We talked at the repair garage and he's contacting Ben at the Joint Marine Unit."

"You didn't miss much here. Rebecca Pennington seemed shocked by the news about Patrick, and couldn't offer any other insights into who her husband might have crossed. Honestly, she sort of fell apart when I told her about Patrick."

"She hated the bloke yesterday," I wondered aloud. "What changed?"

"No idea," Weatherford replied. "Maybe she felt bad about throwing him under the bus with us, or could be the stress of her daughter missing. Who knows?"

My mobile buzzed, and I took it from my pocket. Shocked to see that Rosie Whittaker had replied on WhatsApp, I read the message to myself. It was short.

"Accidents on jobs? Lawsuits?"

I wasn't sure what to do next. Should I share my new means of connecting with Detective Whittaker with Weatherford? He might have questions of his own. But if Rosie or Roy knew I'd shared our exchange with anyone else, it might bring an end to the help, which had only just begun. But surely they'd assume Weatherford must know. Still, I didn't want to risk it. I messaged "Thanks" back and pocketed my mobile.

We'd already chased down the lawsuit angle and hadn't found anything promising. A few contract disputes, but relatively minor issues with other major companies. It was hard to see how individuals had been hurt in any way. But the injury angle was one I hadn't thought of. And should have. It was another lesson in how Whittaker's experience and savvy was irreplaceable.

"Have we looked at safety records for Pennington's firm?" I asked.

Weatherford looked up from his computer screen. "Good question. I tasked the team with doing background and financial checks, but I didn't specifically mention safety issues. You're thinking aggrieved worker who was injured on the job?"

"Worth a look, sir."

"Agreed," he replied and began typing an email.

My mind whirred as I waited. Of the three lochmen – although there were actually five now including the captain and first mate, plus the women, but I wasn't including any of them – two were former military. Which gave me an idea.

"Patrick's autopsy today, sir?" I asked.

"Mm?" Weatherford murmured as he concentrated on his two fingers pecking at the keyboard.

"We need his fingernail scrapings as soon as possible," I added, impatiently watching the man take far too long to type a simple email.

"Of course," he replied without looking up.

"UK military keeps DNA records of service personnel, sir."

Weatherford firmly hit the return key, so I figured he was done. He looked up at me.

"What's that, Nora?"

"The UK military, sir. They keep a database of DNA."

Weatherford thought my words over for a moment. "Oh, you're thinking of Ness and Lomond."

"If I was being murdered with a piece of wire around my throat, I'd fight the *drittsekker* with everything I had," I said.

"His fingers were chewed up," Weatherford acknowledged. "Good chance he scraped some skin off his attacker."

He picked up his desk phone and called our CSI group, putting the call on speaker.

"CSI."

"Is Rasha there please? It's Detective Weatherford."

"One moment."

It took about two minutes, but the familiar voice of the head of the department finally came on the line.

"Vincent, what's up?"

"Hi, Rasha. I know the autopsy on Patrick Pennington is this afternoon, but did you scrape his fingernails at the scene?"

"Of course."

"Can I beg a hurry-up on looking at that, please? We have DNA references for two of the prime suspects."

Rasha sighed. Not once had any officer ever told her to take her time with anything. Every case was always in rush mode.

"They're already in progress," she replied. "I started on them first, but be aware, the seawater hasn't helped our cause and the man had neatly trimmed, short fingernails. Although one was missing."

"Missing?" I blurted. "Removed or accidentally torn off in the struggle?"

"Hard to say," Rasha replied. "But people who torture don't usually stop at one."

"Unless they learn what they were after," Weatherford suggested.

"That's your side of the fence to figure out," she replied. "I'll let you know when I have something."

Rasha hung up the phone, and we looked at each other.

I spoke first. "That nail went down with the dive boat."

Weatherford nodded. "Probably. Ripped it off, thrashing about. Nasty way to go."

"*Ja*," I replied, but I was thinking more about the sequence of events. "They may not have killed Pennington on the RIB, but they had to have returned to the hotel afterwards. Unless they stopped somewhere to dispose of their clothes and wash everything, they would have carried DNA evidence with them."

"We could get a warrant to search, but unless we wait until tonight when they're gone, they'll know we're on to them," Weatherford said, and looked at his watch. "Cleaners have probably been through by now, too."

"Call the manager," I said. "If they haven't, tell him to stop them."

Weatherford flicked through pages of his notebook until he found the number he was looking for, and once again used his desk phone to call, putting it on speaker.

"Barry Dodson," came a deep-voiced man with a slight Caymanian accent.

"Mr Dodson, this is Detectives Weatherford and Sommer. We were wondering if our suspects' rooms had been cleaned today?"

"No," he replied right away.

"Are you sure? You don't need to check?" the detective queried.

"I know they haven't because all three requested no service until they ask for it, Detective."

Weatherford looked at me and muted the call. "Too risky to go in before six."

I nodded. He was right. As long as the rooms weren't being vacuumed, it should be safe to wait and not risk alarming them.

"Great, thanks for your help once again, Mr Dodson," Weatherford said, after unmuting the phone. "Please keep it to yourself, but you can expect us after 6:00pm this evening with a warrant to search those three rooms."

The manager sighed. "Of course we'll help in any way we can, but could you please keep the fuss to a minimum in respect for the other guests, Detective?"

"We'll be in stealth mode, I assure you, sir," Weatherford replied.

He ended the call and stared at the phone. I knew what he was thinking.

"I have to go. Good luck telling Rasha you're screwing up her evening, sir. I need to sort out Violet and get ready for tonight."

"Sure," he muttered, then frowned at me. "You look dead tired, Nora. try to get some rest."

"*Takk*, sir," I said as I left.

Great. Even my overworked, stressed-out boss noticed I look like *dritt*.

I figured the longer I left Violet at the hospital, the better off she'd be. Jazzy had sent me several updates, saying the patient had been sleeping most of the time, so I decided to go wig shopping on my own. I texted Jazzy back and told her to get Violet ready to leave in half an hour.

There was only one proper wig store on the island, and I knew where it was as my brunette disguise had come from there. Island Wigs and Beauty Supply had also helped us during a past enquiry.

"What you want dis time?" the owner, Miss Rosemary, asked when I walked in.

A large, middle-aged woman, she had a shocking pink afro on her head today, in stark contrast to her beautiful dark skin. It looked like a box of bubblegum had exploded on top of her head.

"How 'bout someting more fun," she insisted, holding up a bright blue wig.

The woman wore so many bangles around her wrists which jangled loudly with every movement, I was surprised she could even raise her arms.

"It's not for me," I said, searching for the few normal wigs she stocked. "My friend needs something that looks…" I searched for the right words, as I wasn't really sure what Violet needed. "Healthy," I finally said.

The woman's face dropped. "She gettin' chemo, poor ting. I got just da ting to lift dat girl's spirits."

Sounding like an earthquake in a pots and pans factory, she hustled over to a rack of plastic heads and lifted a bob-cut silvery-purple wig into the air. It wasn't the silver-grey of old age and dignity, but more of a punk vibe.

"I don't think…" I began, and then stopped myself, walking over to Miss Rosemary.

She handed me the wig, which glistened under her cheap fluorescent bulbs. I slipped it over my head and looked at my reflection in one of the hundred mirrors in the place.

"Dat ting perfect for you, girl," Miss Rosemary enthused. "Got dat science fiction badass look."

My reflection was startling at first, but as I turned and studied the wig, it became more and more engaging. Exactly what Violet needed. A distraction from her now well-earned druggie complexion. Plus, her name matched the colour.

I paid for the wig and was about to leave when I remembered the other part of Violet's makeover.

"Is there any place around here that does that fake tan thing?" I asked. "I think they spray it on."

Miss Rosemary lowered her chin and raised her eyebrows. "I look like I need a tanning booth, girl?"

"*Dritt*," I laughed. "Right. Sorry."

She laughed too. "Dat's okay. I got a friend does dat stuff, but she up in West Bay and it's Sunday. She ain't open today."

I flashed my police badge. "This is an emergency."

Miss Rosemary frowned at me. "Gettin' your white ass tanned is some kinda police emergency?"

"Not for me. Same friend. And it's police business. Undercover operation," I threw in for good measure.

"Hmm," she grunted.

I wrote my mobile number on a piece of paper for her. "Please. See if your friend can help me. I'll be in West Bay in less than an hour."

"I'll give her a call," Miss Rosemary said, but I didn't hold out much hope from her tone.

Jazzy had texted back while I'd been in the shop. The nurses wouldn't let Jazzy or Violet check her out as I'd admitted her as a detainee. I hurried to the hospital and parked the Jeep out front. I had a police sign I stuck in the window but still won myself a bunch of nasty looks.

"I can take Violet Blaze now," I said to the lady at the front desk. "What do I need to sign?"

She handed me a clipboard with half a dozen papers on it and a pen.

"Just fill these out and we'll make sure the doctor has cleared her to leave."

Faen. I didn't have time for this *dritt*.

"Okay, I'll check on her and get the paperwork done," I said, then walked down the hallway with clipboard in hand.

Violet was sitting on the side of the bed in the clothes Jazzy had brought her from the shack. She looked like hell, but still a hundred times better than when I'd dropped her off.

"Can we go?" Jazzy asked.

I scribbled on the top of the first form. *"Sorry, no time. I'll be back to complete paperwork."*

"*Ja.* But we have to leave out the back."

Violet stood and rubbed her forehead. "I'm sorry."

"I know," I replied. "Let's get you out of here."

"I can't miss tonight, Viivi. I need the money."

"Viivi?" Jazzy asked.

"Undercover name," I groaned. "Not to be used."

"Shit. Sorry, Nora," Violet said.

I led her by the arm and checked to see who might be watching in the hallway. It looked clear, so we hurried away from the reception desk. At the end of the row of emergency rooms, I spotted an exit on the right. We shoved our way outside and Violet squinted against the bright sunshine.

"Here," I said to Jazzy. "Get the Jeep. It's parked out front."

Jazzy didn't need asking twice and shot off with the keys.

"She can drive?" Violet asked, watching the kid sprint into the distance.

"I wouldn't trust her driving public transport, but she does okay," I said.

"But isn't she sixteen?"

"*Ja.* I didn't say she was legal."

"You're not like any copper I've ever met," Violet chuckled.

"*Takk.*"

Halfway to West Bay, with me driving, my mobile rang. It was a number I didn't know.

"*Ja?*" I answered.

"Miss Rosemary here. It's your lucky day. She do it for you 'cos she home right now and her studio at her house."

"*Takk,*" I replied. "Just a moment. My assistant will take down the address."

I handed my mobile to Jazzy in the passenger seat.

"Hello?" she said.

I glanced in the rear-view to check on Violet. She was letting the wind rushing over the topless Jeep blow her hair back as she sat there with her eyes closed. I was going through the motions, but I still wasn't sure taking her out to the yacht was the right thing to do. She'd be far safer in the shack or even in a jail cell overnight. Hopefully, we'd nab the lochmen and have them behind bars by morning. Then she'd be safe.

"Got it, thanks," Jazzy said and hung up the phone.

"*Takk,*" I said.

"Assistant?" she questioned, staring at me with that teenager look of disgust.

"Like a deputy," I said.

She grinned. "Okay then."

Jazzy gave me directions and on the way to the house off West Church Street near the four-way stop, I called Jacob and asked him to meet us there.

"What are we doing?" Violet asked as I pulled up the driveway.

"You're getting painted a better colour," I said and helped her from the back.

"I'm what?"

A woman came out to meet us and I guided Violet to her.

"Hi, I'm Josie. What are you looking for?" she asked.

She was a young, slim, very pretty, dark-skinned woman in subtle makeup and wearing jean shorts and a T-shirt. Not the beauty specialist I'd been expecting.

"Lightly tanned white girl," I said.

"All over?"

I laughed and thought about the job we'd been performing in the evenings. It would really look funny if she stripped down to pasty white with a tanned face and arms.

"Definitely all over," I replied.

"I'm getting a tan?" Violet asked.

"*Ja.* Now go with Josie."

Violet wandered away with a look of bewilderment as Jacob pulled in next to the Jeep.

"Hey," I greeted him.

"Hey. Hi, Jazzy," he said, and nodded to the kid, but he didn't look happy. Maybe I'd asked one too many favours of him. I'd done that before in the past. He'd felt taken advantage of, and he'd been right.

Jazzy smiled at my partner. Maybe my former partner, I reminded myself, as Dexley stepped from the passenger seat.

"Do you have the CCTV?" I asked.

Jacob held up a memory stick. "I kept it off the server like you said."

I nodded to the patrol car, and Dexley moved aside so I could sit in the passenger seat where the laptop was mounted to the dash. Jacob reached over and plugged in the memory stick. I used the touchpad to find the file.

"Have you checked it?" I asked.

"Yeah," he replied.

Something about Jacob's tone and demeanour made me glance his way.

"It's queued up at the spot you'll want," he said, without looking back at me.

I opened the file and made it full screen. The video played. Whittaker's Range Rover was parked in a shaded spot of what I recognised to be the car park out front of The Sovereign. The camera mounted on the complex entrance faced the side of his vehicle, and I watched a silver car pull in and park on the far side of him. It was hard to see what was going on now, but a head appeared above the roof of the Range Rover, and it looked like Whittaker. I couldn't see anyone else, and as Whittaker disappeared, I presumed he either got in the car, or leaned down to talk through the window.

A few moments later, a figure I now clearly recognised as Detective Whittaker moved to the back of his Range Rover and opened the tailgate. Leaning in, he placed a pair of brown paper bags in the back.

"*Fy faen,*" I gasped. "This can't be."

"I'm sorry, Nora," Jacob said softly, as I watched my mentor and father figure close the tailgate of his SUV, where he'd just placed what appeared to be the cocaine and cash he'd been accused of receiving.

20

BEANIES, BOMMIES, AND RODE

I paced back and forth beside the patrol car, unable to believe what I'd just seen.

"Is that the only camera?" I leant in the car and asked Jacob.

"Yes."

"How long was he there?" I asked, when I knew I should be verifying the timeline myself if I was being thorough.

But I couldn't bring myself to look at the video again. I'd watched it five times already, and each successive viewing made the situation more of a reality and still left me without a satisfactory explanation. If it was all part of some deep undercover operation, then why would the Chief nab him and Monroe be investigating?

"He waited seventeen minutes before da car arrived," Jacob replied. "About twenty-three minutes in dere from start to finish."

The silver car had a tinted registration plate cover, so we couldn't read it in the poor morning light, but the vehicle was a four-door Toyota of some sort. About as nondescript as you could get. There had to be hundreds of silver Toyotas in the hire car fleets alone.

"What do you think?" Violet asked, walking out the front door of the house.

She looked to be a shade more tanned. From what I could see, Josie was handy with a spray can or whatever she used to paint her customers.

"Good," I said impatiently. "We need to go."

Violet's expression fell, but I was in no mood for niceties and bullshit. I paid Josie and took the memory stick from Jacob.

"I'm sorry," he said again.

"*Takk,*" I managed and got in the Jeep.

"I think she looks good," Jazzy said from the passenger seat.

"*Ja,*" I mumbled and backed out of the driveway.

Part of me wanted to call Whittaker and ask him what the hell he was thinking, but it wouldn't accomplish anything. And now I wondered if the drugs could be connected to the lochmen. We didn't have an abundance of cocaine importers in the islands. Weed was more widely spread, and pills easier to bring in, but not the harder drugs. There had to be a chance Whittaker's exchange had something to do with *Manannán* and perhaps even Patrick Pennington's murder. The more I thought about it all, the worse I felt. The news about Whittaker now piled on top of my growing desperation over Chloe Pennington.

"What's in the bag?" Violet asked from the backseat, shouting to be heard over the wind noise as I sped towards home.

"Wait until we get there," I called back.

"Oh this is… shit!" Violet yelped, and I glanced in the rear-view mirror.

A silvery purple blur flew through the air in the wake of the Jeep. I slammed on the brakes. Jazzy shot forward until the seatbelt caught her. Violet gasped as she hit the back of my seat.

"Jeez, Nora," Jazzy complained.

I ground the gears, finding reverse, then accelerated backwards, twisting around to see down the road from where we'd just come. The brand new wig lay at the edge of the pavement, half in the dirt. Braking hard again, I put the Jeep in neutral and depressed the parking brake with my foot. Cursing under my breath in Norwegian, I leapt out and went and picked the wig up, brushing off the dust and dirt.

"I'm sorry," Violet said, and I tossed the wig into her lap.

"I said wait so you wouldn't ruin it in the wind."

The words tumbled out, and I knew I'd regret every one of them. My anger couldn't be contained despite being aimed at the wrong target. One of the few pillars of strength and truth in my life had been a lie, and now my rage was out of control.

"I'm really sorry," Violet sobbed. "I didn't mean to."

"*Faen ta deg!*" I screamed into the air, stomping down the road instead of getting in the Jeep.

I stopped a few metres away and closed my eyes while I growled in frustration. This wasn't me. I didn't react this way to anything. Sure, I got plenty mad about all sorts of things, but I gritted my teeth and dealt with it. I couldn't remember ever losing my cool in this way before.

I startled when I felt a hand on my arm and whipped around. Jazzy looked up at me, her face full of concern.

"You're being an ass," she said softly.

"*Ja,*" I breathed.

"I don't like it," she added.

"Me neither."

She tugged on my arm and led me back to the Jeep where Violet stood on the dirt verge, tears rolling down her cheeks. I looked at her and didn't know what to say or how to say it.

"Hug her," I ordered Jazzy, pointing to Violet.

The kid took a step forward and flung her arms around the drug addict. Violet hugged her back and sniffed back more tears.

"*Beklager,*" I said shakily, still too full of anger to hug anyone.

"That means she's sorry," Jazzy translated, unwrapping her long skinny arms. "She never says that."

Violet nodded and wiped her eyes. "How do you know what it means, then?"

"I looked it up," Jazzy explained, tipping the passenger seat forward so Violet could climb in the back. "I figured I'd need to know how to say it sometimes."

I let out a long breath. So much for me being the adult and the foster parent.

Like a child letting go of a balloon and watching it fly around the room, the kid's words seemed to vent the worst of my fury. But without the farting sound a balloon makes.

Violet stood before the mirror mounted on the back of the bathroom door, wearing nothing but knickers and her new wig. Considering she'd been stoned out of her head and sexually abused earlier in the day, she looked remarkably good. Amazing what IV fluids, whatever legal drugs they gave her, and a spray tan can do for a pasty stripper. That, and a lifetime of overcoming trauma.

"I love it," she squealed, playing with the wig.

"Looks cool," Jazzy agreed. "Got an outfit to go with it?"

"Yeah, she's got plenty of clothes," I quickly butted in before Violet explained how that wouldn't matter too much.

I'd rather the kid didn't know the lengths to which I was going to for a drug bust. Violet caught my eye and nodded, which I took to mean she understood my concerns. Of course, the two had spent the day together yesterday, so I had no idea what Jazzy had already gleaned. She was wily at finding out what she wanted to know. My mobile rang, and I checked the caller ID. Weatherford.

"Sir," I answered.

"We have a lead," he said, and I could hear the optimism in his voice. "Great idea on the injury reports."

Now wasn't the time to inform him it hadn't been my idea.

"Who?"

"His name's Oliver Warwick," Weatherford replied. "He was an engineer subcontracted to work on one of Pennington's condo developments about a year and a half ago."

"What happened to him?"

"He was seriously hurt when he fell from the first floor. Hasn't worked since."

"Why, sir?" I wondered.

If the man was paralysed or couldn't walk, I didn't see how he could kidnap a healthy eleven-year-old girl.

"He broke both legs and fractured a vertebra, but it appears he recovered from all that. His doctor told me he also suffered a head injury with brain swelling. They put him in an induced coma for a week before they felt it was safe to wake him up. He's had terrible headaches and dizzy spells ever since."

That sounded like a recipe for someone to be pissed off.

"Did he sue Pennington?"

"It doesn't appear so. In fact, I spoke with Warwick's sister in England, and she told me Pennington went out of his way to help the guy. Paid to cover some of the shortfalls in his health insurance."

"Oh. So why are we suspecting him?" I asked.

"Because he's struggled with anger issues. Both the doctor and his sister said he has terrible mood swings. He's prescribed antidepressants, but they think he stops taking them sometimes."

"Okay," I said, looking at my watch. "Have you brought him in?"

"That's the really suspicious part, Nora," Weatherford explained. "No one's seen him in four days. He's missed therapy appointments, hasn't answered his phone, and he wasn't home when we checked."

"Does he drive?" I asked.

"Not since the accident. But he still owns a car, and it's missing from his apartment."

I needed to be at the dock in a little over an hour, so there was nothing I could do, even if they had him in custody.

"Leave me a message on my phone if anything changes, sir. I'll get it when we come back."

The detective hesitated before responding. "I spoke with Williams and Ben Crooks. They're ready to go tonight."

"*Ja.* I talked to them too."

"One way or another, we need to wrap this up tonight, Nora. You've gone above and beyond with this case, but we can't keep sending you out there alone."

"Hopefully they'll be inside the twelve-mile mark, sir."

"Sure, but if they're not, we're grabbing the lochmen when they bring you back to shore."

I thought that over. I'd already been invited to dance more, so I could probably have them use me again during the week. Especially if David was interested in returning. I walked over to the chest of drawers in the bedroom and opened the top one, pulling out a Mermaid Divers beanie my friend AJ had given me.

"If I'm wearing a pink beanie, don't arrest them, sir."

"That's the signal?"

"*Ja.*"

"You own a pink beanie?"

"A gift. I've never worn it."

"But it has to be a damn good reason for us not to nab these guys tonight, Nora. I'm serious. We can't keep putting you at risk."

"I understand, sir."

"Okay. Good luck, and be careful."

We hung up, and I made sure to put the beanie in my bag of skimpy outfits.

Something was different with the lochmen. It was obvious the moment we arrived. A tension I hadn't noticed before. They'd always been serious, but relaxed and confident. Now, an air of paranoia draped over the three of them, and they constantly scanned the dock and street beyond. Everything about them screamed guilty of something, and I wondered which one of the three wrapped a wire around Patrick Pennington's neck and brutally severed his trachea and carotid arteries.

My guess was Lomond.

It would have been an intensely violent and messy death. I wondered what trace evidence we'd find on the man at this very moment. It was hard to scrub away every molecule when the execution would have produced so much blood. Lomond was wearing a lightweight jumper with a high neck, probably to hide the desperate scratches of a dying man.

They searched us and our bags, but with the distracted half-hearted attention of men who didn't suspect us of being a problem. Which was good. Although I was annoyed I hadn't sneaked a mobile with me as I could have got away with it.

Violet's renewed energy was already fading. As the IV fluids and medication from the hospital began wearing off, she was quickly becoming exhausted. I'd bought us both coffee-flavoured energy drinks on the drive to switch the Jeep for the shitty little car, and I hoped that would keep her going until 8:00pm. From there, a little adrenaline should give her a boost once she started performing.

The men seemed to settle down once we'd left the dock, and Violet curled up on a cushioned bench seat and fell asleep. How she stayed that way with the RIB bouncing and jolting over the evening swells, I don't know, but she didn't stir the whole way.

I soon noticed we'd taken a different heading from the harbour, which meant they'd moved *Manannán*. Ness didn't say a word until we arrived, and I noticed the anchor line extended from the bow.

"Captain has struggled to get the anchor to hold," Ness said as I walked past him to board the yacht.

"Which end of the bank are we on?" I asked, quickly thinking over how I could play this to my advantage.

"Fucked if I know," Ness replied.

"West," Lomond said. "To be safe."

That put them outside the twelve-mile range even from the North West Point in West Bay.

"It's silty sand here. Maybe he gets lucky and catches a bommie, but more likely the anchor just drags," I said nonchalantly and stepped onto the swim platform with my bag.

"What's a bommie?" Lomond asked.

"Coral head."

"How do you know so much about it?" Lomond questioned, more pointedly.

"I told him," I said, nodding at Ness. "I dive out here."

"Then how do you anchor here?" Ness asked.

I turned and blew out a breath, like I was annoyed at having to explain something so simple.

"He's probably tried anchoring on the top of the bank. Better to anchor off the slope, up-current. This end, the slopes are more sand, so the farther you move east, the rockier they are and easier to get the anchor to grab."

I was making everything up, but if I could build enough doubt between these two and the captain, they might not believe him if he contradicted me.

"And he needs more rode," I added.

"Rode?" Lomond asked. "Don't you mean rope?"

"*Ei,*" I replied, remembering to say no in Finnish. "Rode is the line to an anchor."

Ness laughed. "And how would you know how much *rode* the bloody captain used?"

I sighed again. "From the angle of the line going into the water. It's too steep," I said, demonstrating the angle with my hand. "More rode, less angle, and harder for the anchor to drag. The rule is seven to one."

Violet rubbed her eyes as she joined me on the swim step. "Jeez, Nor... hmm, Viivi," she quickly corrected herself. "You're a regular nautical encyclopaedia."

I scanned the lochmen to see if any of them had caught her screw-up, but they seemed more engrossed in the anchor talk. I continued in an effort to distract them.

"Depth here is 35 to 40 metres, so 250 metres of rode should do it. For a yacht this size and mass, I'd use two anchors for security, seeing as it's a cat and you could run one from each hull at the bow."

With that, I turned and walked up the steps, putting a hand on Violet's lower back to make sure she came with me.

"Sorry," she whispered. "I nearly screwed up."

"It's okay," I lied. "You should get some more sleep before dinner."

She needed the rest, but it would also be harder for her to put her toes in her mouth when she was asleep. That wasn't right. *Faen.* I needed sleep too.

21

ARSE-SHAKING ANGELS

We both stayed in the berth while I heard the yacht's engines start, and the vessel began moving locations. I wanted to go topside to gauge how far we'd gone across the bank, but it wasn't worth the risk. Ness and Lomond may well have given the captain a hard time about not knowing how or where to anchor, so I didn't want to face him and get into a heated discussion over seamanship. He undoubtedly knew more than I did, despite my earlier bravado.

Violet crashed out again, curled up on the floor using a pile of her clothes for comfort. I tried to sleep, but my mind wouldn't shut up. It hadn't bothered me too badly before about being out of communication with Weatherford and Williams. But with Patrick's murder, and the men who I was sure were responsible now acting strangely, it made me nervous. Each night, we'd had a few of Williams' men on a fishing boat a couple of miles away, but they wouldn't even know if something went wrong. I could be garrotted, and they'd be none the wiser until I didn't return to shore.

A few minutes before seven, Morar banged on the door to alert us dinner was ready. I woke Violet and waited while she splashed water on her face and fixed her makeup. We were waiting for the customers to arrive before presenting her wearing the wig, but she already looked healthier with a fresh coat of spray tan and more rest.

From the upper deck at dinner, I couldn't even tell we'd changed positions. We were in a vast expanse of ocean with no visual references, but walking from rail to rail, I could look forward from either side and see an anchor line from both hulls at the bow. At a lesser angle. I'd wondered if the captain even had enough rope aboard, but apparently he did.

Raven and Shandy were in a quiet mood, no doubt feeling the black cloud over the yacht from the lochmen's demeanour. They did both comment on Violet's new skin tone, commenting that she looked better. If only they knew what she'd been through in the past 18 hours, they'd have been even more impressed.

"I know I made good money off dat Patrick guy," Raven said. "But I'd be fine wit him not showin' up."

"He kinda creepy," Shandy agreed. "And he didn't tip so well, considerin' he all over you."

"True, dat," Raven said, rolling her eyes.

"If you're finished, why don't the rest of you go downstairs and start getting ready," Morar said. "I'd like a word with Violet."

Raven and Shandy stood and sauntered towards the stairs at the rear of the deck. I hesitated, and Violet looked at me with fear in her eyes. I could tell she was desperate for me to stay.

"I think I'll have dessert after all," I said.

Katrine stood and gave me an annoyed look with a slight grin. "I'll get you ice cream if you help me clear the table."

"Sure," I smiled back.

"Chocolate chip, cookie dough, coffee crunch, or vanilla?"

"The coffee one," I replied.

I didn't know if ice cream ever had caffeine in it, but I needed all I could get this evening.

Katrine left to get me a bowl, and Morar beckoned Violet over to the rear rail of the deck. I pretended not to pay attention, but I carefully listened. She wasn't exactly being encouraging, but it sounded like she was complimenting her on making an effort. Violet started to tell the woman about her wig, but my focus shifted to the voices I could hear coming from somewhere else. It was the lochmen, but wherever they were, I couldn't make out what they were saying.

I watched Violet glance down to the lower deck and realised that's where the men were standing. Their tone was urgent but hushed, so they obviously didn't want anyone listening in. It would be too obvious for me to join Morar and Violet, but I looked around for other options. I began to rise from my seat, but Katrine returned up the stairs and slid three bowls across the table.

"I decided to join you," she said and sat down next to me.

Morar was done giving Violet her speech, but now I couldn't hear the men's voices. Maybe I'd missed them talking about football scores, but I couldn't help feeling it had been something more important. Violet sat back down and Morar left us, walking down the steps to the pilothouse level.

"Okay?" I asked Violet.

She nodded. "I guess. She told me she doesn't want the hassle of training someone else, so I'd better do a good job tonight."

Katrine laughed. "Sounds like Morar. I'd like to tell you she's soft underneath that bitch of an exterior, but she's tough as old boots all the way through."

"Screw her," I said, and grinned at Violet. "Wait till she sees you tonight."

"Yeah," she chuckled. "Screw her."

We finished the ice cream, then helped Katrine clear the table and load everything into the dishwasher. Leaving her to prepare for the clients arriving in twenty minutes, Violet and I returned to our berth to get dressed. Once we were inside, she grabbed my arm.

"Hey. The three blokes were on the lower deck talking while the battleaxe was rabbiting on at me."

"*Ja*. I could hear them."

"You heard what they said?"

"*Nei*. I couldn't make out what they were saying."

"I could," Violet said, looking proud of herself.

"Really?"

"I forget when we're out here that you're…" she lowered her voice to a whisper. "You know, a copper. But I remembered when I heard them talking and tried to hear what they said."

"*Ja?*" I replied expectantly.

"Does this sort of thing help me?" she asked. "With my case and whatever happens here."

"*Ja,*" I replied. "Of course. Everything you do to help us nick these *drittsekker* will be taken into account."

I had to be careful. It would be easy to promise her things I couldn't be sure the courts would support.

"You're gonna look after me, right?" she asked, looking me in the eye.

I wasn't sure exactly what she meant. Look after as in keep sleeping on my sofa in my home, or look after as in putting in a good word.

"I will fight to help you with your court case," I said, hoping that would keep things clear.

She nodded. "They were talking about an exchange. Sounded like tomorrow. They mentioned the name Tulla."

"Tulla?" I repeated and reached for my mobile to search the internet for loch names.

But I didn't have my phone.

"Yeah. Tulla. At least that's what it sounded like," Violet explained.

"What else?"

She shrugged. "That was all I heard. But that's good info, yeah?"

"Maybe," I responded, lost in thought. "An exchange tomorrow?"

"That's what they were talking about."

"Where?"

"If they said, I didn't hear," Violet replied, and looked worried.

"What exactly did they say?" I pressed.

"I'm not sure, exactly," she stammered. "I had the bitch yapping in one ear while I was trying to listen to them. It was the quiet one talking the most."

"Maree? The pudgy one?"

She nodded. "He said something about getting the exchange done and leaving as soon as possible."

"Okay, that's good. What else?"

"I think it was the angry-looking one who spoke next."

"Lomond?"

"I guess. Honestly, I haven't paid attention to their names. I know two of them are Scottish, but they have these weird names I can't remember."

"They're codenames," I said impatiently, glancing at my watch. We only had a few minutes until we needed to be in the salon. "What did Lomond say?"

"He's the one who said we'd operate for one more night then leave."

"Hmm," I mumbled as I chewed the information over.

It made sense that Morar wanted Violet to work out, as she only needed one more night from her. Katrine had mentioned Mondays were usually their day off, but their plan was now to take care of business on the island, run the club one more night, then leave. Probably during the night. The question was where this exchange was supposed to take place. Violet nearly fell over when a knock came on the door.

"Time, girls," Morar snapped.

"*Juu*," I called back.

We weren't even ready yet. The next few minutes were a mad scramble.

It would have been nice to take more time to get Violet ready with her new wig, but even in a rush, she looked great. The moment the clients entered the salon, eyes turned her way, and I could see her delight when she drew as much interest as the rest of us.

David was back, but he sat at the bar and watched from a distance for a while. Several other men, one of whom had been out to the yacht before, kept me busy and tipped well. I tried not to show how distracted I was. If the *Manannán* was within the twelve-mile range, Ben and the Joint Marine Unit should have been here by now, so I finally settled down and told myself it wasn't happening. Which meant my next decision would have significant consequences.

Could I rely on what Violet thought she heard the lochmen say? If she was wrong and they pulled anchor during the day, we'd lose them. If I let Williams grab them when we returned but found nothing on the RIB, then they'd leave the moment they were released. My decision could be the difference between catching drug dealers and murderers or watching them sail away free men.

When it was my time to rotate out from dancing, I used the bathroom and put on shorts and a crop-top tee. I grabbed a light-weight sweatshirt from the berth and returned to the bar. David was still there.

"Drink?" he asked.

"Sure. White wine please," I said to Katrine, and sat on the stool beside him.

"How's your evening going?" he asked.

"The usual," I replied with a shrug of the shoulders. "I take things off, I put them back on, shake my arse."

He laughed. "You don't butter the customers up for tips, do you?"

"Is that a problem? Would you prefer me to pretend all the time?"

"No," he smiled. "I like your honesty."

He probably wouldn't if he heard all my honesty, I thought.

Katrine handed me a wine. "Here you go, love."

"*Kiitos*," I said, taking the wine, before turning to David. "Mind if we get a little fresh air?"

He slipped from his stool and took my wine glass so I could put the sweatshirt on as we walked across the salon. Outside, the warm, humid air was soon offset by the cooling ocean breeze brushing across the stern of the yacht. It took a moment for my eyes to adjust to the darkness. I scanned to the east, looking for pricks of light on the water, indicating a vessel. In the far distance, indistinct where water met sky, the lights faintly glowed from several tall buildings on the island.

If Ben Crooks and Sergeant Williams were out there somewhere, I couldn't spot their running lights, although I felt sure they'd be on. For safety, but also because the *Manannán* had radar. My backup would be more suspicious running dark when the vessels could be easily spotted on a screen.

"What do you do when you're not shaking your arse?" David asked.

I could see a grin on his face. He was a nice-looking man with a gentle air about him. Quietly confidant, yet I sensed something vulnerable. He didn't quite fit the profile of the other clients. They were wealthy, arrogant men, or friends doing something daring and dangerous. A few couples exploring a wilder side of their marriage. David seemed like he didn't need any of that. If the man sat at the bar in one of the nice hotels or restaurants, he'd soon attract the attention of well-maintained divorcees and gorgeous younger women. He'd pay for their time in different ways, but save himself a boat trip which ended up alone.

"Bartender," I replied. "Save money. Travel. Work some more."

I leaned against the gunwale, and he stood closer, while maintaining a respectful distance between us.

"What about you?" I asked, making an effort to converse, and because I was curious.

"I'm an investor," he said.

I laughed. "That can mean anything."

He nodded and grinned again. "It could. But maybe it's just boring."

"Maybe," I replied. "Or you're hiding something."

He laughed softly again. "Perhaps. But I bet you could find out if you had dinner with me."

"We're not allowed to associate with guests away from the boat."

"This yacht will move on soon, and you and I will still be on the island," David replied. "It'll be none of their business."

If I was looking for a man to take care of me and provide security, then David was probably the best version I'd ever come across. He was more than twice my age, but handsome, sexy, and genuine, unless I was misjudging him. But having been coerced into an affair with a teacher at fifteen, and brainwashed into a sex-trafficking men's club at sixteen, I'd had my fill of older men thinking they could do what they wanted with me.

"You should talk to Violet," I responded. "She needs someone like you."

"But I'm interested in you."

"You don't know me."

"Which is why dinner would be a good idea," he said, unwavering.

Part of me wanted to warn the man that he shouldn't be on the yacht. Especially tomorrow night. But arresting the lochmen meant more to me than saving a man who I suspected was kind with good intentions. He was still paying sizeable sums of money to watch young women take their clothes off in an illegal floating strip club, so as innocent as he seemed, he was no angel.

A burst of light bathed the aft deck as the sliding door opened. Violet stood there and smiled at us.

"You're up, *Viivi*," she said, emphasising my fake name.

"Consider it?" David asked as we walked to the door.

"*Juu*," I replied, as I put an arm around Violet. "You too."

22

COCAINE AND THE TICKING CLOCK

"That's better," Morar said, as she handed Violet back fifty percent of her tip money. "Third best tonight."

Shandy rolled her eyes.

Morar ignored her and continued. "You can both work tomorrow night."

"Wait," Raven snapped. "What about our day off?"

"You'll get one," Morar replied firmly. "Just not tomorrow."

"When we gettin' it, den?" Shandy persisted.

Morar glared at her. "When I tell you. Or you can have every day off if you'd prefer?"

Shandy looked at the floor and shook her head.

"Can we work all week?" Violet asked, and I wanted to kick her, but it would have been too obvious.

"We'll see," Morar replied. "Now, you two go to the tender. They're back."

I heard the outboards approaching, so I whisked Violet away to get our stuff from the berth and put my jacket on.

"Maybe we'll get a few more nights," she babbled as we gathered our things.

I paused and looked at her, raising an eyebrow.

"Oh, right. I keep forgetting. Can you wait until after shift tomorrow? I made great money tonight."

"Let's go," I said, then stopped by the door. "Here." I handed her my tip money.

"I can't take yours," Violet replied, looking from me to the enticing wad of cash.

"I can't keep it. I have to hand it in as evidence every day."

She still didn't reach for the money I held out. Instead, she took her cash and offered it to me.

"I don't need to put your cash in evidence. That just sort of slips through the cracks."

"Bugger that," she said. "I'm not giving it to you to hand over to the old bill. Just keep it for me."

With my mind elsewhere, I wondered what she was talking about, but then I realised. I took her money and shoved it in my pocket. Taking half of mine, I put it with it, then placed the balance in my other pocket.

"Thanks," she whispered. "I don't trust myself, you know?"

"*Juu*," I said, still accidentally in my Finnish guise.

I also made a mental note to hide the money when we returned to the shack. Just in case her good intentions failed her completely.

As we bounced through the darkness with the lights from shore growing brighter, I still had a decision to make. It was only Ness and Lomond who'd returned after taking the clients back, and I ticked that as another vote in favour of waving off the arrest tonight. I wanted all of them, and we already had one manhunt going on. We didn't need another one searching for a missing lochman.

I'd been wearing the beanie to keep my head warm anyway, so now nearing the harbour, I made a point of standing up and moving to the centre console. Hopefully, I'd be easy to see. Ness turned to make sure Violet wasn't with me.

"Think about what I said?" he asked.

I nodded. "Sure."

"Sure, you've thought about it, or sure you'll do it?"

I considered the best answer to learn something more without raising his suspicions. The men had calmed down throughout the evening, but I sensed them tense once more as we neared the harbour.

"When would we leave?"

Ness looked at me, and Lomond, standing on the far side of the console, looked at Ness.

"How much notice do you need?" Ness asked.

I shrugged. "Depends. How long would I be gone? Decent-priced digs are hard to rent here, so if it's only weeks, I'll keep mine. If it's months, then I wouldn't. But I'd be screwing my roommate."

"If you keep bringing in good tips, it could be a lot of months," Ness said.

Lomond was still keenly paying attention to the conversation. I imagined what his solution would be to the end of my tour aboard the *Manannán*. Would he garrotte me like Patrick Pennington, because that was how he got his kicks, or simply toss me overboard in the middle of the Caribbean Sea? He had the air of a cold-hearted killer. Trained by the military to take lives. An adrenaline-packed thrill he couldn't move on from.

"I can fit my life into one suitcase, a dive bag, and a rucksack," I replied. "Tell me the day and I'll be ready."

It was subtle in the dark on the bouncing boat, but I knew Lomond nudged Ness in some way. Ness flinched and looked at his fellow lochman before realising he shouldn't have reacted.

"You got it," he said to me. "I'll let you know. But not a word to anyone. Understand?"

"*Juu*," I replied, and made sure I was clear of the windscreen in front of the centre console as Ness slowed the RIB, entering the natural harbour.

I scanned the shoreline and caught a glint off somebody moving near the dive shops behind the guest dock. Lomond must have seen it too as his head whipped in that direction.

"Hold up short," he growled to Ness, who quickly shut down the throttles.

I put a foot forward as though stopping myself from falling. To make absolutely sure I was seen, I then took a few steps towards the bow before turning around.

"Six again tomorrow?" I asked, looking at the two men.

They were on high alert, searching the edges of the harbour for more signs of trouble. We all swung around when a rubbish bin crashed over. A man stumbled from the shadows of the dive shop, clearly drunk. Barefoot, with his shirt untucked, I nearly didn't recognise Sergeant Williams.

"That bloke's sloshed," Violet laughed from the stern, completely unaware of the tension.

"Okay," Lomond said quietly, and Ness reengaged the throttles, idling gently to the dock.

***

"Hey, you look like the drunk guy at the dock," Violet said when Williams met us in the car park at Central Station.

"Nice save, sir," I said as he grinned. "Wait, do I still call you, sir? I'm at least an *acting* detective. Doesn't that make us equals?"

"Hell no. Keep da sirs goin', Beanpole."

"Why did you call it off?" Weatherford asked, joining us next to my Jeep.

"Violet helped us get information on their movements, sir," I replied, making sure she heard me give her the credit.

I didn't know if it would make any difference in front of a judge, but I needed her to know I'd tried on her behalf.

"There's an exchange happening tomorrow," I continued. "Then they're leaving."

"Where?" Weatherford asked.

He looked absolutely worn out, which wasn't a surprise as it was now the early hours of Monday.

"We don't know. But they're running the club for one more night before they leave, so some time tomorrow and it will have to involve the tender unless someone else takes a boat out to *Manannán*."

The detective scratched his head and frowned. "Damn. Okay. So they have to bring their clients back to shore, then you two, right?"

"*Ja*. And one more thing. The exchange is with someone named Tulla."

"Is dat another loch name?" Williams asked.

"I think so. Look it up," I replied.

Williams dug out his phone and typed in an internet search, scrolling down the list he found.

"Yeah. It's a loch."

"But that's not anyone you've met on the yacht?" Weatherford asked.

"*Nei*."

"Could there be someone out there you haven't met?"

"*Nei*. I don't think so."

Although I considered the fact that I'd never set eyes on the first mate.

"But it's an exchange, sir. Why would they exchange something with someone who's already with them?" I asked, thinking it through out loud.

Weatherford put his hands on his hips. "So, they're meeting someone codenamed Tulla, sometime tomorrow, and we don't know where or when. That about it?"

"*Ja*," I replied, undeterred. "We follow the lochmen all day and watch the yacht. If the tender doesn't make any other trips and no one else visits the *Manannán,* then the exchange must be during the routine shuttle runs."

"Maybe dey brought da drugs ashore tonight?" Williams said.

"I didn't see them carrying anything more than a rucksack," I replied, "and Ness was very casual about it if it was full of drugs. He had it hung on the back of the helm seat."

"It didn't appear to be heavy," Weatherford agreed.

"What came of the search, sir?" I asked.

Weatherford shook his head. "Nothing. Rasha's team went through each room with a fine-toothed comb and never found a trace of anything suspicious. No blood, at least. They'll test hair fibres they collected tomorrow, but I'm not confident they'll link them to Patrick."

"Hair fibres won't help, anyway," I muttered, for the first time questioning whether the lochmen were responsible for Pennington's murder.

"True. He could have been in their rooms at some point," Weatherford agreed.

"*Faen,*" I swore under my breath.

It felt like we were nowhere with any of the cases. The yacht, Whittaker's situation, or the hunt for Chloe Pennington.

"Did you find the injured bloke?" I asked.

Weatherford paused before speaking, looking at Williams. "Thank you, Sergeant, and please pass on our appreciation to Ben and his men. Let's regroup in the morning when we've all had some rest."

"Yes, sir," Williams acknowledged, and grinned at me.

"Try to sober up before then," I said.

He grinned wider. "Sober up, *sir.*"

I tried not to, but I couldn't stop myself from laughing a little.

Detective Weatherford beckoned me to one side after Williams had walked away.

"We haven't found him," he said once we were distanced from Violet.

I looked back and could see she was too tired to care about being left out. She climbed into the passenger side of the Jeep, tipped the seat back, and closed her eyes.

"We're about 36 hours away from a young girl being murdered, and we're clutching at straws," Weatherford continued. "We have to chase down this Oliver Warwick guy, but his only connection to the case is a tenuous one, promoted by the fact he's unaccounted for."

The detective's frustration mirrored my own, and I sensed our shared desperation growing. It wasn't a path that would help us find Chloe, but I didn't have encouraging words or an idea to share that would give us hope.

"Did Rupert get another message?" I asked.

Weatherford nodded and took out his mobile, found the recording, and hit play.

"I'm starting to think you value your secret more than your daughter's life, Pennington. Chloe is very disappointed that she only has two days to live."

The kidnapper seemed so adamant that Pennington knew the reason Chloe had been taken. It was hard to imagine that Rupert couldn't fathom it out. So perhaps his secret was indeed more important to him than his daughter. Maybe I was completely misreading the father, but I believed he was genuinely confused, so it didn't fit in my mind.

"I'd give anything to be able to talk to Roy about this," Weatherford muttered as he rubbed his forehead, no doubt nursing a stress and exhaustion fuelled headache.

"He gave us the injury victim idea," I said, too tired to think through any explanations I'd need to come up with.

"What?" he questioned, frowning at me. "You spoke with Whittaker?"

"*Nei.* I texted with his wife."

"She relayed a message from Roy?"

I nodded.

"Why didn't you tell me?"

"Because I promised it would be between the two of us."

Weatherford walked around in a circle, looking at the ground and shaking his head. He finally stopped.

"Did he give you anything else?"

"*Nei.*"

"Do you think he'd respond again?"

"I don't know," I replied. "But what would we ask him?"

Weatherford groaned. "That's the problem, right? He's cut off from all the details we know. Roy immerses himself in his cases and sifts through the evidence to find the best way to move forward. Unless we can show him everything, I don't see how he can help at this point. Shit, I don't even know what I'd ask him."

I knew what I'd ask him. What the hell was he doing putting cash and cocaine in the back of his SUV on Thursday? But that wouldn't help us find Chloe Pennington.

"Don't you think it's strange that it's all related?" I said, as the idea wandered into my sleepy mind.

"How do you mean?" Weatherford asked.

"Whittaker, the lochmen, and the Penningtons," I replied. "The common thread is cocaine."

The detective thought it over for a few moments.

"We both know Roy's innocent, and so far, we don't have any proof that the lochmen are dealing drugs," he said, taking a moment to think again before continuing. "And it's only Patrick Pennington we've found in possession. There's no link at all to Chloe or her parents."

Weatherford didn't know about the CCTV, so he still thought our boss was innocent.

"Whittaker had cocaine in his SUV, regardless of how it got there, sir," I responded. "And Patrick had a connection to the lochmen, an argument with one of them, cocaine in his house, and he was executed. Not a stretch to figure the drugs were the link."

Weatherford let out a long sigh and nodded. "I don't disagree, but we don't have a stitch of evidence, and Chloe's only got 36 hours left." He looked at his watch. "We all need sleep, Nora. Go home. I'll see you in about five hours."

"Sir," I acknowledged, and walked towards the Jeep.

"And Nora," he whispered just loud enough to stop me.

I looked over my shoulder.

"Keep her ladyship locked up. We have enough to worry about without chasing that kid around town."

"*Ja*," I replied, then looked at Violet.

She was slumped against the roll hoop of the Jeep, fast asleep.

23

COFFEE AND A KISS-ARSE PASTRY

I went to bed frustrated. I woke up mad. In between were bursts of fitful sleep which left me unrefreshed to face the new day. The new week. One in which Chloe Pennington would only see less than a day and half unless we found her, or her father confessed to a sin. Rolling out of bed, I tried to stay quiet, so I didn't wake the other two. Jazzy briefly stirred, rolled over, and was soon back in a deep sleep. Violet was cocooned in a lightweight blanket on the sofa and never even moved.

The island acted as though it was just another Monday. Traffic was busy out of West Bay as people made their commute to offices, restaurants, and tourist activities. The sun had risen from its familiar spot in the east, and the usual heat and humidity made my back perspire against the Jeep's seat. The farther I drove and the more life appeared to be normal, the angrier I became.

And then I did something really dumb.

Banging on the front door, I waited, pacing back and forth on the front step. Finally, it opened and Rosie Whittaker looked at me.

"Nora. What are you doing here?"

"I need to talk to him," I replied, my voice stripped of patience.

She looked over her shoulder, then back at me.

"You know you can't," she said, pulling her dressing gown tighter across her chest.

Undoubtedly, I'd woken her up or at least caught her before her day had started. A day that wouldn't be feeling normal to her either.

"I need five minutes," I insisted.

Rosie shook her head. "You'll both be in more trouble if…"

"It's okay, love," I heard the detective's voice from inside the home. "Let her in."

Rosie glanced around the street, as though making sure we weren't being watched, then stepped aside. I moved inside the house and she quickly closed the door behind me.

"This way," the detective said, and I followed him into his study.

I'd only been inside his home a couple of times before and never in the study. It reflected Roy Whittaker's personality perfectly. Neat, tidy, a wall of books, a comfortable yet simple office chair behind an elegant but not ostentatious oak desk. A clock on the wall and a view of his well-maintained back garden. He closed the door behind us.

"This is inappropriate and ill-advised, Nora," he said, leaning against his desk.

"I've seen the CCTV," I blurted, and watched his face.

His expression didn't change. Not an eye twitch, tensing of muscles, or movement of lips. Nothing. He didn't respond.

"Why?" I asked, exasperated.

He finally sighed. "Nora, you have to believe me when I tell you to let this go. Let Monroe do his job."

"He's an arse."

"He's doing what he's supposed to do."

"What aren't you telling me?" I asked, searching for anything that made sense of what I'd seen.

It couldn't be true. There had to be an explanation. I was caught in the spin cycle of bouncing between believing my own eyes and certain there was something more to the story. I'd woken up furious, and now I'd hurtled around the washing machine a few times until I was hanging on my mentor's next words to give me a justifiable reason he'd loaded drugs and money into his SUV.

"I'm not telling you anything, Nora, because I'm not allowed to discuss this in any way."

"You're really pissing me off, sir."

"I can see that," he replied, as calm as always. "It's not my intention, but my hands are tied, Nora. Please don't put your own career in jeopardy. No more attempts to reach me."

"We're desperate on the kidnapping case," I said, my voice reflecting our frustration.

"I simply can't help you," he said before a short pause. "Directly."

I started to question his answer, but stopped before saying anything. We were in his private study in his house. How would anyone know what was said in this room? I stared at his face. His expression was unwaveringly blank. Deniability? He wouldn't have to lie if asked whether he had encouraged or authorised communication. My eyes flicked around the room, then back to Whittaker. Almost imperceptibly, he nodded. *Fy faen. His study was bugged?*

"I should go."

"You should, and please do not try to make any contact again, Nora."

"No, sir. I'm sorry."

Whittaker opened the study door, and Rosie swiftly showed me out. I nonchalantly searched the street as I turned the Jeep around, but didn't see any unusual or suspicious vehicles or people. I left, still thoroughly confused, but less aggravated, although I wasn't sure why.

I stopped for coffee and something to eat on the way to Central Station, and just as I'd wedged the two drinks into the makeshift cup holders in the old Jeep, my mobile rang.

"Sir," I answered, seeing it was Weatherford.

"I was hoping I wasn't waking you," he said. "Are you at home?"

"*Nei*. I'm ten minutes from the station."

"I'll text you a location. Oliver Warwick's been sighted near Safehaven Drive."

"Okay," I replied, thinking that was a strange place for a man on the run to be.

Safehaven ran between North Sound Golf Club and a canal which led to the North Sound itself. On the south side of the canal was the Ritz-Carlton's golf course. All that was in the area were fairways, a hotel, and expensive homes. But picturing the road, I realised what else. The canal was busy with charter boats at the east end, but along its length stretching west were mainly empty lots which had never been developed. A few nice homes and a condo building were situated closer to the west end. It would be easy to tether a small boat somewhere along the middle of the canal, and no one would notice. At least not at night.

"Seen on a boat?" I asked.

"No, but my guess he's staying on one close by," Weatherford replied. "Meet me there."

"*Ja*," I replied.

"Hey," he said, before I'd hung up. "You didn't happen to stop for breakfast, did you?"

"*Ja*. I have coffees and pastries."

"I'm starting to feel like a scrounger," he laughed. "But thank you."

"I'm starting to feel like a kiss-arse, but you're welcome," I replied, and hung up.

I was closer than Weatherford to where Warwick had been seen, but it was still a pain to get to. There was no right turn from the northbound lane off the bypass, so it was a toss-up whether continuing to the next roundabout and coming back to Safehaven was faster, or staying on West Bay Road with the heavier traffic but eliminating the U-turn. I chose the bypass and was tempted to use the big off-road tyres and lift on the CJ-7 to jump the centre reservation, but I resisted. Officers had been chasing false sightings of Chloe Pennington all week, and this could be a similar wild goose chase. And I had that saying right. I know because I'd screwed it up before and looked it up afterwards.

Once I'd made it to Safehaven, I turned left and grabbed my mobile, clicking the link in the text to see where Weatherford had dropped a location pin. Driving slowly, using my thighs on the underside of the steering wheel, I zoomed in on the map that had opened. The mark was by one of the two homes on the north side of the canal. They were right next to each other, and large. A resident must have recognised Oliver Warwick from his picture the RCIPS had circulated online and in the news.

Putting my mobile down, I steered the Jeep left and then right around the curves which doglegged the road around the end of the canal, and I wondered where the man might have been going when he was spotted. It was a long walk to the shops or somewhere to get breakfast. But I didn't know which way he'd been heading, so perhaps he was returning from getting something he needed. This was all based on the theory he had a boat in the water, but I couldn't imagine why he'd be in this part of the island if he didn't.

I drove slowly by the two homes, with the golf course on my left, and jolted over the ridiculous number of sleeping policemen in the road. I couldn't see anyone wandering about, except for the people swinging sticks at little balls. There was also no sign of a boat along the middle stretch of the canal.

As I neared where the canal kinked right on its way to the sound, I scanned the square shaped cut-out, which served as a small marina accessed from Safehaven. Most of the commercial boats used the opposite side of the canal where a parallel road fed into a car park for customers, but a few ran from the side I approached.

Surveying the vessels, I spotted a couple of dive boats and two fishing charters, as expected. I drove on, waiting until I was past a stand of trees where the road kinked left, before turning right onto a stretch of scrub land. Maybe he'd already taken the boat out into the sound. Or, more likely, it wasn't Oliver Warwick at all. Grabbing my mobile, I returned to the satellite view and then looked up what lay directly ahead of me. A line of trees obscured my view of another marina style cut-out off the canal. This one was larger and probably made for a development that had never happened or was planned for the future.

Driving the Jeep towards the trees, I parked and jumped out, strapping on my utility belt. I loosened the security snap holding my Taser in place, but left my radio turned off. I didn't need sudden chatter on the walkie-talkie to give me away. Walking to the treeline, I stayed in the shade behind a sea grape from where I could see all of the marina. There was only one boat: an old red-and-white cabin cruiser moored to the sea wall on my left, facing away from me. I figured Weatherford would have mentioned if Warwick owned a boat, so if this was where he was hiding, then he'd borrowed or stolen it.

I was tempted to approach the vessel, but I knew protocol dictated that I wait for backup. Chloe Pennington could well be aboard. It all fitted. Warwick, disgruntled at Rupert having been hurt on his job site, persuades the man's young daughter to skip school and play on his little red-and-white boat. Why Warwick, after being helped financially by Pennington, would turn on him was a question we'd have to ask the kidnapper when he caught him. But head injuries could do strange things to a person. So could the drugs to treat brain and behavioural issues. If Warwick needed someone to blame for his life being ruined, Rupert Pennington was at the top of the chain of events, despite having nothing personally to do with the accident.

The rising sun from the east cast long shadows across the still water of the cut-out. In the distance, I heard a voice announcing a group was next up to tee off on the golf course. The undecipherable babbling of excited tourists resonated across the canal from a Stingray City charter, getting ready to head out into the sound. Seagulls squawked as they hunted for humans' discarded scraps instead of the fish nature intended for them.

I texted Weatherford. "Suspicious boat. Large cut-out east end canal. Standing by."

I waited, watching the little boat for signs of movement. My mobile vibrated.

"3 mins away."

When I looked up, gentle ripples emanated in a widening semicircle from the cabin cruiser. Just as I wondered if the remnants from the wake of a passing vessel had created the movement, the red-and-white boat rocked and a figure appeared on deck.

From 50 metres away I couldn't tell if the man I was watching matched the picture of Oliver Warwick I'd seen on a computer screen, but the medium height and scrawny build were right. I shrank behind the tree as he surveyed the area. When I peeked again, he was facing away from me, standing at the helm to the right of the cabin entrance. I heard the inboard engine turn over and eventually catch with a haze of dark grey smoke from the stern.

"Boat leaving," I hurriedly texted.

The man jumped to the dock and freed the bow line first, gently shoving the front of the boat away from the sea wall. He then walked to the stern, freed the second line, and tossed it ahead of him as he stepped aboard. My phone vibrated with a reply text, but I didn't have time to check. Visions of the young girl in the cabin of the boat sent me sprinting along the concrete sea wall.

He was facing away, and I watched him slip the motor into gear. He then eased into the throttle, and the cabin cruiser moved away from the dock. Already too far out for me to leap to the deck, I continued running, hoping to meet him at the rock wall forming the front of the sheltered marina.

Which was when he glanced over his shoulder and saw me. Closer now, I could see it was definitely Oliver Warwick. Startled, he frantically looked around for the backup who hadn't arrived yet, then pushed the throttle farther forward, accelerating away from me.

24

———

SEE-THROUGH KNICKERS AND
BALLS IN THE WATER

I plucked the radio from my belt as I ran and switched it on.

"This is PC277," I panted into the microphone while I held the broadcast button down.

I used my constable number out of habit, and because I didn't have an ID number as a detective yet.

"In pursuit of suspect. He's aboard a red-and-white piece of shit..."

"*Dritt,*" I swore after releasing the mic, then remembered Whittaker wouldn't be the one listening to my broadcast. Not that swearing over the radio was approved by anyone else, but he'd always call me out about it.

"It's a small cabin cruiser, maybe seven or eight metres..." I quickly made the conversion in my head. "Twenty-two to twenty-five feet. Eastbound, exiting the canal between golf courses. Request Marine Unit response."

Turning the corner, I kept running along the eastern shore of the cut-out, watching Warwick swing out into the canal exit, causing a big catamaran to veer to port and hit reverse on its engines. Tourists tumbled like bowling pins and various items launched over the side. Which gave me an idea.

Sprinting as hard as I could, I reached the rock jetty which protected the cut-out marina. Waving my arms in the air, I tried to pick out the captain of the catamaran. Crew and passengers were moving about chaotically and pointing to towels, sunglasses, and whatever other crap had gone into the water. Holding up my badge, I yelled at the top of my lungs.

"Police! Pick me up!"

I frantically waved with one hand and pointed to the rock jetty with the other, and the captain finally saw me. For a moment he hesitated, no doubt wondering how the tip jar would look if he abandoned customers' gear they hadn't held on to. I watched him take a microphone off a hook and his voice blared over the cat's speakers.

"Everyone sit down," he ordered in accented English. "We will return for anything lost overboard. Crew, get me a head count. We're now under direction of local authorities until further notice."

I scanned the clear water lapping against the jetty, looking for the deepest spot where the captain could bring the big boat close enough for me to board. The very end looked better, so I scrambled along the big limestone boulders while the captain skilfully manoeuvred his boat closer. Nudging one hull of the 65-foot fibreglass cat near the rocks, I took a long step and leapt towards the boat.

My leading foot just made the top of the narrow hull and my momentum sent me tumbling onto the trampoline-like netting strung taught between the hulls. Scrambling to my feet, I caught the captain's eye.

"Chase that red-and-white boat!"

He nodded, already backing away from the rocks. By the time I reached his side, we were aimed at the sound and he was already bringing the big boat up to speed.

"Captain Maldini," he introduced himself with what I now recognised to be an Italian accent.

"Detective Sommer," I replied. "Thanks for stopping."

"That *idiota* nearly hit me," he said with a flourishing gesticulation. "I have words for him."

"Are we going to be late for the stingrays?" some kid asked from behind us.

I turned around. He was around twelve and pudgy, with the kind of fat he was unlikely to grow out of. His parents were both heavy as well, suggesting a household diet promoting their child's bloated appearance. The red hue of his sunburnt flesh didn't do him any favours either.

"We'll email them and tell them to stick around," I said, then turned to the front.

Maldini snickered. I could have told the kid they'd still be there because that's what wild creatures did when humans regularly fed them. Finding their own food was much harder work. But the lad had enough challenges in life without being burdened with the ethics of our interactions with wildlife.

The cabin cruiser had exited the mouth of the canal and was heading straight for the middle of the sound. We were 500 metres behind, but the catamaran, with its sails furled and twin engines throbbing, was easily catching the smaller vessel. But something was odd.

"Do you see anyone at the helm?" I asked the captain.

"No," he replied, as we both squinting to see.

He reached into a cabinet below the helm and pulled out a pair of binoculars, handing them to me. I found the little boat in the lenses and rolled the thumbwheel until it came into focus. I couldn't see anyone aboard. What I did notice with a startle were flames shooting from the cabin, and within seconds the cabin cruiser was engulfed in a mini inferno.

"*Merda*," Maldini muttered as I handed him back the binoculars.

I grabbed the radio from my belt and keyed the mic as I swung around and scanned the island beyond our wake. "Suspect boat on fire in North Sound. Approaching now. Suspect believed to have left boat. Repeat, suspect now believed to be on foot near the canal."

It was a clever move, as he'd obviously jumped from the cabin cruiser as he'd left the canal with perfect timing while we were all distracted. He'd set the little boat ablaze, which would destroy almost all evidence aboard. But my biggest fear was that Chloe Pennington might still be aboard.

I faced the front, where we rapidly gained on the burning vessel. It had lowered into the water and began slowly rotating, the motor having succumbed to the fire. I kept hoping to see the young girl appear from the cabin and jump overboard, but there were no signs of life.

A slew of chatter returned over the radio, but it mostly sounded like Weatherford directing officers back at the canal. I put the radio aside and unbuckled my utility belt. Maldini took it from me and shoved it onto a shelf under the helm. Kicking off my trainers, I quickly removed my socks and unbuttoned my blouse. Fortunately, I was wearing a sports bra today. And white knickers, which might be more of a problem when wet, but I wasn't about to dive in wearing trousers.

The captain slowed the catamaran as we neared the cabin cruiser, which was beginning to sink. The flames licked from the upper surfaces, but the incoming seawater had doused much of the fire inside the cabin.

"Woah," the chubby kid blurted as I dropped my trousers.

Mobile phones had been clicking a few pictures and shooting the odd video when we'd began, but now every passenger on the catamaran was aiming a device at the burning wreck – or me.

"*Fy faen*," I groaned. It would be just my luck that one of the lochmen would see a shot of me on some stupid social media site.

But dealing with that would have to wait. My concern was for the girl. I turned to Maldini, and he nodded his understanding of my plan, so I trotted between passengers towards the bow of the port hull. On the way, I snatched a dive mask from a lady, unclipped the snorkel and tossed it back to her. I didn't need anything snagging underwater. By the time I reached the bow, the captain had the cat lined up five metres from the boat, which was already sitting on the sand in three metres of water.

Nothing remained above the surface, but I could clearly see what was now truly a wreck, resting on the sea floor. Clouds of sand hazed the water around the crispy hull, and anything that could float was on the surface or making its way there. Charred pieces of upholstery and plastic bobbed on the sound. Slipping the mask in place, I dived off the cat and swam down.

Without a weight belt or fins, the air in my lungs fought to keep me from descending, but I grabbed the helm wheel and pulled myself down. Light from above filtered into the first few feet of the cabin, but beyond that was dark and full of junk and particulate. Now deep enough to be neutrally buoyant, I took hold of the edge of the step with my left hand and reached into the void with my right, searching the blackness. All I cared about was finding Chloe, and I tried my best not to imagine what my hand was bumping into and grazing against. Not that barbecued human would be any better, but I still foolishly hung to the idea that the girl might be alive.

With my lungs burning after a minute and a half of foraging blindly, I pushed off the scorched deck and surfaced. A row of curious faces lined the port side of the catamaran, which was now anchored in place thanks to the crew.

"What you find?" some kid shouted.

"Are there bodies in there?" a man asked.

"Will this take long?" a woman asked.

"Hey," Maldini shouted, pushing passengers aside. "Here."

He threw an underwater torch my way as I took deep breaths to clear my lungs of carbon dioxide and bring in oxygen-rich air. Looking along the row of faces, I once again saw a parade of mobile phones capturing the moment. In the distance, sirens wailed.

After a long, steady inhalation, I dropped below and swam down, using the wheel to pull myself into the entrance to the cabin. Turning on the torch, I shone the beam around. It didn't help much, as the detritus suspended in the water reflected most of the light, but I caught the outline of a small sofa on the port side and a tiny galley on the right. In the bow was a V-berth. I spotted various pots, pans, cushions, cups, glasses, and clothing, but no bodies.

Surfacing, I picked out the captain, and he nodded towards the stern. Swimming to the back of the port-side hull, I found a drop-down ladder, which I climbed.

"Nobody in there," I said as Maldini greeted me and took the mask.

"Nice," a teenage boy said from nearby, and I heard the clicking of pictures from his mobile phone camera.

I looked down at myself. The sports bra covered more than most bathing suits, but my soaked knickers were almost transparent, so a boat full of tourists now knew I was a natural blonde.

"Here," the captain said, handing me a towel, which I wrapped around my waist.

I looked up at the crowd, who were most definitely all looking at me.

"I am a police detective working several cases, some of which require me to work undercover," I shouted. "Do not post any pictures or videos showing my face online. You'll be putting my operation and life at risk."

I scanned the crowd, hearing a variety of murmurs and snickers.

"Too late," a teenage girl grinned.

"You have to try," the captain said, shrugging his shoulders.

"Likes and views are far more important than someone else's life," I muttered. "I hate people."

Maldini nodded.

"But not you," I said quickly. "You seem okay."

"*Grazie*," he replied.

It took more than an hour for me to catch a ride back to shore from the Marine Unit, by which time my underwear was mostly dry and

I'd traded the towel for my clothes. Thankfully, the catamaran had a freshwater shower on the deck, so I'd rinsed the salt water away to avoid being itchy all day in parts I'd prefer didn't itch.

The radio had been busy with reports from all over the place, none of which announced they'd caught or even seen Warwick. It was an impressive getaway. My best guess was he'd swum to the spit of land jutting out from the south side of the canal entrance and made his way along the far edge of the Ritz-Carlton golf course. Or maybe he'd drowned, and we'd find a bloated body in the mangroves in a few weeks. In which case Chloe Pennington would likely starve to death wherever he'd hidden her away. There was a possibility that he hauled her from the cabin and made her swim with him, but it seemed unlikely to me that no one on the catamaran had seen them. Dragging a hostage around made him far less nimble. Which left a nagging thought in the back of my mind. Maybe she wasn't a hostage. Could an eleven-year-old be complicit in something like this?

After chatting with Weatherford on the phone for a few minutes, I laid my utility belt in the passenger side footwell of the Jeep and kept the radio with me. Returning to the road, I looked to the right at the golf course clubhouse. I wondered if a soaking wet man could sneak into the locker room unnoticed. It seemed unlikely given the number of people milling about, but it was now mid-morning. It would have been quieter earlier.

I swore under my breath at every sleeping policeman which I slowed to bounce over, and felt exhaustion consuming me again. Every day was getting worse than the last and I wondered when I'd be able to sleep for more than a few hours. If this little girl was murdered in a case I was at least partially responsible for, I wasn't sure I ever would.

A group of four stood around at a tee to my right as I made the left kink, thankfully clear of the stupid bumps in the road. One of the men was lining up to tee off while his friends watched. I couldn't help but follow his ball as it sailed through the air. The fairway doglegged around a large pond, but it looked like Big

Swinger had gone for the green, which had to be nearly 300 metres from the tee. I chuckled when his little white ball made a splash five metres from the edge of the pond. The man swung his club in frustration and shook his head. His friends laughed.

I was returning my attention to the road when I caught sight of another golfer. He was beyond the green. I'd never played the game in my life, but I was pretty sure you shouldn't tee off if other players were still on a green you might reach. But this guy was alone. And walking towards the next tee. Where four women were gathering their little trolleys which they pulled their bags of clubs along with.

Slowing the Jeep, I watched the man, wondering what he was up to. Maybe walking home after playing a round? But he only carried one club in his hand. He turned and looked behind him, pausing on the Jeep for only a moment. He appeared to disregard me as passing traffic. But I recognised him.

Shielded by a row of trees, I sped ahead, then turning hard right beyond them. That got Warwick's attention. Along with shouts from the men teeing off. Accelerating hard across the grass, the big off-road tyres flung wads of damp dirt and sod into the air behind me. I avoided the green itself, but the rough around it would require the groundskeeper's attention.

Warwick took off in a run, zigzagging while he tried to decide which direction to head. The Trolley Women screamed and bellowed, but whatever they were saying was lost over the roar of the inline six-cylinder engine. I slid around a tree and saw Warwick, who had chosen to run straight at the Trolley Women. They nervously watched, now unsure who to yell at. For a moment I thought he might be grabbing a hostage, and I wondered if he had a weapon with him, other than a sand wedge. But he sprinted through the middle of them, figuring I wouldn't risk running the women over.

He was right, and I braked, turned hard left to miss the nicely groomed raised tee area, then sped up again as the Jeep found the cart path on the far side. Warwick was now short of options. To our left was Pinehurst Road, on the right the pond, and straight ahead, the cart path continued alongside the fairway. He hesitated, and I quickly closed on him, wringing out second gear as the CJ-7 fishtailed while I tried to keep it mostly on the concrete cart path.

Warwick realised his best evasive manoeuvre a moment too late. He could change directions much faster than the Jeep, and he cut left to run towards the road. At the very moment I reached him. I winced at the sound as the big tubular bumper of the Jeep clipped the man, tossing him to the ground. I braked hard and skidded to a stop, grabbing my utility belt as I engaged the parking brake and hopped out.

Dazed, but alive and seeming to have all his limbs intact, Warwick moaned and rolled over, clutching his shoulder. Something didn't look right.

"You're a bloody maniac!" a woman shouted from behind me.

"Stay back," I warned. "I'm a police detective. This man is wanted in connection with several crimes."

"You're a copper?" another one of the women questioned. "No bloody way. If you're a detective, then my husband's Bradley Cooper."

The other women laughed. I didn't know who Bradley Cooper was. Pulling my badge from my pocket, I flashed it to them.

"Stone the crows," the first one said. "She is a copper."

"My shoulder," Warwick moaned from the ground.

"Hold still," I told him and grabbed his wrist in one hand while pinning his shoulder down with the other.

"Argh," he screamed. "What are you doing? That hurts like hell."

I pulled really hard on his wrist and felt something move in his shoulder. The man bellowed in pain, but when I stood back, it looked like his dislocated shoulder was back in place. He rubbed his arm and carefully moved it around.

"I can't believe that worked," I muttered, and then wondered if handcuffing him would break him again.

"That's a pretty slick technique you got, love," the first woman said. "You run 'em down, then fix 'em up and arrest 'em."

"He ran into my Jeep," I replied, already worried about how the report would look.

"Why you after him?" the second woman asked.

"He kidnapped a young girl," I replied.

"What?" Warwick gasped.

"Sod him, then," the woman said. "Ran right into you, just like you said."

"Yeah. Saw it with our own eyes," the first woman agreed.

25

SO MANY WAYS TO HIT THE GROUND

It took hours to get Oliver Warwick into the interview room. He had to be checked out at the hospital, including an X-ray, all for the doctor to say that his shoulder appeared to have been reset successfully. Which was obvious when we walked in there. Then we waited for a solicitor to show up, and they always dragged their feet. Finally, Weatherford and I stood in the viewing room behind the one-way glass, with Rupert and Rebecca Pennington alongside us.

"I helped the bloody guy," Rupert complained. "The idiot wasn't watching where he was going and walked straight off a balcony. He didn't actually work for me. He's a bloody contract worker."

"We all visited him several times in the hospital," Rebecca added. "Ungrateful bastard."

Rupert leaned closer to the glass. "Where does he have Chloe?"

"We don't know," Weatherford replied. "He's not said a word yet."

"You *all* visited him after the accident," I said. "Including Chloe?"

The two parents looked at each other.

"Not every time," Rupert responded hesitantly.

"No, but maybe twice, I think," Rebecca said.

The detective and I shared a knowing glance.

"When was the last time you saw or spoke with Mr Warwick?" Weatherford asked.

Rupert shrugged his shoulders. "Been a while. Six months. Maybe a little longer."

"Okay, you'll need to wait in the conference room while we talk to him," Weatherford said, and reluctantly, the Penningtons followed me out of the viewing room.

After what had seemed like forever, Weatherford and I sat down across from Warwick and his solicitor, Marlon Rankin, a public defender I'd met before. After we went through the usual BS explaining the suspect's rights and the recording of the interview, we began.

"Where is Chloe Pennington?" Weatherford asked, leading with the ultimate question without hesitation.

Warwick shook his head. "I have no idea," he replied.

The man was small framed and pale, with short brown hair, unkempt from his morning's activities. His voice was quiet and uncertain. He had a slightly dazed demeanour like he was in a different world to the rest of us. Perhaps from his medications. Which were currently sitting on the sea floor in North Sound, so if he needed them anytime soon, he'd need a refill.

"Can I ask how you're connecting my client to the Pennington girl's disappearance?" Marlon asked.

A portly dark-skinned local man, I'd found him relatively reasonable to deal with in the past, considering he was usually defending a guilty client. He kept us honest without trying to pull far-fetched stunts.

"Mr Warwick is a former contract worker on a Pennington project where he was hurt on the job site, which leads to motive. He was found on a boat we believe to be stolen, and a boat was used to abduct Chloe from nearby her school. And Mr Warwick disappeared around the same time the girl was taken."

Marlon looked at his client, then back at us. "That's a lot of circumstantial rhetoric, Detective. I don't hear a lick of actual evidence mentioned."

"Where did you get the boat?" Weatherford directed at Warwick.

"I borrowed it," the man said, looking at no one.

"From whom?"

Warwick shook his head.

"You don't know from whom you borrowed the boat?" Weatherford persisted. "How does someone give you permission if you don't know them?"

"I was going to take it back."

"Bit difficult now," I replied.

Marlon held up his hands. "So, there's some question over whether the boat was borrowed with or without permission, but I still don't hear anything suggesting my client was involved with the girl's disappearance."

The solicitor was clever with his words, using disappearance instead of abduction, leaving a suggestion that she might not have been taken by someone. Of course, he hadn't heard the daily messages sent to the family.

"So, to be clear for the record, Mr Warwick," Weatherford said. "When was the last time you saw Chloe Pennington?"

"I don't think I've ever met her," he replied with a thoughtful frown.

"We know that's not true," the detective pounced. "Please don't lie to us. When did you see her last?"

Warwick's eyes darted around the room before settling on Marlon as though he'd just landed in the chair and needed help.

"It's okay to answer," the solicitor encouraged.

Marlon was smart enough to realise from the question that we did have proof of a meeting at some point, so it was better to be honest than raise further suspicion. Plus, he had to determine what he was up against to defend the man.

"I think she came to the hospital to see me," Warwick said.

"Okay, thank you," Weatherford responded. "See, better to tell us the truth. So when have you seen her since then?"

"My client just told you the last time he saw the girl," Marlon quickly intervened. "Can we move on?"

Weatherford blew out his cheeks. "Okay. The boat, Mr Warwick. Why did you run, and why did you set fire to a boat you claim to have borrowed?"

"I was scared," the man replied. "She was chasing me."

"I announced I was police," I pointed out. "But you still took off."

"She ran me over," he said. "I was right to be scared."

"You hit my Jeep while running away. Again," I said. "There are four witnesses."

"Why did you set fire to the boat, Mr Warwick?" Weatherford asked.

The man looked up at him. "I didn't. It caught on fire and I leapt out to save myself."

I looked at Weatherford. He reflected my look of resignation. Warwick had either planned or stumbled across the perfect excuse for what he'd done. At least the part about the boat's demise. It would take us weeks or even months to get analysis back from the wreck. With the amount of fire damage mixed with the sinking, it would be a tall task to figure out how the fire started.

"Where did the boat come from?" I asked, turning back to the suspect.

He shrugged again.

"Don't give me that," I snapped. "Fine, you borrowed the piece of shit from someone you can't remember, but you have to know where it was before you took it."

His eyes wandered around for a few moments and then seemed to focus on me. "North Sound Estates."

"From a dock at someone's house?" I asked.

He shook his head. "It was tied up at an empty lot."

North Sound Estates was a development area east of the airport on the south east corner of the sound. A latticework of canals made just about every lot waterfront. It was a mixture of older homes, new builds, and empty parcels. Years ago, it had been a relatively inexpensive area for locals to build homes with water access. Now, like everywhere else on the island, the prices had skyrocketed and most locals cashed out of the lots.

"Let's take a break for a few minutes," Weatherford said and paused the recording. "We'll be right back. I'll send an officer in here in case you need anything."

We left, and the detective directed a constable into the room to look after Warwick while we chatted in the viewing room.

"What do you think?" Weatherford asked me.

I looked through the glass at the diminutive figure in the interview room, asking to use the bathroom.

"If he has Chloe held somewhere else, why was he on the boat by the golf courses?" I replied, trying to organise what we knew in my mind. "If she's well hidden, why not stay with her?"

Weatherford nodded. "It all fits except for the girl not being on the boat."

"Unless…" I began, then paused.

I wasn't good at stopping the words coming out of my mouth, but even I choked on what I'd been about to say. I looked at Weatherford.

"Yeah," he said sullenly. "Unless he's already got rid of her."

I wasn't ready to accept that scenario.

"You've been to his apartment and searched there, right?"

Weatherford nodded.

"So, if Warwick took Chloe," I began, "and used the boat he stole, then we need to figure out from where."

"Because we'll find his car there," the detective said, continuing my thought.

"*Ja*, which will mean his only transport has been the boat, unless he's been going back and forth."

Weatherford started for the door. "Which may mean he has Chloe somewhere accessible by boat and not too far away."

"*Ja*," I agreed. "That piece-of-shit cabin cruiser wasn't going anywhere fast, and he couldn't risk showing up at a petrol dock. Chances are he would keep her within a mile or so of where we found him."

The constable escorted Warwick back from using the bathroom a few moments after we sat down. Weatherford restarted the recording.

"Interview continued at 1:32pm, same people are present."

The detective slid his mobile across the table, open to the maps app showing North Sound Estates.

"Show us where you took the boat from."

"Borrowed," Marlon said.

Weatherford gave the solicitor a glare before focusing on his client. "Where, Mr Warwick?" he repeated.

The suspect leaned forward and picked up the mobile phone. He used his fingers to zoom in and scroll around. He then shoved the device back across the table.

I leaned over to see the screen as the detective picked it up. Warwick hadn't exactly pinpointed a lot, but he'd narrowed down the area to maybe a square kilometre. A manageable size to search for a vehicle.

Weatherford rose to his feet. "I'll be right back."

He left the room to get officers on their way to the location, but left the recording running.

"Why the boat?" I asked.

Warwick looked at me with a confused expression.

"What did you need the boat for?" I asked, rephrasing.

I got another shoulder shrug.

"Had to be a reason. You have a perfectly good apartment you're paying for. Why disappear without telling anyone to hide on a boat?"

"I needed to be alone," he replied.

"Don't you live alone?"

"People know how to find me there."

"Why didn't you want anyone finding you?"

He began shaking his head. "Because they're always asking me shit like you're asking me shit."

Warwick rocked in his seat and began breathing harder. He was getting wound up. I wondered whether a wound-up Warwick would be more forthcoming than zoned-out Warwick.

"You mean you didn't want anyone to find out Chloe was with you?" I challenged.

He vigorously shook his head. "No!"

"Detective," Marlon said, "you're agitating my client."

"Am I?" I responded. "I'm just asking questions. This is an interview. It's what we do. If he's nothing to hide, he should be able to answer the questions, right, Warwick?" I said, thumping the table with my fist.

"No!" he yelped.

"Where's Chloe?" I asked.

"You need to stop," Marlon protested.

"Where do you have Chloe?" I continued.

Warwick began to groan as he rocked and continued shaking his head. Marlon stood.

"This interview needs to stop. My client needs medical attention."

"He's had medical attention," I shot back. "Stalled us for hours while they checked him over. He's fine. Where is she, Warwick?"

"I don't know!" he screamed and shoved his chair back, which then tipped and fell over backwards, slamming into the concrete floor.

"Oh my goodness," Marlon fussed, as he knelt down to help his client.

"*Fy faen*. Pausing interview because the idiot fell off his chair," I groaned and hit stop on the recording.

It was the second time in one day I'd put the dumb-arse on the ground without touching him myself.

Weatherford chose this moment to return.

"Nora, what happened?"

"I can confirm that Warwick has anger issues," I said, standing up. "And talking to him's a waste of time."

The suspect was upright again, rubbing the back of his head, with his solicitor squawking about unfair this and that.

"I'll meet you outside in five minutes," Weatherford said. "Leave me to sort this out."

I nodded and was happy to leave the room. Warwick had issues because of the accident eighteen months ago, and I could sympathise with his struggles, but I had a far stronger desire to save Chloe Pennington. It didn't matter if the voices in his head told him to do it or he was simply overwhelmed by a misguided need for revenge. Or an accurately guided need, for that matter. Perhaps Rupert Pennington was a *drittsekk* who deserved anything coming his way, but I was certain his eleven-year-old daughter didn't. And I found most kids annoying little brats.

Walking down the hall, muttering to myself under my breath, I almost walked into the door to the viewing room as it swung open.

"Hey!" I called out, my outstretched hand loudly thumping the metal door.

"Constable Sommer," Chief Inspector Leonard Monroe said, as though my name left an unpleasant taste in his mouth. "This doesn't fall under my current purview, but I suspect badgering a suspect until he falls to the floor is not how an interview is supposed to be conducted."

"If it's not under your current purview, then why are you here?" I replied, guessing at what purview meant. "Sir."

"Because I'm keeping an eye on you, young lady," he said, and walked away.

It was a good job my Taser was in the Jeep. In the foul mood I was in, watching that *dummenikk* flop around on the floor felt like an acceptable way of leaving the police force.

26

GUNG-HO GIRL

I leaned against Weatherford's Bronco while I waited for him and thought about my run-in with Monroe. If he knew I'd met with Whittaker, there was no way he wouldn't have at least brought it up. More likely, he'd have reported and probably suspended me. *But why was he checking on me?* Maybe he thought I was complicit in Whittaker's drug deal, but watching me interview a suspect was hardly a great way of learning anything about that. The encounter bothered me, and my sick feeling over Whittaker's situation had returned. When I'd left his house, I'd felt slightly reassured, although he'd said nothing to lead me to believe he was innocent. Now, with the anger and bitterness returning, I figured it was just the calming effect he'd always had over me.

Weatherford arrived, and we drove out of George Town. Getting to North Sound Estates was a pain in the arse. As a seagull flies, our destination was 8 or 9 kilometres due east from the station, but driving there meant going south on the bypass to wrap around the airport, then along the southern coastline until finally turning north and winding through a warren of streets making up the estates. The trip took thirty-five minutes, which included a stop at Hurley's market to get a coffee-flavoured energy drink and a sandwich. I was famished and dead tired.

Warwick had guided us to a section of the estates covering eight side streets off Leeward Drive. They were all cul-de-sacs, dead-ending at the main canal which divided these side streets from a mirror image version to the east. Between each cul-de-sac were short branches of canals making every lot waterfront. One day the area would be really nice, but for as long as I'd been on the island, North Sound Estates had been a work in progress. Shipping containers of construction materials and equipment littered empty lots between finished homes and uncleared wooded properties. The roadway was old, patched-up tarmac covered with a scattering of dust and gravel.

Systematically, we began searching the area the constables who'd been dispatched earlier hadn't covered. They had been delayed as North Sound Estates actually fell under Bodden Town's jurisdiction. It had taken longer to send a patrol car than hoped, but with two vehicles now looking, we quickly covered the area. And found nothing.

"Maybe he didn't drive his car here?" Weatherford speculated.

"Then where is it?" I countered.

"It was on my list of things to ask him."

The detective's unspoken part read something like 'until you put him on the ground and brought the interview to a halt'.

"We should keep searching," I said, keen to avoid further discussion of the chair incident. "Widen the area. He's stoned on meds so he could be confused."

Weatherford radioed to the constables and sent them around to the east side of the estates. We took the remaining west side. After five minutes, we were three side streets from the area Warwick had indicated when we spotted a sickly green coloured Suzuki Jimny SUV.

"That's it," Weatherford said and pulled over next to the vehicle.

He double-checked the registration number before we got out

and I peered through the driver's side windows, careful not to lean against the door. The Suzuki was filthy, with the dirt scuffed away around the door handle. I suspected it had sat unused for a long time before Warwick drove it here. Inside was an untidy mess. I checked the door. It was locked, and I wondered if his keys were resting on the sea floor in North Sound.

Weatherford made a call and asked Rasha to send her team to examine the car, and was now talking to Sergeant Hadley about organising a search for likely places Warwick may have hidden Chloe along the shore of North Sound. I was opening my map app to look as well when my mobile vibrated. I had a WhatsApp message from Rosie, Detective Whittaker's wife.

"Can I call you?"

"*Ja*," I replied without hesitation, but I was stumped why she'd want to talk to me.

Rosie had been reluctant to let me in and keen to broom me out the door that morning.

I answered the call when it rang, noting she was using WhatsApp for the call, which was good.

"*Ja.*"

"I didn't know who else to reach out to," Rosie blurted, sounding upset. "If everything's okay, he'll be so mad at me, but I'm really worried."

"What happened?" I asked, waving Weatherford over as he'd hung up his call.

"Something's not right," Rosie replied. "He was up really early and shut in his office most of the morning, but when I took him breakfast, I could tell he was not himself."

We both got back into the Bronco and I put the call on speaker, holding a finger to my lips. Weatherford nodded an acknowledgement.

"What do you mean, not himself?" I asked.

"Distracted, but anxious," she said. "Lord, I don't know how to describe it," she added, flustered. "I just know Roy, and I've never seen him like this."

"What can I do?" I asked, still puzzled as to why she was calling me.

"I know I'm asking a lot, Nora, but I also know how much he means to you. Can you make sure he's okay?"

"You mean come to the house again?" I replied. "He made it clear I was not to come back."

Weatherford looked at me sternly and was about to say something, but I held my hand up in front of his face.

"Not here," Rosie replied. "He left in a big ol' hurry."

"Where did he go?"

"That's why I'm calling you. I don't know," Rosie gushed.

I shrugged my shoulders at Weatherford. *What could we do?* Then a thought occurred to me.

"Do you have that finding app on your phone?"

"A what now?"

"Find My Phone app," Weatherford said, then grimaced and mouthed *sorry* to me.

The line was quiet for a moment. "Hello, Vincent," Rosie finally said. "I didn't realise you were there. I was hoping to keep this quiet."

"You know I'd do anything to help Roy," Weatherford replied. "This stays with Nora and me. No one else needs to know."

"Okay, thank you. Now, what am I looking for on my phone?"

"It's an app called Find My Phone. If you have it set up to do so, it'll show the location of Roy's mobile," Weatherford explained.

"I've never set anything like that up," Rosie replied. "But you know, I do remember Roy messing with something on my mobile and telling me I could see where he was anytime. That was ages ago when I got a new phone. Let me look."

We waited while Rosie searched the apps on her mobile. Weatherford looked at me and mouthed, *What can we do?*

I shrugged my shoulders. *Let's see where he is,* I mouthed back.

"Oh, I do have it!" Rosie declared. "So what do I do now?"

"Open the app and it may take a moment if you've not used it in a while," Weatherford explained. "But it should show any devices that are linked, and a map."

"Okay, yes. It says Roy's Mobile."

"Great, click on his device and it'll show you where it is on the map."

"Hmm, yes. Let me zoom in. Well, that's strange," Rosie muttered.

"What?" I asked.

"It show's he's near the water, just outside George Town."

"In a car park or restaurant?" Weatherford asked.

"No. Looks like a house or a business," Rosie replied. "But I can't think what's there. A little north of The Lobster Pot."

"Take a screenshot and message it to me," I said. "Is he moving?"

"Doesn't seem to be. Give me a minute. I'm not great with all this mobile phone technology."

As we waited, I tried to picture what was along that section of coastline. The Lobster Pot restaurant was an iconic landmark which had been in business forever, and the Coral Sands was a small time-share resort about half a kilometre north. Between the two wasn't much. Maybe a home or two and a couple of businesses.

My mobile buzzed, and I selected the message portion of the app. Holding the phone so we could both see it, I realised where Whittaker had gone.

"*Fy faen*," fell from my mouth.

"I'm sorry, dear?" Rosie asked.

"I know where that is," I said, trying to think how to explain it to the wife of my mentor.

"It'll take us twenty minutes to get there, Rosie," Weatherford said, and I was glad he took over. "We'll call you once we know more, and let us know if that signal moves, okay?"

"Sure," she said, somewhat uncertainly. "I'll keep an eye on it."

I hung up and looked at Weatherford.

"You know where that is, don't you?" he asked.

I nodded. "I've been there before."

Weatherford started the Bronco and sped down the lane. "But that doesn't make sense," he muttered as he drove. "Brenda McGinnis is involved in just about every shady deal you can imagine, but I've never known her to be connected to drugs."

"Maybe the old cow learned a new trick," I replied.

Weatherford drove even faster down Leeward Drive. "Dog, Nora. The phrase is you can't teach an old dog new tricks."

"I prefer cow," I replied. "It fits Brenda McGinnis."

Weatherford scoffed. "That's an insult to cows."

Traffic was heavy but moving, and we made it to the north-west side of George Town in seventeen minutes. Weatherford used his grille-mounted flashing lights and siren for the busy sections, but turned everything off when we reached North Church Street along the waterfront. He pulled into the car park next to Trisha's Roses, the local flower shop, and we got out of the SUV. I checked my phone, but no message from Rosie, so I presumed Whittaker was still nearby.

"What are we doing?" I asked, as Weatherford began walking towards the pavement.

"We're checking on Roy like we said we would," he replied.

"*Ja*, but what's the plan?"

He paused and looked at me. "Miss Gung-ho, charge in and figure it out later, is asking me for a plan?"

"*Ja*," I replied. "But we can gung-ho-the-shit out of it if you prefer. Sir."

Weatherford grinned, then frowned. "Yeah. We should probably come up with something better than *Where's Roy?*"

Across the road from us was McGinnis's property, which her family had owned forever. The single-storey house on the right had received a much needed coat of paint since the last time I'd paid attention to it, but it was still old and ugly. Like Brenda.

I didn't see Whittaker's Range Rover, just an old Mercedes

outside the bungalow, and an older centre-console fishing boat tied up at a concrete pier. On the left stood her warehouse, which had been built within the last quarter of a century and was far tidier and cleaner looking than her dwelling. At least from the outside. I'd been in the office once before, and it was a pigsty inside. Two large roll-up doors flanked her office. One of them was open, and I watched a white delivery van slowly pull out.

We both moved back behind the Bronco. Once clear of the door, the van stopped, and the driver went back inside the warehouse. The roll-up door began closing and a few moments later, the man reappeared from the office, which he locked behind him. The guy was big and brawny with buzzed hair. He climbed back in the van and pulled to the road. I could now see the hulk of Brenda McGinnis in the passenger seat. She was lighting a cigarette. The stench of her office came back to me and made me want to cough.

The van turned right towards town and we ducked farther behind the Bronco to stay out of sight. I quickly called Rosie.

"Is it moving?" I asked.

"Oh, hello. No, I don't think so," Rosie replied. "It hasn't moved at all or I would have… oh, wait a second. Yes, it's moving now!"

"Which way?"

"Along the waterfront towards the harbour," she replied.

"Stay on the line and tell us where he goes," I urged as Weatherford unlocked the Bronco and we climbed in.

I took another look across the road. "I don't see Whittaker's Range Rover."

Weatherford backed out of the spot and squealed the tyres pulling up to the road.

"We can always come back and look inside the warehouse," he said, sharing his thoughts aloud. "But if we don't go now, we'll lose the van."

"*Ja,*" I agreed, and he accelerated onto North Church Street, drawing an annoyed horn honk from the car he dodged in front of.

"What's going on?" Rosie shouted over my mobile's speaker.

She sounded close to tears.

"Is the signal still moving?" I asked in response.

"Yes, yes. Along the waterfront. Did you see Roy?"

"*Nei*, but his mobile is in a van we're following," I explained. "So he might be too."

"In a van?" she questioned. "What's he doing in a van?"

"We don't know…" I began, but Rosie interrupted.

"It's stopped!"

"Where?" I asked, trying to see the van up ahead, but there were too many vehicles between us.

"Near Rackhams," Rosie said. "It's stopped. No, wait. Something's wrong. It says I've lost the signal."

"*Fy faen,*" I groaned. "They've pulled the SIM."

27

GIANT BACKSEAT SNAIL

Weatherford couldn't turn on the lights or run the siren without alerting McGinnis and her thug, but we were losing them. With too many vehicles in between and the way North Church Street wound left and right, following the contours of the shoreline, the van could easily turn somewhere without us knowing.

"Pass him!" I urged, seeing a gap in traffic coming the other way.

"Jeez, Nora," Weatherford growled. "I'm not risking the public chasing a van which may or may not have Whittaker inside."

"*Fy faen,*" I muttered. "He's in there."

The car in front slowed as the tourists gawked at the pretty turquoise ocean on their right and the shops selling overpriced trinkets on the left.

"Go around them!" I fumed. "Sir."

Weatherford pulled out and accelerated the Bronco, just as a car coming the other way appeared around the corner. After a series of horn honks and gesticulations from all involved, we were one vehicle closer to the van.

"You're a terrible backseat driver," Weatherford moaned. "You know that?"

I looked over my shoulder and wondered how anyone could reach the pedals from back there.

"You drive like an old snail," I replied. "Sir."

He shook his head. "Adding *sir* to your orders doesn't negate the fact you're *giving* orders to a senior officer, Nora."

"Sorry, sir."

"And it's *drive like an old lady* or *move like a snail*," he corrected me once again.

"Then an old snail would be really slow, sir."

He laughed. Briefly. "Is that the van?" he blurted. "I think it turned. Up there at Fort Street," he added, pointing out the windscreen.

"I didn't see," I replied, wishing we'd been closer.

"Damn it," Weatherford cursed. "I'm not sure."

With the curve in the road, buildings on our left blocked our view, so I wasn't sure how he'd even seen any vehicle turn, and as we neared Fort Street, I could only see the traffic a hundred metres in front of us.

"I'm turning," the detective said, making his choice.

"No!" I shouted, and he jerked the steering wheel to stay on the waterfront road.

"You saw the van?" he asked.

"Maybe."

"Maybe?" he ranted. "If they turned on Fort, we've lost them."

I waited until we rounded another left curve opposite the commercial dock entrance where our view opened up. The road, which had magically become Harbour Drive, followed the edge of the natural harbour, turning right a few hundred metres ahead.

"There," I said, pointing to a white van in the line of traffic slowly making its way around the bend in the distance.

"Good job," Weatherford said, as we approached the curve ourselves. "We should call in backup."

"And tell them what, sir?" I quickly replied. "Detective Whittaker is in a van with a known criminal."

"Fair point," Weatherford muttered. "Let's see where they're going first." He looked at his watch. "I can't believe we're on a wild goose chase instead of searching for the girl. We don't have time for this."

But the detective didn't stop following the white van, so I figured he was venting his frustration more than wrestling with a decision. He'd worked with Whittaker for a long time and respected him as much as I did. At least until now. I wondered if Weatherford was mulling over the same thoughts as I was. Were we chasing Brenda McGinnis and her accomplice, or the detective we thought we knew all this time? Whichever it was, it felt like we'd have an answer at the end of this drive.

For every car that turned off the main road in front of us, another seemed to join, so we remained a dozen vehicles back. I brought up the map on my mobile and looked ahead, trying to think about where we might be going. Staying on the coast road around the south-west corner of the island was certainly more scenic, but not as fast as taking the bypass which cut off the corner.

"They're pulling over," Weatherford said, and I looked up.

Sure enough, the van had stopped on the left side of the road and the traffic was streaming past. The detective kept driving too, and I swung around in the passenger seat to watch the van as it grew smaller behind us.

"They just stopped," I said. "No one got out."

Weatherford slowed and turned left into the entrance to the Palm Springs Condominiums, an older development of two-storey homes. He quickly turned the Bronco around. It took a minute to get clear traffic in both directions so we could pull out and return north.

"They're gone," I said, searching the southbound lane for a white van.

"Maybe they turned around," Weatherford suggested.

We reached the spot where they'd pulled over, with no van in sight. Weatherford slowed and pulled over to the left, coming to a stop. Large homes lined the inland side of the road, and I looked out the passenger window at a huge undeveloped piece of land stretching from the road to the waterfront. Although I couldn't see that far, as it was mostly wooded, but the satellite view on my mobile confirmed the fact. Fifty metres ahead, a dirt trail disappeared between the trees and shrubs. I open the door and stepped out, squinting to look at the trail.

"They went down there," I said, certain I could see a light haze of dust settling.

"You sure?" Weatherford asked.

"*Nei*, but they came this way for a reason. They didn't go past us south, and why would they backtrack north?"

"Maybe she left the lights on in her office," Weatherford joked as he stepped out of the Bronco, although his expression remained serious. "We really should be calling in backup."

"Then Monroe will find out, and we don't know what's going on here yet, sir."

Weatherford nodded.

An idea came to me. It wasn't a great one, and I doubted the logistics would work, but it was worth a try. I dialled a number on my mobile.

"Dis better be a social call, girlfriend," Jumbo answered.

"*Nei*. Where are you?"

"Da Annex, 'bout to watch a game."

The Annex was the name of the football stadium in George Town. I couldn't believe my luck.

"Do you know where Palm Springs and Windsor Village condos are?" I asked.

"Way down South Church, right?"

"*Ja*. Just before them, on the ocean side, is a vacant property. The gate's open. You'll see a Bronco parked on the road nearby. Text me when you're here, and hurry."

Weatherford held up his hands like he wanted to know what I was doing. I ignored him.

"Wait up now, blondie," Jumbo laughed. "I bought a ticket to dis game, man. Why I missin' it to drive all da way down dere?"

"All the way? It's about four kilometres. Get moving."

"What's dat in real numbers?" he asked. "And I still don't hear what in it for me."

"About two and a half miles," I replied impatiently. "What have you got right now?"

"Fix-it for a noisy exhaust."

"Have you fixed it?"

"Nah. Waitin' for dis pimpin' system comin' in from Miami, man. Ain't gonna pay to fix it den replace da ting."

"*Faen.* Fine. I'll sign off on it," I replied. "But if you get pulled over again, tell them it fell off again. Now hurry."

I hung up before he could ask me anything else.

"Who was that?" Weatherford asked.

"Backup, sir," I replied. "What do you have in your truck?"

"How do you mean?" the detective asked.

"Weapons."

He frowned at me, but then looked at the woods for a moment before moving to the back of his SUV. Opening the tailgate, he pulled out a tactical vest and a Taser.

"It'll be a bit big, but try it on," he said, handing me the vest.

"*Nei.* Give me the Taser. You can wear the vest. You're a bigger target, sir."

He glanced down at his portly stomach before accepting the trade and handing me the Taser.

"Please don't hit me with that thing," he muttered as he put the vest on.

"Don't get between me and somebody who needs shooting, sir," I replied and jogged towards the trail.

He caught up with me at the entrance, already breathing heavily. It was probably time Vincent Weatherford thought about getting a gym membership. A pair of gates in the tall chain-link fence protecting the property were open, and by the way the undergrowth consumed them, I guessed they'd been that way for a while. Although there couldn't be much here worth protecting.

"Think that goon is carrying?" he asked.

"*Ja*," I replied. "For sure. Maybe we sneak in and take a look before doing the gung-ho thing, sir."

"That would be prudent," he said and walked between the broken-down chain-link fence gates. "Why bring him here?" he whispered as we moved along the trail.

"I can think of several reasons, sir."

"None of them good," he finished for me.

"*Nei.*"

The trail turned and disappeared to the left while dropping over a ridge. When we reached the corner, the roof of a building came into view. Weatherford held up a hand. In the distance, waves could be heard meeting the ironshore coast and birds tweeted from the trees, but I couldn't hear the van's engine.

Weatherford pointed to the trees to our right. "We'll see if we can approach through the cover," he whispered.

The brush looked too thick to wade through, but I followed him anyway. Stepping over branches and getting swiped in the face by twigs, we made it a few metres in before he stopped.

"I see the building," he said. "Looks abandoned. There's a grassy area behind it. Let's try this way."

He turned farther right and continued pushing his way through. I tried not to think of all the bugs and spiders joining us on our trek through the woods. After a few minutes, we reached less dense foliage. We were only five metres from the north-east corner of the building.

Abandoned was being kind. It was one big storm away from falling down. All the windows were boarded over, and by the look of them, they'd been patched up several times. Part of the roof was still in place, but it appeared an entire section had collapsed. I could just see the front of the van on the west side of the old single-storey house, so it seemed likely McGinnis and her thug were inside. We needed to see if Whittaker was with them.

Weatherford carefully moved to the side of the building and edged along to the first window. I followed closely and could now hear muted voices from inside. The detective tried looking through cracks in the wood, and while he did that, I moved around him to the next window. It had a knothole in one plank which made a perfect peephole. I waved Weatherford over, then took a better look.

The open roof cast plenty of light inside the place, which was a mass of rubble, discarded junk, and rubbish. Sat on an old rusty metal chair in the middle of what had probably been the living room was Whittaker. His hands and feet were zip-tied. Brenda McGinnis sat on a wooden crate a few metres away from the detective. She took a long drag from the cigarette resting between her lips and blew a trail of smoke out through her nostrils. She hadn't got any lighter or more pleasant looking since we'd met before.

A noise came from off to the right, out of my view, before the thug stepped forward with a rope in his hands. He was wearing gloves. Now closer to him, he seemed even larger. He had to be at least two metres tall and 110 kilos. None of it fat. What we'd call *jötunn* from Nordic mythology. A giant. I stepped back and let Weatherford take a look.

As he leaned forward, I heard McGinnis speak. "How long we ken each other? Gotta be 30 years or more, surely."

Her gravelly voice had a thick Scottish accent, and the smell of her office filled my senses once more.

"I couldnae risk you buggering up my new venture, now could I?"

"It was a clever set-up," I heard Whittaker respond, which made me happy to hear, despite the circumstances.

"Aye, I'm a canny one when I need to be."

I leaned closer to the detective. "She's Scottish," I said, pointing out the obvious. "Do you think there's a connection to the lochmen?"

"I don't know," Weatherford hissed, pulling back from the peephole. "But we have to do something, right now."

I could still hear Brenda rambling on between coughs and pauses, which I assumed were drags on the cigarette.

"We should wait for Jumbo to get here, sir. Her heavy's enormous."

"Jumbo Flowers?" Weatherford growled disapprovingly. "That's who you called?"

I nodded.

"No matter, we don't have time to wait for anyone," he urgently whispered as he took out his mobile and furiously typed a text. "Look for yourself."

I leaned forward and peered through the peephole.

"Shame it's come to this, but you've been a royal pain in my arse for too long, Roy Whittaker," McGinnis said, as Jötunn threw the rope over the one remaining sturdy roof beam. The other end was draped in a noose around Whittaker's neck.

28

MUSIC BOXES FOR THE UNDEAD

"What do we do?" I whispered to Weatherford.

"Where's Jumbo?" he asked.

I quickly texted as Brenda continued to babble on about how Whittaker had made her life difficult for decades. At least her coughing and raucous voice helped hide any noise we were making on the other side of the wall.

I held up my mobile with Jumbo's reply.

"Smith's."

Smith's Barcadere was a small public beach less than half a kilometre from us.

I typed a reply. "Drive in. Make noise. Loud."

He returned a thumbs-up emoji.

I looked through the peephole again.

"Stand on the chair," Jötunn ordered, his voice deep with a northern English accent.

Opposite our window was a side door, hanging open, still barely attached by one hinge. To our right was the main entrance into the little dwelling, its door missing completely.

"I'm not going to help you do it," Whittaker replied.

"How about I start breaking fingers until you do?" the thug threatened.

"Ye cannae break anything, you fuckin' eejit. The man dinnae break his own fingers before he topped himself. Haul him oop. He'll be beggin' for the chair."

Jötunn took the slack out of the rope, then with a firm grip, began pulling. The old beam resisted with a lot of friction, but using all of his mass, the thug soon had Whittaker on his tiptoes. The noose began choking the detective.

"We have to move," I spluttered, turning to Weatherford. "There's a side door on the far side. Cover it and I'll draw him out front."

Weatherford hesitated for a moment and then nodded, hurrying around the end of the building to our left. In the distance, I heard a strange bang, almost like a gunshot. From inside the building, Detective Whittaker's guttural gasps echoed around the derelict room. There was no more time. With Taser in hand, I picked my way through the undergrowth and rubble hidden in the long grass to the west side of the house which faced the water.

As I mentally tried to picture how much ground I'd need to cover before firing at Jötunn, a mixture of raucous engine noise and music filled the air.

"What the fuck is that?" Brenda rasped.

"A car," Jötunn replied.

"I ken it's a car, ye eejit. Drop him and go see!"

I turned the corner and peeked through the front doorway to see Jötunn heading for the side where Weatherford was about to be. Jumbo hadn't lied about his exhaust. It sounded more like a diesel truck approaching, with reggae music at full volume adding to the ruckus. I watched a mainly red vehicle pass by the side door, and Jötunn ran outside after it.

Chaos reigned. Jumbo's car came around the front of the derelict house and stopped behind the van with another backfire, making me flinch. A moment later, another bang echoed off the walls, sounding exactly like a gunshot. A man let out a cry. Brenda screamed unintelligible orders to her henchman, and I ducked back. Jötunn had reappeared through the side door and ran towards the front entry. I'd only have one chance to hit him when he appeared through the opening, so I set my feet and aimed a metre in front of the doorway.

Brenda yelled something else I couldn't understand and a large blur shot from the house. I fired and expected Jötunn to drop like a rock. But he didn't. Stopping, he turned towards me with his gun raised to my chest.

"Police!" Jumbo bellowed, and Jötunn swung his way, firing at the voice.

I took a step forward and kicked him between the legs with everything I had. Air left the giant's lungs in a gush and he crumpled to the ground, clutching his crotch with both hands while still holding the gun.

"She's getting away!" came Weatherford's voice from behind the building, but he sounded winded, struggling to force the words out.

My brief hesitation gave Jötunn time to raise his gun again, and this time I kicked his arm, sending the pistol flying through the air. The giant staggered to his feet, and I quickly stepped back, clear of his mitt-like hand swiping at me. Jumbo barrelled into him, and the impact shuddered like two trains colliding. Both men careened into the side of the building and I wondered if the hit might be the last straw in knocking the dilapidated structure down.

"Nora?" Weatherford hoarsely shouted.

Jumbo was now on top of Jötunn, pounding the side of his head with his fist. Each blow would have knocked a normal human into next week, but the giant just growled and blinked, still conscious and struggling. I ran inside the building and found Whittaker slumped on the metal chair, bound, but the hanging rope lay on the floor.

"Go after McGinnis," he gasped, rubbing his throat.

Running out the side door, I found Weatherford getting to his feet, a bullet embedded in his vest over his heart.

"Are you okay, sir?"

He nodded and waved a hand up the trail in the direction of the road. "Get her. I'll help Roy."

Breaking into a sprint, I took off up the trail, and as soon as I rounded the bend, I saw Brenda McGinnis. I slowed to a walk as I came up beside her. The old woman was hunched over, throwing a foot out front with each step, barely preventing herself from toppling over. Wheezing as though she was trying to breathe through a straw, she coughed and spluttered more than she drew in fresh air.

"Where are you going, Brenda?" I asked.

"Fuck you," she choked.

Sirens wailed, barely audible over the music still coming from Jumbo's car.

"Attempted murder," I said nonchalantly. "That'll put you away for the rest of your life. Which might only be a day or two, anyway."

"Fuck you," she squeezed out again.

"From what I've heard, you've always stayed away from dealing drugs, but now these Scottish blokes show up on the island, and you're planting bags of cocaine on the detective. Are they your supplier?"

"Fuck…" was as far as she got, before dropping like a sack of carrots to the ground.

On her knees, she grabbed her chest, made an awful gurgling sound, then fell to one side and lay perfectly still.

"*Fy faen,*" I muttered, staring down at her, unsure what to do.

Apparently, the exertion had brought forward her expiration date. I knelt beside her. Her eyes stared at the blue sky and her mouth hung open with a wisp of cigarette smoke curling into the air. Or perhaps it was her rotten soul escaping.

I rolled her bulky body over onto her back and began chest

compressions. It felt more like I was pushing into an overstuffed pillow than a human being, but air rasped from her mouth with each pump of my hands. I looked at her mouth. There was no way I could bring myself to perform full CPR with rescue breaths. My lips were not going anywhere near that foul hole in her face.

A cracking sound came from her chest and I realised beneath the fat I'd broken a rib. I stopped pressing and figured I'd throw in a few more compressions for show once the cavalry arrived. The world was a far better place without this woman, but it would have been nice to learn if she truly had a connection to the lochmen.

The sirens grew louder, and I was wondering if Jumbo had successfully subdued Jötunn, when Brenda's body twitched and scared me to death. A gasping screech emanated from her mouth, and she blinked a few times.

"Ferrrk," she moaned and clutched her chest again.

"You're not dead?" I mumbled.

"You.. Scrawny… little… bitch," she spluttered.

With the police getting close, I only had a matter of seconds before standard operating procedure would need to be strictly followed.

"Are you Tulla?" I asked.

Her eyes narrowed. "Fer…" she began, but I pushed on her hands, which she still held against her chest.

Brenda let out a rasping wail of pain.

"Are you Tulla?" I repeated.

She tried uttering something, but I could barely hear her. The sirens filled the air, and I looked up to see a patrol car turning through the gates. I leaned over and put my ear next to her stinky mouth.

"Who's Tulla?"

"Fer…" she began again, but I leaned my forearm on her chest and she couldn't finish the word, sucking in a breath instead.

"Are you Tulla?" I asked once more.

"Fuck," she wheezed. "Baker."

"Baker?" I questioned, unsure I'd heard her correctly.

"Decker," I thought she said the second time.

Her eyes clenched shut, and she fought to draw air into her lungs. The patrol car skidded to a halt a few metres from us. Both constables leapt out. I sat up, taking my arm from her chest.

"Acting Detective Sommer," I said, looking up at them. "She's a suspect and needs medical attention immediately. One more suspect by the building. He was armed, but shouldn't be now. Two more detectives and a civilian aiding us. One of you tend to her, and the other with me."

The two officers must have recognised me, as neither questioned my orders and one of them followed as I leapt to my feet and ran down the trail.

"Police!" I shouted as I neared the building.

"Clear!" Weatherford called back, his voice sounding better.

I entered through the side door and found Whittaker and Weatherford standing next to each other, with Jötunn on the ground, his wrists bound with a mass of zip ties. Jumbo watched over him.

"Get her?" Weatherford asked, his vest hanging loose on his body as he'd released the straps. The bullet glinted in the light from the open roof. It was lucky Jötunn had instinctively gone for a body shot, despite the vest.

"*Ja*," I replied. "She died for a bit, but she's alive now. Or was when I left."

"Died?" Weatherford asked. "What happened?"

"She exercises less than you, sir."

Jumbo snickered. The two detectives shook their heads.

"Constable, take this man into custody please," Weatherford said, and I automatically stepped towards Jötunn.

"Nora," Weatherford said, and I looked at him. "Not you."

The constable who'd followed me pulled the giant to his feet with Jumbo's help.

"Oh," I muttered, and stepped back out of the way while the suspect was marched away.

"Nora," Whittaker began, still rubbing his neck, which bore a nasty-looking red mark around his throat. "I was just thanking Vincent and Mr Flowers. If I may offer my apologies for the events over the past few days, and extend my sincere thanks to you too. I would certainly be..." he paused and looked up at the old beam, "swinging from the rafters, it appears, if you hadn't intervened."

"You should thank your wife, sir," I replied. "She raised the alarm. We just followed up."

And while I thought of it, I took out my mobile and messaged Rosie, letting her know we had her husband and he was safe.

"You missed," Jumbo said to me with a big grin. "Maybe you needed a bigger target?"

It was the first time I hadn't hit my intended victim with the Taser, and it didn't feel good. I should have tracked the man as he appeared instead of trying to time him arriving at the spot I was aiming.

"It's Detective Weatherford's Taser," I replied. "I think the sights are wonky."

Jumbo laughed.

I turned back to Whittaker. "Why were you in the van, sir?"

Whittaker blew out his cheeks. "Because I made a stupid mistake," he replied. "After making an innocent mistake."

I waited for him to explain, as his answer didn't tell me much.

"We heard her admitting to setting you up," Weatherford said.

Whittaker nodded. "It's Rosie's birthday in a few weeks. She collects music boxes, and I responded to an advert online offering these beautiful handmade music boxes. I chatted via text with the person and even spoke to the man on the phone once. He said he's in East End but had a cousin coming west to deliver to another customer at The Sovereign who could meet me. I ordered two different styles, and the guy showed me the music boxes when we met, but obviously did a very clever switch when he bagged them and handed them to me."

"I've seen the CCTV," I said.

He nodded at me. "Of course. Well, they even told me in which spot to park so they'd know it was me. Seems suspicious now, but perfectly logical at the time."

"*Ja.* Clever. Only one camera view and they positioned themselves perfectly to stay hidden."

"I suppose I shouldn't ask why you were looking at the CCTV after being told to leave my situation alone," he said, peering over his glasses at me.

"*Nei*, sir. Best not. But why go to her warehouse?"

He wrinkled his brow. "I'm afraid that was the stupid part. I'd explained the situation to Chief Inspector Monroe, but I didn't have a single shred of hard evidence. My text exchange was to a burner phone that had been turned off, and as you know, the CCTV looks pretty conclusive. I visited McGinnis with my mobile on record, and of course her goon patted me down and found it. As I'd hoped. The other recording device was in the lining of my jacket, and hopefully recorded everything," he said, brushing a hand over his lapel. "None of which would have mattered if you three hadn't shown up. So, thank you again."

"Do you suspect McGinnis has a connection to the lochmen, sir?" I asked. "The men from the boat," I added, unsure if he was up to speed on the codenames.

Whittaker shrugged his shoulders. "I've never known Brenda to be involved in drugs up until she framed me using them, so I don't know."

"You're right, though," Weatherford added. "There's the Scottish angle. But that's more than thin."

"I asked her who Tulla is, sir."

"Did she tell you?" Weatherford asked.

"Maybe," I replied. "She answered, but she'd only been undead for a minute or so. I couldn't really understand what she said."

"Who is Tulla?" Whittaker asked.

"We believe it's the lochmen's contact on the island," Weatherford explained. "What did you think she said, Nora?"

"Decker," I replied. "But I thought it was Baker before that."

Whittaker looked at me curiously. "Why would she tell you?"

"Probably the delirium, sir. The just died and woke up again thing."

The detectives looked at each with raised eyebrows. Jumbo stifled a laugh.

I thought my story sounded believable.

29

CHOCOLATE MARGARITAS

It was going to take hours to sort out the mess and paperwork at the derelict building, so I gave a brief statement before Weatherford helped me sneak away. I saw the Chief with Chief Inspector Monroe arriving as we pulled out, so my timing was fortunate. Jumbo gave me a ride to Central Station. I signed off on his fix-it ticket while his broken exhaust had everyone in our path jumping aside and covering their ears.

My mobile had multiple missed texts and calls from Rosie, but they were from before I'd informed her Whittaker was okay. I also had one missed call from Jazzy. If Violet had gone missing again, she was on her own. I didn't have the energy or the time to chase her addicted arse all over town. There wouldn't be time to switch the Jeep later, so as I pulled out of the station in the shitty little undercover car, I called.

"Hey," Jazzy answered.

"Hey," I said. "You called."

I cringed and held my breath.

"Yeah. Just wondering where you were, as we hadn't heard from you all day."

I sighed a long breath of relief.

"On my way now."

"Okay, bye," Jazzy said, and hung up.

My next call was to Sergeant Williams to make sure everything was ready to go for tonight. If Brenda McGinnis was Tulla, her meeting with the lochmen wouldn't be happening, so we needed a fallback plan. Weatherford had someone at the station searching all the databases for Bakers and Deckers to see if anyone stood out as a person of interest, but it was a long shot. The further away I got from her stinky breath whisper, the more I questioned what she'd been trying to say. It could have been just another expletive directed at me. *Fucker, perhaps?* I attempted a Scottish accent as I chewed it over in my mind. Maybe.

Violet was in a great mood when I arrived. Jazzy had taken her swimming and freediving on the reef, and they were both excited about seeing a hawksbill turtle and a nurse shark. Although Violet said she'd been scared to death of the shark at the time. She looked like a completely different person than the one I'd run into at the hotel interviews, and especially the version I'd found on the couch at the repair garage.

A long shower felt good, and after changing and shoving a sweatshirt into my bag, we left the shack. Stopping on the way to the harbour, I bought a much needed coffee-flavoured energy drink and a large bar of chocolate. Carefully unwrapping the treat, I split it with Violet and we hurriedly ate the chocolate before it melted in the island heat. I then made sure my mobile was set to silent with no vibration, and placed it inside the wrapper. A couple of small pieces of double-sided Sellotape secured the disguise.

The lochmen were waiting on the tender, and they appeared to be nervous again. Maybe they'd heard about McGinnis being arrested, although that seemed unlikely. The RCIPS were certainly trying to keep it quiet. The lochmen had been tailed all day, and from what Williams had told me earlier, they hadn't left the hotel grounds. They'd eaten meals there and lounged by the pool for a few hours in the afternoon. The sergeant hadn't called to say different, so I assumed they'd also come straight to the boat without meeting anyone. So, if Violet had heard correctly, their rendezvous was yet to happen. Regardless, waiting until they returned to shore was now our Plan B. Plan A was on me.

I asked if it was okay to put my bar of chocolate in the ice chest. Ness joked about being okay with it as long as I shared it with them. Lomond then searched us both and our bags. Violet was still clearly nervous, and I wished I'd been able to disguise the mobile without her knowing. But it was another half-hearted search, and I slipped the chocolate bar back in my bag when they weren't looking. I didn't need one of them picking it up and realising it didn't feel like a bar of Cadburys.

The RIB was loaded with shopping bags, several of them the insulated kind to keep things cold, so I guessed they'd made a grocery stop on their way. I knew from what Katrine had told me that she was usually the one shuttled to shore and tasked with stocking their food supplies, but she wasn't aboard. It further supported what Violet had overheard.

Once we cleared the harbour, I sank into my seat and napped the rest of the trip, until Violet woke me with a shake. After boarding and putting our bags in the berth, I returned to the galley where Katrine was putting away groceries.

"Sorry we couldn't dive today," I said.

She shrugged her shoulders. "Comes with the territory. I never know what's going on until it happens."

I made sure no one was close by before speaking again. "Like when you'll leave here?"

She looked up at me. "Like that, yeah." She now checked for anyone within earshot. "They haven't said, but I'm guessing we're going tonight or tomorrow."

"They've been preparing?" I asked.

She nodded. "You probably saw all the supplies on the tender. I didn't even get to go. Just sent them a list. Wankers got half the wrong things."

"How much longer do you think you'll do this?" I asked.

She scoffed. "If there was a way to quit today, I would," she replied, then shook her head. "But I'll have to wait until we're done with this loop." She placed several loaves of bread in the freezer, then leaned closer to me. "These aren't people to piss off, if you know what I mean."

"*Ja*," I replied, forgetting to use Finnish. She didn't appear to notice. "Especially the Lomond bloke. He looks mean."

Katrine raised her eyebrows. "He carries a gun. I've seen it," she whispered.

"And what's with all the codenames?" I asked, "Scottish lakes, right?"

She rolled her eyes. "Took me weeks before I'd realise they were talking to me. They're full-on about it too. At least mine is feminine."

"So, what's your real name?" I asked.

Katrine looked around nervously again.

"Mine's Nora," I whispered. "Viivi is a stage name. Stole it from a Finnish model."

Katrine grinned. "Siobhán."

"Are you working on dinner yet?" came Morar's voice as we heard footsteps on the stairs.

We both startled, and I grabbed a couple of cans of soup from one of the bags.

"Cupboard on the far right," Katrine said, picking up on my cover.

Morar arrived at the galley doorway.

"It'll be a quickie tonight by the time I'm done here," Katrine said.

Morar grunted, looked at her watch, and moved on.

When the RIB returned, we had more customers than any of the previous nights. David was one of the first through the sliding doors, and he didn't wait at the bar this time.

"Hey," I greeted him.

He smiled. "Good evening Viivi. I have even more competition for your attention tonight."

"You won't need to worry," I replied.

His smile broadened, but that was because he didn't know what I really meant. I hadn't given much thought to what we'd do with the clients if we were successful in taking down the *Manannán*. I didn't give a shit about most of them. They were creepy and treated all the girls like pieces of entertainment meat for their consumption. But David and one or two others were different. A couple who were back for a second night seemed like they were simply exploring ways to excite their marriage.

But none of that would be up to me, and wouldn't be an issue at all unless I managed to enact Plan A. For which I would have to wait. Raven started on break, which meant she drew a crowd at the bar and Katrine was kept busy serving drinks. My break was on the third rotation. Which seemed to take forever.

I was tired of taking my clothes off and dancing around this stupid brass pole. For the first few nights, I'd passed the time by trying different tricks and testing my skills in various ridiculous poses and positions while spinning around. The customers loved it. But now I was tired, bored, and full of nervous anticipation. I was also keeping a much closer eye on the lochmen and Morar. It was critical I knew where they were. Morar was always in the salon, but tonight, Lomond was also hanging around more than before. Maybe because there were extra customers. The place felt packed with eighteen clients, and I wondered what the maximum legal capacity of the yacht was. Hopefully, over-capacity would be the least of their charges later tonight.

When my break time finally came around, I went to our berth and dressed in Lycra shorts and a T-shirt, then unwrapped my mobile. The cell signal was weak, but enough to send a text. I hoped. Returning to the bar, David was already waiting.

"Drink?" he asked.

"Sure," I replied, as it might seem strange if I didn't accept the offer. The house made money when the clients bought us drinks. "White wine, please," I directed to Katrine.

While she made our drinks, I checked around for anyone watching before palming the knife Katrine used to slice limes. She'd left it where she always did, next to the salt tray for margaritas. I could easily have taken a knife at dinner, but hiding weapons in skimpy outfits, which I then took off, wasn't easy.

Katrine returned and slid the wine glass to me.

"*Kiitos*," I said, but she kept hold of the glass.

Our eyes met, and she frowned, nodding to her margarita salt tray. *Dritt.* She'd noticed. I hadn't been as covert as I'd thought. Putting my hand around hers on the glass, I winked with a smile. I had no way of controlling what she might be thinking, but all I could hope for was her trust. *And why would she do that?* A few casual conversations wouldn't be enough for her not to think I was about to do something crazy with a knife. *Why else would I need it?*

"It's okay, and thank you," I said, keeping my eyes on hers.

She took a few moments to consider my message, then nodded and took her hand away.

"Come and get some fresh air with me," I said to David, and he followed me to the sliding doors.

Lomond and Morar watched us, but didn't say anything. They probably thought David might proposition me, but I didn't care what they thought as long as they didn't see the knife I'd slipped into David's jacket pocket. Once we were on the aft deck with the door closed, I moved to the starboard side and leaned against the gunwale. I figured David was about to extend his dinner invitation again, but I spoke first.

"Would you mind waiting here while I use the bathroom?"

He looked confused. We had just left the bar with a toilet only a few metres away to come outside.

"Stand right where you are as I'd prefer they thought I was still talking to you," I explained.

"What's going on?" he asked, instantly concerned. "Are you in some kind of trouble?"

"*Nei*," I replied, forgetting my Finnish again. "But they watch us all the time. I need to do something for a friend. It'll only take a minute."

"Violet?" he asked with a look of concern.

"*Juu*. I told you she needs a guardian angel."

He smiled. "I'll be right here."

Leaning in closer, I kissed his cheek and took the knife from his pocket before moving quietly forward. Unfortunately, the yacht didn't have an exterior walkway to the bow, so instead, I had to step over the gunwale and use my toes to grip a trim line running along the side. Above the salon windows, which were all blacked out from the inside, was a feature line in the hull. The ridge was subtle and smooth, but using my fingertips, I began shuffling along, clinging to the side of the yacht in the dark.

"Jeez, Viivi," I heard David mutter.

"Face the other way," I hissed back.

"Alright, alright," he replied, and I focused on not falling in the water.

When I reached the foredeck, I pulled myself onto the stylish overhang roof which sheltered the door from the salon level, and slid down to the deck. Peeking up behind me, I could see the pilothouse. A dim glow from the instruments barely lit the figure sitting in the helm chair. The captain was reading a book.

The foredeck was dark, with the only illumination coming from the pilothouse. The navigation lights on the end of both hulls faced forward and away from the yacht, shielded from the deck to avoid confusing other vessels.

Hunched over, I scrambled forward to the large cleat where the anchor line was tied, keeping the yacht from succumbing to the surface current. Taking the knife, I began sawing through the taut line, strands fraying with each cut. I stopped halfway through and moved to the port side. Cutting more aggressively, I hacked all the way through, feeling the yacht lurch backwards. It yawed as the remnants of the starboard line held for a brief moment, then snapped, setting the *Manannán* adrift.

I swung around and looked up. The captain was already on his feet. An experienced seaman, he would have sensed as much as felt the movement in his vessel. The current ran south-east. I had precious seconds before he'd fire up the diesel engines and regain control of the yacht before it drifted into Cayman Islands waters. Unless I stopped him.

30

UNBEARABLE

I knew going in that my plan was far from perfect and had plenty of moving parts that could go wrong, but I didn't think it would be this soon. I had no easy way to reach the pilothouse. It was usually accessed via the stairs in the salon, which meant going inside and being instantly discovered by everyone. I looked up. The sundeck, where we ate dinner each evening, was open at the front with a hardtop shading the forward half.

Scrambling up the overhang roof, I looked straight into the windows of the pilothouse and saw the captain furiously working through the sequence to start the engines. He must have heard me as he glanced up and squinted into the darkness. I didn't wait to find out if he'd realised what I was up to or not, but pulled myself over the top onto the sundeck. The stairs were at the stern, and I raced past the dining table to reach them, striding down the steps three at a time. A hallway ran between the crew berths to the pilothouse, passing the stairway leading down to the salon on the way.

I could hear and feel the vibration from one of the diesels already running, and the captain was about to start the second. Sprinting down the passageway, I caught him by surprise.

"Shut them down," I hissed, pushing the handle of the knife into his lower back, hoping he'd mistake it for the barrel of a gun.

He startled and froze. "What are you doing?"

"Police. Shut the engines down. Now."

He reached forward and hit the kill switch.

"We're in international waters," he said, raising both hands.

I could see a faint reflection in the front window, and his eyes were darting around, trying to fathom a plan. He'd have help arriving at any moment, and outside was nothing but pitch black darkness. Not a flashing light anywhere. Which meant we hadn't reached Cayman waters. From behind me, I heard a door opening. I shuffled us both sideways, out of view of the hallway.

"Did I hear the engines, Captain?" Ness asked, and soft footsteps fell on the faux wood flooring.

Ness could well be armed, and all I had was a paring knife. I didn't stand a chance against the two of them. *Where the hell were Ben and the Marine Unit?* We could argue the twelve-mile mark later, but if they didn't show up soon, I wouldn't be around to tell my side of the story. I had to do something.

Shoving the captain against the console, I ducked through the doorway and lowered my shoulder. With accidentally perfect timing, I crashed into Ness. Windmilling his arms, he couldn't stop himself from tumbling down the stairwell on the starboard side. Grabbing the railing, I just caught myself from flying after him. I heard gasps over the music from the salon and looked down at the man slumped against the wall with his legs trailing up the curved steps. He moaned, barely conscious.

Hearing movement behind me, I turned just in time to dodge to one side as the captain swung a long, heavy torch at me.

"No way you're a copper," he spat, stumbling forward after missing.

I punched him hard in the stomach, and he doubled over. Gripping both hands together, I brought my fists down on the back of his neck, and he dropped to the floor at the top of the steps.

Outside, the world lit up with flashing blue and red lights.

Sirens wailed into the night air, and Ben Crook's voice boomed over a loudspeaker.

"Cayman Islands Marine Police! Prepare to be boarded!"

Shouts echoed up from the salon, and another door opened down the hallway behind me.

"What the hell's going on?" a man asked. "Who the bloody…"

I didn't wait around to find out whether he was the first mate or Maree. Jumping over the groaning captain, I landed halfway down the stairwell, then picked my way over Ness. Across the salon, I saw Lomond with a gun in his hand. Customers gasped and babbled unanswered questions as the girls gathered up anything they could find to cover themselves. The scene was loud, crowded, and chaotic. Morar was already heading towards the stairwell, pushing people aside to help Ness. She abruptly stopped and pointed at me.

"It's her!"

Lomond began raising his gun, with anyone in his way frantically scattering. Behind him, the sliding door opened, and David stood there, stunned, silhouetted by the bright flashing police lights. Lomond instinctively turned, but seeing it was a customer, swung back and levelled the gun at me.

"It was me!" I heard Violet scream as I dived for cover behind the bar.

The report of two gunshots echoed around the salon, followed by more screams as people ducked or dropped to the floor. Using Morar as cover, I grabbed her and pushed her in front of me across the salon. We dodged around Violet, who'd dropped to the ground like the others.

"Get out of the way!" Lomond yelled as I glanced down.

Two red blossoms spread across the front of Violet's T-shirt, and she coughed and wheezed, clutching her chest.

"Nora!" Katrine screamed from behind the bar, and I looked up at Lomond.

From the determination in his eye, I could tell he'd decided to fire regardless of Morar being in the way. I shoved her forward once more and her body jolted twice, then crumpled aside out of my grip. David lunged at Lomond, smashing into him as another shot rang out, deafeningly loud within the confined space. In three steps, I was on top of Lomond as David struggled to his feet. The lochman desperately raised the gun still clutched in his grip, but he was too slow. My hand slammed into his chest, the paring knife plunging through flesh.

My hand jerked as the blade deflected off a rib bone. Pinning him to the floor, I sat astride Lomond, my fingers still tightly wrapped around the handle. His jaw hung open, and his eyes met mine. I watched disbelief slip away to a distant, empty stare as the life drained out of the man.

"Police!" Williams bellowed, charging through the sliding door with his assault rifle held ready. Several of his men poured in behind him.

Leaping to my feet, I ran across the salon and slid to my knees by Violet. Cradling her head, I looked at the two gunshot wounds in her chest. One bubbled as her strained breaths wheezed from the punctured lung.

"Violet," I muttered, unable to find anything else to say.

Her distant eyes found mine, and her muscles tightened. Finding my arm with her bloodied fingers, she squeezed with the meagre strength of an infant. Her lips quivered as she tried to speak, and her eyes finally focused. I could sense the fight in the petite, frail body which had already endured so much. Around us, orders were barked, people shouted in response, the music stopped, and officers surged past us.

"I've got you," I said, because somewhere at sometime maybe I'd heard that said. Comforting words as a friend or loved one fought for their life.

But I didn't have her. Violet's body went limp in my arms, and the focus ebbed from her gaze.

"Nora!" Williams was shouting. "Are you okay?"

I looked up. The room was bright. Someone had turned all the lights on. The customers were seated in the booths or on the floor with their hands on their heads. Morar's body lay in the middle of the salon, a pool of blood trickling back and forth as the yacht rocked in the swells. Lomond lay in the corner where I'd left him, the knife buried to the hilt in his chest. Nearby, David sat on his knees with his hands on his head.

"Nora?" Williams asked again, leaning down and resting a hand on my shoulder.

Adrenaline-fuelled trembles emanated through his firm but caring touch.

"I'm okay," I muttered and pulled Violet to me, cradling her in my arms.

Williams left me. He vanished into the melee as I closed my eyes and let the commotion continue around me. I didn't want to let her go.

There was no way to know what Violet Blaze's life had held in store for her. She'd proven time and again that she was her own worst enemy. But now we'd never know. Dougal Blair, known on the yacht as Lomond, had taken that from her. I'd robbed him of his future, but that was a gift to the world. Violet had still been in with a chance of becoming someone useful. I guess I'd invested in that future, as the pain I felt was unbearable.

"Nora, we need to leave her," came a voice I hadn't expected.

Hearing Whittaker pulled me from my stupor. I had no idea how long I'd been sitting on the floor with my new friend, but Weatherford stood next to our boss with two paramedics waiting behind them. They were ready to attend to Violet, but it was hopeless. And I didn't want to let her go. While I stayed on the floor with her in my arms, we were locked in the moment. The second I stood up and walked away, I'd be leaving my friend behind. Our paths would fork, never to meet again. My life would go on, yet hers would forever have ended on the *Manannán*. Where she died saving my life.

31

EXTRA ARSE-KISSING COFFEE

It was almost midnight when I arrived home. Jazzy should have been in bed, but the living room light was still on. I found her reading a book on the couch.

"You have school tomorrow," I reminded her. She'd already skipped a day to babysit Violet.

I'd hoped to delay giving her the news until the morning, but she was looking around me to see where her new friend had got to.

"I thought I'd be off again tomorrow," Jazzy replied.

Closing the door, I dropped my bag and walked over to the couch, sitting down next to her. She reached out and touched my hair, which was pulled back in a ponytail.

"What's that?" she asked, then yanked her hand away. "Is that blood?"

I touched my hair and felt the matted strands. I'd washed as best I could in the bathroom on the yacht and given my blood-soaked clothes to Weatherford to bag as evidence, but apparently I'd missed some. There'd been so much blood.

"Where's Violet?" Jazzy asked, beginning to panic. "What happened?"

I didn't know where to start. I was completely shit at talking about anything sensitive or difficult, and I knew this was an important moment.

"Things went badly," I began, and her hands shot to her face in horror.

"Violet's dead," I said, ripping off the plaster.

My delicate approach was an immediate disaster, and I was too exhausted to figure out a better way to tell a teenager the person she'd just become attached to had been killed.

Jazzy slowly shook her head, and a tear ran down one cheek. Her mouth opened, but she couldn't find any words.

"This *drittsekk* was trying to shoot me, and Violet jumped in the way."

I might be terrible at delivery, but I wanted Jazzy to know how Violet had died trying to do the right thing. A point my mind had been wrestling with since she'd died in my arms. *What if she hadn't got in the way? Lomond had been aiming at me, but being twice the distance away and already diving clear, would he have hit me?* The possibility that she'd died for nothing was too much. I knew I couldn't dwell on something that might have been, but the obstinate, self-destructive part of my brain wasn't about to let it rest.

"That's her blood," Jazzy whispered, pointing to my hair.

"Maybe," I answered too quickly.

Her eyes widened, and she gasped. "Is it yours? Are you hurt?"

"*Nei*. But I killed the *drittsekk*. It could be his blood."

Once again, the talking thing caught me out. It used to be I would have shrugged my shoulders in answer. Now, I have to be parent-like and actually converse, which rarely works out well for me.

Jazzy leaned over and hugged me. "Thank you," she sobbed in my ear.

Five hours of sleep wasn't enough, but I was surprised I'd

managed that much. Pure exhaustion won. I crept out of the house quietly, having left Jazzy a note on the kitchen counter.

"Your choice on school today."

It would probably be perfect evidence against me if someone tried to prove I was unfit to foster a kid, but I trusted Jazzy to do what felt right. Unless they were teaching *Coping with the death of a friend* in class today, she wouldn't miss anything critical.

I stopped for coffees and pastries on the way to Central Station and walked upstairs to Weatherford's office. He wasn't there. I found him down the hallway in Whittaker's office. It was a good job I'd bought an extra coffee and a treat.

"Hey," I greeted them both.

"I told you last night you didn't have to come in today, Nora," Weatherford said, before taking the coffee I handed him.

"Get anything out of the lochmen or crew?" I asked, ready to get on with the day.

I slid a coffee towards Whittaker and tore open the bag of pastries for everyone.

Whittaker shook his head. "No, but we brought the *Manannán* into port and had officers searching all night. They found a large quantity of cocaine."

"Cleverly hidden in a fake water storage tank in the port hull," Weatherford added.

"Any reaction to the name Tulla?" I asked.

"The brother, Iain MacLeod, who went by Maree," Whittaker replied. "He reacted to the name, but clammed up. None of them would say anything beyond demanding their lawyer be present."

Weatherford picked up one of the pastries. "They're all well coached on what to do."

"I suspect the three main men and Morar might be the only ones who really knew what was going on," I said. "The bartender, Katrine, helped me. We need to cut her a break."

"We'll revisit the yacht once we get through today," Whittaker said. "We only have until noon to save this girl."

"What's the plan?" I asked.

"We have a debrief in 20 minutes," Whittaker said. "We were just making a list of how best to despatch everyone."

"Anything come from the Baker, Decker searches?" I asked, knowing it was a long shot at best.

"Nothing actionable, I'm afraid," Whittaker replied.

"Here's yesterday's message," Weatherford said, setting his coffee down and holding out his mobile, hitting play.

"I knew you'd let her die. Your own flesh and blood. You have until noon to do the right thing."

The digital voice had changed slightly again, but remained flat and unemotional despite the words. The kidnapper was using a digitised voice service to read the message he'd inputted. Free resources to produce a file were easily found on the internet.

"But how could Warwick have sent that message if we have him in custody?" I wondered aloud.

"Set them all up in some form of automation," Weatherford replied. "We interviewed him again, but he won't say anything. Marlon Rankin has him off limits now for medical reasons."

"It's him, Nora," Whittaker said. "They pulled up the boat from North Sound yesterday evening. It's a complete mess, as you can imagine, but they found this scratched into the woodwork."

He unlocked his mobile and held up a picture to show me. It looked like a zoomed-in shot of the inside of the cabin. Charred fibreglass and wood surrounded a piece of trim which had been spared from the flames. Scratched into the surface was a short message.

"CP help."

"Chloe Pennington," I murmured.

"We're sending officers door to door, focusing on the west and south shores of the sound. All we can do is search everywhere he might have hidden the girl," Whittaker said. "Or hope he'll break and tell us."

"Everyone is on hand this morning," Weatherford added. "We have him, so now it's just a matter of finding Chloe."

"Unless he already set something up to happen at noon," I

pointed out. "If he automated the messages, maybe he's rigged everything."

Whittaker frowned and thought it over. "Then he was always going to kill her. Unless he was using his mobile to control these automations. Which went down in the boat. It's been recovered, but it's ruined. Short of having an accomplice, he can't manage or change anything remotely anymore."

"Damn," Weatherford muttered. "Then we still only have until noon."

Whittaker nodded and began gathering notes to carry downstairs.

I turned to leave the office, but paused. "I'm glad you're back, sir."

"Not as happy as I am," Weatherford scoffed.

Whittaker looked at us both. "All thanks to you two."

"I'll meet you in the briefing room," I quickly replied on my way out. My sentimental blathering tolerance had already peaked for the day. Maybe year.

The detectives were no doubt going down early to prepare for the meeting, so I found an open computer and accessed the interview video from the night before. Ness sat in the uncomfortable metal chair with a piece of gauze taped across his left temple. It was easy to fast-forward through most of the interview as he simply ignored the questions. I watched the only section in which he spoke carefully. Weatherford asked who Tulla was, and he stared blankly back. After letting it play for another minute, I rewound and watched the follow-up question for a second time.

"Do you know Brenda McGinnis?" the detective asked.

Ness's face barely registered the question. Barely being the key. I watched it a third time and zoomed in, although the picture became a little blurry. On hearing the name, I swear I could see the beginning of a frown. I wanted to check Maree's interview tape, but it was time for the briefing, so I closed the windows and logged out.

The room was packed with officers from every department. The air conditioning couldn't keep up with this many bodies emanating heat in a confined area, and the air was already stuffy and smelled of sweat. Whittaker began with a recap of the case, emphasising the urgent need to find Chloe Pennington, although we had a suspect in custody. He talked about the scratched message from the cabin cruiser, but then added more detail.

"The boat is unregistered, and we checked with the lot owner from North Sound Estates, but it doesn't belong to him. No one has reported a boat matching that description missing."

I chewed that over while Whittaker continued, and just as he wrapped up his summation, Rasha from our CSI group walked in. She looked tired and frazzled. I wondered if she'd slept at all.

"Rasha," Whittaker said upon seeing her. "I know you're swamped, so please give us anything new to share so you can get back to your group."

She puffed out her cheeks in a long exhalation. "I think everyone knows about the markings scratched into the cabin cruiser pulled out of the sound. If you don't, check your email. It was circulated overnight. Beyond the message we presume being from the girl, we've been unable to pull anything useful so far." She rubbed her brow, then looked at a notebook in her hand. "Speaking of boats, I could only spare one tech, but we obtained a warrant to look at Brenda McGinnis's centre console moored at…"

"Sorry to interrupt you, Rasha," Whittaker said. "But we should focus on the Pennington case this morning, please."

Rasha nodded impatiently. "Yes, sir, I know. If I may?"

Whittaker nodded for her to continue.

"We were primarily looking for traces of drugs, which we haven't found yet, but my tech did discover blood. She suspects the boat had been washed down, but she was able to take samples from the backside of the wheel, along with prints."

"It's a fishing boat, isn't it?" Weatherford asked. "Wouldn't you expect to find traces of blood?"

"Human blood," Rasha said.

"*Fy faen*", I muttered to myself. "Patrick Pennington's?" I asked aloud.

Rasha took a moment to reply. "We believe so, but we're testing again. There's a lot of contamination and only a small sample, so we want to be certain."

I looked at Weatherford who stared back at me. This added a layer of confusion to the lochmen case. We'd been sure they'd killed the Pennington brother over something to do with the drugs found in his condo. In some ways, this further supported our theory that Brenda McGinnis had ventured into drug dealing and she had a connection to the yacht. It looked like Brenda's boat might have been the one used to steal the dive boat and execute Patrick Pennington.

I'd convinced myself Brenda McGinnis wasn't Tulla after seeing Ness's reaction to her name, *but what if he only knew her by her codename?* That didn't make perfect sense as they would have assigned their contact the codename. But they would have to have known her by something else before that.

Whittaker was thanking Rasha, who hurried back to her team to continue, and the detective moved on to assignments. Slipping out the door, I rushed upstairs to Whittaker's office. I logged into his computer using my credentials and found the background check information on Rupert Pennington. I then brought up the same reports on his brother, Patrick. They'd both been arrested and charged with drug possession at the same time back in 2011. Charges were dropped on both men. The possession was for a few ounces of cocaine. They'd been pulled over together in the same vehicle on their way to a party, according to their statements. It didn't say why they'd been dropped.

Something still didn't sit right with me about Warwick. He was an engineer, so obviously an intelligent man, but the bloke we interviewed certainly didn't seem like someone who could put an elaborate kidnapping plan together. *And why would he stay on the dilapidated boat he'd used to snatch the girl?* But he had run. Although people ran all the time from the police for all kinds of reasons.

The sports coach, Garner, had given me the creeps, but now we'd found the boat used to take Chloe, it felt safe to rule him out.

"Nora?" Whittaker said, walking into his office.

"Are the Penningtons here, sir?" I asked.

He nodded. "We have them in a conference room downstairs. Why?"

I explained what I'd read about the arrests as Weatherford joined us.

"You think the Penningtons are connected to McGinnis and the yacht?" Whittaker asked.

"They are," I replied. "If Brenda had the brother killed, who was in possession of a large amount of cocaine, maybe Rupert still likes a snort or two."

"But what would that have to do with Warwick taking their daughter?" Weatherford asked. "I get that there's commonality in the drug aspect, but I don't see how that's any concern or motivation for Warwick."

I thought it over. He was right.

"Nora?" Whittaker said, and I realised I was still sitting in his seat.

"Sorry, sir," I said, jumping up and moving out of the way.

"You brought coffee and breakfast so I'll let it slide," he said, and managed a momentary grin as he took his seat.

"But wait a second," Weatherford said, pacing back and forth, deep in thought. "What if Rupert was involved with his brother in something involving the drugs?"

"You already made your own argument against that being relevant, Vincent," Whittaker responded. "What would the connection be to Warwick?"

"What if Warwick's not the perp?" I blurted.

"Why would Chloe scratch help in the cabin of the boat?" Whittaker countered.

I didn't have a good answer for that.

"What if Rupert is Tulla?" Weatherford said, verbalising what

I'd been thinking. "I know. What's the Warwick angle? But maybe it's worth pressing him about the drugs."

"Rupert?" Whittaker questioned. "When his daughter is…" he looked at his watch. "Less than four hours from being executed."

"The kidnapper is adamant that Pennington has done something wrong, sir," I pressed. "We've been focused on his legit business interests, but what if he has other businesses on the side?"

Whittaker chewed it over for a few moments. "Okay. But go easy on the guy, Vincent."

Weatherford nodded, then looked at me. "Sitting in?"

My mind was whirring like a top, trying to put all the pieces together. Nothing made sense in any order in which I placed them.

"Start without me, sir. I'm going to visit Eileen in TSU."

"What do you need technical support for?" Whittaker asked.

I shook my head. "I'm not sure, sir, but I'm hoping to have a better idea by the time I get down there."

The two detectives looked at each and shrugged their shoulders. I guess that meant that they didn't object.

32

KITTY-FOOTING AROUND A TECHNICALITY

It was over half an hour later when I opened the door to the conference room. From the heated questions being fired at Detective Weatherford, it appeared he was yet to get around to the interview part of the proceedings.

"And what the hell have you been doing to find our daughter?" Rebecca blasted at me before I'd even taken a seat.

I ignored her and sat next to Weatherford. "What does the name Tulla mean to you?" I asked, looking at Rupert.

He glared back at me as though I were a lowly employee speaking out of turn.

"What?"

"Tulla," I repeated. "Know who that is?"

Rupert threw his arms up. "What does this Tulla person have to do with finding Chloe? You have the man responsible in custody. Give me five minutes with him and I'll get the location out of him."

I kept looking at Rupert while Rebecca fussed and squawked about us wasting time.

"How did you beat the possession charge in England?" I asked next.

Rupert's face turned red, and I sensed Weatherford shifting

uncomfortably in his chair. Whittaker had told him to *go easy on the guy*, but he hadn't given me the same instruction. A feeble technicality, but we didn't have time to kitty-foot around. We needed to find a crack in whatever Rupert was hiding. If the kidnapper was convinced he had a hidden secret, then we had to assume the same.

"What could that possibly have to do with Chloe?" he ranted.

"It wasn't just your brother who liked to get high," I said, knowing I was tormenting the man.

"My brother's dead! Why would you bring up some stupid mistake we made decades ago?"

"This is ridiculous," Rebecca chimed in. "How old are you anyway?" she aimed at me before turning to Weatherford. "Why are you letting this girl treat us this way?"

The detective didn't flinch. Instead, he looked at Rupert. "When we searched your brother's condo, we found a large quantity of illegal narcotics."

Rupert didn't look shocked. His shoulders slumped.

"Patrick has a problem. Had a problem," he corrected himself. "It was a constant battle for him. He had the coke when we were pulled over back in the UK. I had no idea. I pulled a few strings and was able to make it go away."

"But what does any of this have to do with finding Chloe?" Rebecca said, looping her arm through her husband's.

"Because there's a chance Chloe's abduction might be connected to a drug operation we've been investigating," I responded.

Weatherford shifted uncomfortably again and looked at me, but I was too busy watching Pennington's expression. He looked perplexed.

"I simply don't get it," he said. "I don't know anything about any drugs, I swear. My only involvement with narcotics has been trying to keep Patrick off them."

"I believe you," I said.

"Thank you," he replied, slapping his hands on the table. "Now, can we please focus on finding Chloe?"

I turned and pointed at Rebecca. "But she's Tulla."

Weatherford grunted something incoherent, and Rupert swung around to face his wife.

"What is she talking about, Becca?"

The woman stood up and glared at me. "I've no clue what this idiot is babbling about!"

"Sit down, Mrs Pennington," Weatherford barked, and Rebecca looked stunned. Angry, but stunned.

My phone vibrated in my pocket, and I quickly looked. It was a message from Eileen in our Technical Support Unit. She'd tried to brush me off at first, but once I'd explained what I was looking for and why, she'd set about the task.

"We need to step outside for a moment, sir," I said to Weatherford.

"Stay here," he ordered the Penningtons and followed me out of the room.

"Was that just a guess?" he asked once he'd closed the door.

"Sort of," I admitted. "Her expression hearing the name Tulla was weird every time. She was trying too hard not to have a reaction."

"Can we prove any of this?" he asked.

"I don't know, but it doesn't matter, sir."

"What do you mean?"

I held my mobile up. "Because we have the name of who I think took Chloe."

The next ten minutes were pure chaos, juggled and somehow managed into an organised effort by Whittaker and Weatherford.

"Explain to me how you found this name again," Whittaker said as Weatherford drove his Bronco at high speed through town with lights blazing and the siren making it hard to hear each other.

"I asked Eileen to search for drug arrests and incidents over the past five years, here on the island or in the UK," I explained. "Which returned a bunch of names."

"Okay," the detective said. "That had to be an extensive list."

"*Ja.* But then she cross-referenced with visitors currently here in the Cayman Islands," I continued. "Which narrowed it down to six people."

"How did you rule out the other five?" he asked.

"They're all under thirty, here on work visas, and came up in the search because of minor pot or pill possession in the UK, sir. Timothy Henshaw is 46 years old, lives in Kent, and has visited the island multiple times in the past eight months."

Whittaker was looking over his shoulder at me in the back seat as we rocked from side to side in the speeding SUV.

"And we think he's at this address in North Side?"

"*Ja.* He rented the house for a month, starting three weeks ago, sir."

Whittaker faced the front and studied the paperwork in his hand. "Computer systems engineer. Lives in Kent. Divorce finalised earlier this year," he read aloud.

"See the part about his daughter, sir. Her name came up in the search too, but didn't show as currently on the island."

"Died of a drug overdose here in Grand Cayman a year and a half ago," Whittaker read. "I remember that case. Kid was only eighteen. Here on a three-week holiday with a friend. Very sad. The girlfriend was in the hospital too. They'd been on quite a binge. Couldn't tell us anything about where they'd bought the cocaine. She was flown back to the UK as soon as the hospital released her, so the case went cold."

"Looks like the father managed to find out more than we could, sir," I said. "We've been trying to get the wrong Pennington to own up to something."

Weatherford killed the siren but kept the lights on as he cleared town and traffic thinned along the newer stretch of bypass named Linford Pierson Highway.

"So, if Rebecca Pennington is Tulla, how do we think she fits in with the lochmen?" he asked.

I shrugged my shoulders. "Not sure, but my guess is she was

the contact between McGinnis and them. Which is odd, as they're all Scottish. But I think we might find a link between Rebecca and Ness going back to the UK."

"She was a model and actress," Whittaker mentioned. "Maybe she had ties to drug supplies back then. A bit cliché, but illegal narcotics often run in those circles."

"So why was Patrick Pennington executed?" Weatherford asked.

"Oh, I have conformation from Rasha," Whittaker said. "It is Patrick's blood on McGinnis's boat. Only a trace, but it's his."

I waited a moment to see if he'd answer his fellow detective's question, but he just turned and looked at me again.

"It was a message to someone," I replied. "Maybe the lochmen sold directly to Patrick, and Brenda let them know the island was her turf. It's only a trace because her thug garrotted Patrick on the stolen boat before sinking it. Didn't clean himself up as well as he thought."

"That could be," Whittaker replied. "We'll see if we can learn anything more from McGinnis now she'll be going away for more than attempted murder."

I looked at my watch. It was 10:35am. The drive would take us another half an hour, at least. I watched Whittaker do the same thing. It was only 15 kilometres in a straight line, but double that by road. We had to drive most of the way to the east end of the island before Breakers Road cut north through the mangroves and woods covering the middle of the oddly shaped land mass.

"Put the siren back on, Vincent," Whittaker said. "We need to push it."

The police helicopter was inflight to Rum Point with Sergeant Williams and his firearms team aboard, landing several miles from the house Henshaw had rented on the north side of the island. Whittaker had determined we could get there by road in the same time it would take to drive to the airport, fly across North Sound, and then use a local patrol car to reach the destination. He was probably right, but at least we would have been more active that way. It felt painfully long driving all the way there, despite the speed we were going, and we all kept looking at our watches.

"Hello, Mrs Henshaw?" Whittaker said when his call went through on the Bronco's hands-free system. "My apologies for calling you at this hour in the morning. I'm Detective Whittaker with the Royal Cayman Islands Police Service."

Weatherford switched the siren off again so we could hear.

"Margate," an English woman replied. "I went back to my maiden name after the divorce. But Beth is fine."

"Okay, Beth, thank you. I have two other detectives in the car with me. We're en route to the house your ex-husband rented here on the island."

"Is Tim okay?" she asked.

"We believe so, ma'am, but I'm afraid he may be involved in the kidnapping of a young girl."

The line went quiet for several moments.

"Tim? Are you sure, inspector?"

Whittaker looked at me and raised his eyebrows. "We won't know for certain until we get there, ma'am. Can I ask when you last spoke to Timothy?"

"I haven't seen him or spoken to him since the day our divorce became final," she replied. "To be honest, I've not answered or returned his calls."

"I'm terribly sorry to be blunt in my questioning, Beth, but we're very short on time. May I ask why you two divorced?"

I heard a sigh into the phone. "I assume you know about our daughter's passing, inspector?"

Whittaker didn't bother correcting her from the UK term inspector, although we used detective in the Cayman Islands.

"We're aware, yes, ma'am, and my sincere condolences. I feel awful this happened on our island. We don't see many incidents like your daughter's, but drugs are an ever-growing issue."

"Yes, well, Lucy made a poor decision. From her friend's description of the events, no one forced her or coerced her into what she did. And that's at the core of why Tim and I divorced, inspector. He refused to accept that Lucy was responsible in any way. He had to find a culprit. It's completely consumed him and he's been obsessed ever since her death."

"Were you aware he was currently here in the Cayman Islands, ma'am?" Whittaker asked.

"No, not at all. But like I said, we've not spoken."

"I'm afraid I need to ask you, Beth. Has Timothy ever been violent in any way? Either with you, or anyone else?"

The woman laughed, but with little humour in her voice. "Have you seen my ex-husband, inspector?"

"Only a passport picture, ma'am," Whittaker replied.

"He's shorter than me, weighs about the same as I do, and I'm not a large woman, and his idea of sports is playing Wordle. Timothy hasn't thrown a punch, or anything else, his whole life, inspector. He looks just like you'd imagine a stereotypical computer programmer to look."

"Okay, thank you, Beth. We may well reach out to you again shortly, but for now I think we have what we need, unless my associates have any questions?" Whittaker said, looking at us.

Weatherford shook his head, focused on driving, but I leaned forward.

"Has Timothy ever been a member of a gun club, archery, martial arts, anything like that, ma'am?"

"No, no, not at all. At least in the time I've known him, and we met in uni. He carries spiders outside on a piece of paper and will only use those mousetraps which allow you to release the pesky things," she replied and then paused for a few moments. "But, I will add that the man changed when we lost Lucy. Although I still can't imagine he'd turn to violence. We had a few big shouting matches around the time we separated, but he never raised a hand or even threw anything across the room."

I looked up and saw we were following the road left out of the little town of North Side.

"Thank you again, Beth," Whittaker said. "Please stay by the phone for the next hour or two."

He hung up the call and Weatherford turned the flashing lights off. I looked at the satellite navigation on his dashboard and it showed us three quarters of a mile from our destination.

"How are we playing this, Roy?" Detective Weatherford asked.

Whittaker looked at his watch one more time, then checked his phone, which had just beeped.

"Well, we have 50 minutes until his deadline. First things first, let's establish whether he's here, and if he has the girl. That's Williams, letting me know they're a few minutes out." He turned to face me again. "If we drop you short of the house, can you cover the back but stay hidden?"

"*Ja*," I replied, and Weatherford finally slowed down as we neared the house.

Two hundred metres away, he pulled over, and I got out.

"Nora, you'll have to use your mobile to communicate. Williams is bringing the radios. Stay out of sight and let me know when you're in place. Don't do anything until I get backup sent your way, okay?" Whittaker instructed.

I nodded and closed the door. Weatherford pulled away. I looked at the satellite view I'd brought up on my mobile, then the street view. The home was a two-storey on stilts, set back 30 metres from the water's edge, which was ironshore with sandy patches. Between the stilts below the home was a small concrete storage room. A wooden dock extended into the ocean, which I knew to be quite shallow in this area. Woods surrounded the lone home on both sides. I ran through the trees until I reached the sand and turned west along the shore. Once the home came into view, I ducked back into the tree coverage until it ended where the lot had been cleared. I texted Whittaker.

"In place."

"Stand by," he sent in reply.

Crouching down, I settled in behind a few shrubs and scanned the house. The water lapped against the beach to my right and the breeze whistled through the trees. An air-conditioning compressor whirred from the side of the home. An iguana, the invasive green kind, skittered across the concrete pad where the six beefy stilts supported the home. The sweet, citrus scent of plumeria filled my nostrils.

As I waited, I began to wonder if I'd brought all our resources to the house in which Chloe Pennington was being held... or to an empty home rented by a broken-hearted but innocent man who couldn't move on from the death of his own daughter. Either way, we'd be here when the clock ran out.

33

HITTING THE BEACH IN TACTICAL BLACK

It had been a while without anything happening, and I was getting spikes and needles in my legs from crouching. According to my mobile, it was 11:25am. I couldn't see the road, but I heard several vehicles approach the area then stop. Patrol cars would have Rum Point Drive blocked in both directions by now, and hopefully Williams and his team were here. Constables bringing the Penningtons would also be here, or at least close by.

My mobile vibrated. It was a text from Whittaker. "Knocking on the door."

I'd already messaged and told him the back of the house was clear with no boat on the dock, so I sat tight and watched, trying to get the circulation back into my legs. Through the underside of the home, I saw Whittaker's legs as he walked to the front steps. A moment later, I thought I heard three knocks, then after a few moments, I definitely heard three more, when the detective rapped harder. From behind me, the trees rustled, and I spun around. A man in black tactical gear carrying an assault rifle appeared. I returned my attention to the house as the officer scurried over and crouched next to me.

"Black doesn't work so well at the beach," I whispered.

"Badass is always in style," Williams replied, and handed me a radio with a single earpiece and lapel mic kit.

I threaded the wiring under my shirt, put the earpiece in, and secured the radio to my belt. Whittaker was already talking when I switched on the unit.

"…establish whether the suspect is in the house."

I looked at Williams. "What are we doing?"

"Need to get a look in the windows without alertin' da guy if he in dere," he replied.

"That rules you out."

He rolled his eyes behind his goggles.

"This is Sommer. Approaching rear," I said into the mic, holding down the little button on the side.

There was a brief hesitation before Whittaker replied. "Copy. Proceed."

"Copy," I acknowledged and moved around Williams, heading along the hedge line towards the road.

The midday sun wasn't helping me out much with shade, but approaching from the side offered more cover. The house had been designed to enjoy the ocean view and not the neighbour who would undoubtedly build at some point. I counted only four small windows on this side, two of which were frosted, indicating they were bathrooms.

Breaking cover, I ran to the house where I went under the structure. The stilts raised the home a few metres off the concrete base to allow storm surge to flow underneath, but it meant I had no chance of seeing into the ground floor window. My only option to view inside the home would be from the full-width deck facing the water, which had steps to the path leading to the dock. Using the steps would make me easily visible to anyone looking out the rear from either floor.

I moved to the corner of the building and searched for a way to climb the deck. Reaching up, I grabbed the wood planking, and using a brace in the framework to push with my foot, peeked over the top. By shuffling towards the water about a metre, I could see into the living room through big double sliding windows. A man stood with his back to me, and sitting on the couch was Chloe Pennington.

Lowering myself back down, I keyed the mic, speaking softly. "Suspect inside living room at back of house, ground floor, with the girl. I didn't see a weapon. Girl is not restrained. Over."

As I waited for instructions, I replayed what I'd just seen in my head. It hadn't been what I'd expected. Maybe I'd dreamed up a crazy situation after the madness on the *Manannán*, but I thought the kid would at least be tied up.

"Are you sure there's no weapon, Nora? Over." Whittaker asked.

"*Nei*, sir. Not 100 percent sure. He had his back to me. But no visual on a weapon."

He could have three guns and a samurai sword tucked in the front of his trousers, but I doubted it.

"Okay, we're taking the house," Whittaker said. "Three men in front. Break through the front door first. Three men round back. Go through the rear once the front door is breached. Copy?"

A series of verifications came back over the radio, then Williams began giving his men orders, organising them into position. I scrambled up the side of the decking and looked inside once more. Timothy Henshaw had moved to where he could look through what appeared to be a dining area to the front of the house. No doubt he was checking for movement outside. He spun around and said something to the girl.

Henshaw's ex-wife had been right. He was a small man with thinning hair and a slight frame. I watched him nervously adjust the glasses perched on his nose several times. He moved towards Chloe and I shifted my weight to free up a hand and grab the mic, ready to broadcast over the radio. But he turned and walked back to where he'd been standing. They appeared to be in conversation. I squinted to see beyond the living room. The kitchen was open to the ocean view on the right, and a short hallway led to what I assumed was the front door. Where I could just make out a stack of furniture in the shadows.

I keyed the mic. "Hold, sir, hold. Front door is blocked from inside. Over."

"Blocked?" Whittaker came back. "How?"

"Looks like furniture, sir. Over."

"Copy," he replied. "Hold team, hold. Over."

"Holding," Williams repeated.

"Sir. I think I can talk to him from the back. Over," I said, questioning why I'd want to try such a thing.

"Talk to him how? Over."

"I see a way in, sir. Over."

"That'll give him two hostages, Nora. Over."

"I'll stay outside then, sir. But I believe I can talk to him. I'll jump off the deck at the first sign of a weapon, sir. Over."

There was silence over the radio for more than a few moments.

"Can you take a picture with your phone? Over," Whittaker asked.

"I'll rest my phone on the deck and start a video call. Over."

"I need to see the situation before I can clear you to approach. Over."

"*Fy faen*," I muttered to myself and fumbled with my mobile until I held it in one hand and snapped a photo.

It was mainly glare from the sliding glass, but I could vaguely make out the two figures inside, so I texted the picture to the detective. I waited for a response.

"Are you sure about this?" he texted back.

My brain told me no, but my gut seemed pretty enthusiastic to give it a try.

"I think it's worth a shot before force," I texted back.

The next message came over my earpiece. "Tactical, please closely cover rear while remaining hidden. Be ready for immediate response. Detective Sommer, you're cleared to approach with care. Please provide video feed. Over."

"*Dritt,*" I mumbled. *What had I got myself into now?* But I liked hearing the title he used.

I video called Whittaker, making sure my mobile was muted. Once he answered, I carefully reached up and rested the camera against one of the balusters.

"Too much reflection off the glass. We can't see inside. Over."

I swore under my breath. What could I do about that? "Copy," I replied over the radio, then carefully pulled myself up, moving as close to the building as possible.

Hoping they wouldn't notice from inside, I swung both legs over the railing and landed softly on the deck. Again keeping tight to the wall, I edged along the few metres to where the sliding glass began. I risked another quick glance into the living room. They were turned towards the front of the house, so I tiptoed to the middle of the doors and tugged on the handle.

To my amazement, the glass slid open. They hadn't locked it. To Timothy Henshaw and Chloe Pennington's amazement, they spun around to see me standing at the entrance to the house.

"Hey," I said. "I'm Nora, a police detective. I'm unarmed."

"Get out!" Henshaw said, moving in front of Chloe.

The girl had jumped to her feet and now peeked around the kidnapper, her hand resting on his waist.

"We can see with the door open. Be careful, Nora," Whittaker said softly over the radio.

"I can help you," I said, and cringed at my own words.

Henshaw scoffed. "Of course you can," he said sarcastically. "You need to get out."

"I'm unarmed," I assured him again. "But my friends outside have a shitload of big guns. You're better off talking to me than dealing with them." I looked at my watch. It was 11:42am. "They'll be inviting themselves in before noon."

Henshaw looked nervously around. "Are the Penningtons here?"

"Should be by now," I replied.

"She needs to confess," he said.

I let out a sigh of relief. If I was wrong about Rebecca Pennington, then we were both wrong.

"Hi, Chloe," I said, seeing her show herself more. "You okay?"

She nodded.

"Tell me to close the door," I whispered, and Henshaw frowned at me.

"Tell me!" I hissed.

"Close the door," he said hesitantly.

I reached back, gave an okay sign to my mobile, and slid the glass closed.

"We can't see, Nora," Whittaker said into my ear.

I keyed the mic while holding up a finger to Henshaw. "All good. Hold. Over."

"What on earth are you up to?" Henshaw asked.

The man looked tired.

"I'm helping you," I replied.

"Bullshit," he responded, looking around again.

Chloe stepped out from behind him. "How?" she asked.

"By getting your mother to confess," I replied. "That's what you both want, right?"

They looked at each other, then back at me.

"That's all I've wanted all along," Henshaw said, and Chloe nodded.

"How did you find out it was Rebecca?" I asked.

Henshaw shrugged his shoulders. "I went to the seediest places I could find and asked where I could score drugs. After two muggings and a beating for asking the wrong person, I found a bloke who could get cocaine. I paid him £5,000 to give me the name of his supplier."

"And that was Rebecca?"

He shook his head. "No. Cost me another £10,000 to get her name from the second guy. That was three months ago. Then I started talking to Chloe."

He rested a hand on her shoulder.

"Okay, here's what we're going to do," I said, and he looked at me suspiciously.

"She needs to confess!"

"*Ja.* Now shut up and listen."

Chloe gripped his arm. "She's going to help us."

He looked down at the girl. "That's easy for her to say, but she's a bloody copper. She's scheming something."

"I am," I said. "I'm scheming how to get you what you want. Because I want it too."

I had no idea if we could find evidence to convict Rebecca of anything. Presumably, she'd been running a drug operation behind her husband's back, so she'd covered her tracks well. A confession would certainly help our cause. But we needed more than a straight admittance. A good solicitor would have that tossed out. She was simply saying whatever it took to get her daughter back.

I keyed the mic. "Are the Penningtons here, sir?"

"Yes. What's going on, Nora?"

"Henshaw will settle for a private confession from Rebecca, sir." I quickly released the button. I knew what was coming next.

"No, no!" Henshaw yelped. "It has to be public!"

"It will be," I replied. "She'll confess in front of you with two police witnesses. You'll then demand that she reveal her partner."

"She has a partner?" he asked in surprise.

"How do you propose we do that?" Whittaker asked in my ear.

"My dad isn't involved," Chloe claimed.

My head felt like a crowded room of babbling people.

"Not your dad. Another woman by the name of Brenda McGinnis. We have her in custody on attempted murder and probably a full murder charge. When Rebecca names her, McGinnis will then throw Rebecca under the bus and give us what we need. Hard evidence."

"But if she confesses, you'll have that," Henshaw said.

"No, we won't. That'll get thrown out without supporting evidence. But when we nick her, it'll all be made public."

"Nora?" Whittaker asked.

"Hold, sir. Get Rebecca ready."

"Look," I continued to Henshaw. "You're obviously not going to hurt Chloe, so come noon, your game is up."

"I could never harm her," Henshaw admitted, looking down at the girl.

"Right, so either the cavalry is galloping in at 11:59, or it rolls past noon and all your leverage is gone. Do it my way and we all get what we want."

"Is Tim going to jail?" Chloe asked.

"I don't care as long as your mother does," he responded.

"Not up to me, but the fact he didn't do anything against your will is certainly going to help."

Henshaw winced. "Not entirely."

"Okay, well, you two figured it out, right?"

They both nodded. I felt exhausted from the lack of sleep, but more from all the bloody talking. I was ready to wrap this shitshow up.

Henshaw looked at his watch. "Okay. But we're trusting you."

"*Ja*," I replied, and keyed the mic. "Sir. You and Detective Weatherford bring the parents to the rear deck. Take off your jackets. No weapons. Over." Then I quickly opened the mic again. "Those are his final demands, sir. Over."

I almost forgot that it all needed to be Henshaw's idea. For now.

"Ops switch to backup," I heard Whittaker say.

He was keeping the chatter out of my ear. It would be nice not having the distraction, but now I'd rather listen in to make sure they weren't planning something else.

"Chloe. Get a knife from the kitchen. A big one."

"What?" she and Henshaw both asked.

"If she's not under threat, why would Rebecca say anything?" I urged. "The detectives will walk right in like I did. Now get the knife."

Chloe ran to the kitchen, and I noticed movement along the side of the house.

"We're approaching. Over." Whittaker announced on my channel.

"Slowly, sir. Henshaw has a knife, but there is no immediate threat. Repeat. No immediate threat."

I moved closer to the side window and made sure the detectives were still moving. Whittaker hesitated for a moment, then continued.

"You need to get ready," I told Henshaw. "Stand with Chloe in front of you. Hold the knife in your right hand."

Chloe had made her way back with a blade that looked more like a machete in her little hands. She passed it to Henshaw and moved in front of him. The eleven-year-old had her wits about her far more than the revenge-seeking adult.

"Okay, this is very important, Timothy," I said and waited until he looked at me. "Don't hold the knife against her. Hold it by your side, understand?"

"Wouldn't it seem more real if I had it to her throat?" he asked. "Chloe knows she can trust me."

"Yup, that would be more believable, but they'll shoot you."

He swallowed hard and kept the knife firmly against his own thigh.

"We can do this," Chloe encouraged.

Henshaw nodded, then tensed as the two detectives escorted the girl's parents up the steps to the deck. I slid the glass open again.

"Chloe!" Rupert called out.

"Are you okay, sweetie?" Rebecca asked, her face full of concern.

But it wasn't the scared, nervous parent concern, like her husband. Or perhaps I was projecting.

"Mr Henshaw," Whittaker said. "This will go much more smoothly if you'd put that knife down."

"No way," he blurted and waved the knife at them, then immediately realised what he was doing and quickly brought it back down to his side.

"Let's stay calm," I said. "We need Mrs Pennington to admit her role in Lucy Henshaw's death, then we can all go home."

"I've never met a Lucy Henshaw, and I don't know what this man is talking about," Rebecca ranted. "Same as your ridiculous accusations earlier," she added, pointing at me. "Now somebody stop this extortionist and get our daughter."

"Please, Mummy," Chloe pleaded. "Tell him whatever he wants to hear so he'll let me go. I'm scared."

I hoped the kid was enrolled in drama at school. She was a lot more convincing than her mother.

"Fine, I'll say whatever you want if you'll release her," Rebecca responded.

Rupert looked at his wife. "Go on then."

"Okay, okay. I apologise for what happened to your daughter."

"That was weak," I said, because Henshaw didn't.

"Is that your apology for what happened to Lucy?" Henshaw woke up and shouted. "And what did happen to her, Pennington?"

Rebecca threw her arms up. "I don't know. I never met her. Now give us back our daughter."

"You imported and supplied the drugs which killed her," Henshaw stammered, his voice breaking. "Admit it, or Chloe pays the price."

I watched the man's hand holding the knife twitch, and for a moment I wondered if I'd completely misread the situation and he'd tricked Chloe and me both.

"Why does this man think you sell drugs?" Rupert asked, taking a step back from his wife. "I'd like to hear this too, Becca."

She glared at him. "Why would you believe this rubbish?"

"I think you know why," he replied.

"You could ask your brother if he hadn't been murdered," I said, which caused them both to turn their attention on me. "Ask her about Patrick."

"What does she mean?" Rupert snapped.

"She's making shit up," Rebecca retorted. "You know your brother mixed with the wrong sorts."

I turned to Henshaw and subtly nodded. Which had zero response.

"Partner," I hissed under my breath, and he frowned at me.

He finally figured it out. "The wrong sorts like your partner?"

"They're all spouting bullshit," Rebecca said. "Are you two just going to stand around and let my daughter be held at knifepoint?" she directed at the two detectives.

"Seems pretty simple, ma'am," Whittaker replied. "Tell the man what he wants to know and he'll let Chloe go."

"Why would anyone believe him?" Rebecca responded. "He's a kidnapper, for Christ's sake."

"Because he's only ever asked for one thing," I pointed out.

"And you let me think it was something I'd done all this time," Rupert said, shaking his head. "Tell him, Becca. For fuck's sake. It's our daughter."

"None of this would stand up in court," Rebecca ranted.

"Then where's the harm in saying it?" I countered.

"Rebecca?" Rupert urged.

"Please, Mummy," Chloe said, and struggled against Henshaw's gentle hold on her.

"Fine! I supplied the cocaine which Lucy Henshaw overdosed on. There. Everybody happy? Now give me my daughter back!"

"Who's your partner?" Henshaw asked. "You forgot that part."

"My husband," Rebecca replied curtly.

"What?" Rupert blurted.

"Stop lying, Mummy!" Chloe yelled.

"You might as well say her name, Mrs Pennington," I said. "We have her in custody. She'll be charged with Patrick's murder."

Rupert looked like he'd been punched in the face. "You had something to do with whoever killed my brother?"

"Your brother was an idiot!" Rebecca snarled.

"Name your partner," Henshaw demanded.

"Please, Mummy," Chloe begged again.

"McGinnis," Rebecca said flatly, regaining a determined resolve. "Brenda McGinnis."

I nodded to Henshaw, and he dropped the knife, releasing his arm from the girl. Rupert shot forward to meet Chloe, but he wasn't fast enough. Rebecca bowled him aside as she flew past the outstretched hands of the two detectives, sending her husband crashing into me. By the time I picked myself up, Rebecca Pennington held the knife to her own daughter's throat.

"Stop! Everybody calm down!" Whittaker ordered.

"Rebecca?" Rupert groaned from the floor. "What are you doing?"

Chloe wasn't acting terrified now. The kid was visibly shaking.

"Here's how this is going to happen," Rebecca said without a stitch of emotion. "I'll need a ride to the airport and a private plane, fuelled and ready. Chloe will be released when I land the other end."

"Change in target? Over." Williams asked over the radio.

I nodded once.

"That a confirm, Sommer?"

I nodded again.

"Need target where prior target stood. Copy."

I nodded once more, then began sidestepping towards the couch. Rebecca had ended up closer to the dining area.

"Stay where you are," she ordered.

"I just need to sit down. Been a shitty day," I replied.

"Careful, Nora," Whittaker warned.

"Timothy, come over here and sit down with me, so Rebecca can see everyone."

"What are you doing?" the woman growled, her eyes flicking around the room.

Henshaw tentatively moved my way, and I waited to sit until he reached me.

"Stop!" Rebecca shouted as she moved forward and to her right, keeping everyone in clear sight. And then her head became blurred in a red mist a moment before the shot rang out.

I bolted across the floor and swooped Chloe up in my arms before Rebecca Pennington's limp body hit the living room floor.

Keeping the kid's head pressed into my chest, I ran outside through the sliding door and down the steps. Williams' men stormed past me on their way in.

Once I'd run past the hedgerow where I'd crouched earlier, I stopped and gently put Chloe down. She was shaking like a leaf. All I could do was hope I'd spared Chloe from seeing her mother's gory corpse, even if she knew what had just happened. Regardless, the kid was going to need serious therapy to help her through this trauma. Rupert and Weatherford arrived beside me, and the girl's father lifted her into his arms as they both sobbed.

I turned to look at Weatherford, and his expression tensed. He raised his eyebrows.

"I'm covered in blood again, aren't I?"

He nodded.

"*Fy faen,*" I groaned.

34

FIRED, BOLLOCKING, OR COFFEE?

I faced days and days of torturous paperwork, but it would all have to wait. I'd slept for eight hours straight, which was unheard of for me. Now I sat on the deck enjoying coffee with Jazzy, listening to the water slap against the ironshore and watching Edvard munch on the lettuce leaves we'd given him.

"How can you miss someone you only knew for a couple of days?" Jazzy asked.

I'd slept past the time she should have left for school, and apparently the kid had decided to take another day off. She claimed it was to keep an eye on me after a rough couple of days. I had to admit I welcomed the distraction of her chatter, although I'd prefer it if I didn't have to participate.

"I don't know," I admitted. "I never have before."

"But you miss her too, don't you?" she asked.

"*Ja.*"

"Maybe because we said we'd watch out for her," Jazzy said.

"*Ja,*" I responded, with a lump in my throat. I'd done a shit job of that.

We sat quietly, sipping coffee for a while before she spoke again.

"So, is this kidnapper guy going to jail?"

"He'll be charged with something," I replied, hoping the system would be kind to the man. "He never had any intention of actually hurting the girl. But he did kidnap her initially. Once they talked more, and she pieced together some of the strange things her mother had done, then Chloe helped Timothy with his plan."

"That's crazy," Jazzy laughed. "She plotted against her own mother. You'd better watch out," she added, raising her eyebrows at me and giggling.

"I'm not your mother."

"You're sort of like one."

"*Nei.* You're just renting my services."

"Does that mean I can send you back for a better model?"

"It means I'm funding you until you get a fancy job and start paying me back," I said.

We grinned at each other.

My mobile rang inside the shack, and I slumped in the chair. It would be work, or my friend AJ calling to see when I could help on her dive boat. I wasn't up for either at the moment. Jazzy got up, and I handed her my coffee cup.

"Refill please."

She took the mug, went inside, and returned a moment later with my phone to her ear.

"Yes, sir, she's here."

I glared at her as she handed me the device.

"*Ja?*"

"I hope I'm not disturbing you too early?" came Whittaker's voice.

"*Nei.* Slow start, but I'll be in later, sir."

"No rush," he replied. "But I was wondering if it would be too much of an imposition if I dropped by to talk to you for a few minutes?"

"*Nei,*" I said, surprised. "When?"

"Well, I'm actually parked on the road right now."

Another surprise. "Oh, okay. Do you remember the way in, sir?"

"Around the side to a hole in the fence?"

"*Ja.* Jazzy will meet you there in just a minute."

I jumped up and went inside. "Can you meet Whittaker at the fence? I should put a bra on."

Jazzy gave me the pissed-off teenager look, but she got another coffee cup out, then ran out of the house. She returned a few minutes later with the detective in tow. I had three coffees lined up and more appropriate clothes on. I'd shown enough of myself to other people in the past week.

"I'm sorry to invade you at home, Nora. I know you must be exhausted after the past few days."

"That's okay," I replied, although whether I was okay with his visit or not really depended on what he wanted to talk about. "Please sit down. There's a coffee for you."

Edvard had scurried across the deck with the stranger's arrival, but he began carefully stepping towards his last leaf of lettuce. He looked like he was moving in slow motion.

"Thank you," Whittaker said, taking a seat and watching the iguana.

"Should I go?" Jazzy asked, looking at me.

I, in turn, looked at the detective. "Am I getting fired or an embarrassing bollocking, sir?"

He laughed. "Neither. And I don't mind Jazzy staying as long as she's sworn to secrecy."

Jazzy dropped into the wooden chair and pulled a zipper motion across her lips.

"I wanted to update you on a couple of things which happened after you left yesterday, and have you help me understand a few details from the cases you were involved with," he said. "Obviously, I missed several key days, and I thank you and Vincent for doing a fine job filling in."

I didn't feel like we'd done a fine job. Or at least I hadn't. The answer sat under our noses for five days and it was only a tiny slip on Rebecca Pennington's part that led us in the right direction. It seemed Henshaw had no intention of hurting Chloe, but I wasn't sure what would have happened if the clock had run out.

"They pulled the tube from Brenda McGinnis's throat last night, so we were able to speak with her. We made a deal to drop the attempted murder on me in exchange for her giving us key details about Rebecca. Based on what she told us, we found her cocaine supply in a tanning room in the Penningtons' house. Hidden behind a panel, right under her husband's nose."

"Was Rebecca some kind of middleman with the lochmen?" I asked.

Whittaker finished taking a sip of coffee, then nodded. "According to McGinnis, Pennington knew them and made the contact. She wouldn't admit to having Patrick killed, but she did say that she met Rebecca two years ago and they formed an alliance. Pennington had money but couldn't access it without causing suspicion, so Brenda bankrolled her to get started and provided a local dealer network. Swears she never handled any drugs."

"Except the bag she framed you with," I pointed out.

He shrugged. "We're letting her off those charges anyway."

"So Rebecca had the international contacts?" I asked.

"We're still digging into how and when," Whittaker continued. "But Brenda said Pennington knew one of the lochmen from the party scene in London back when she was an actress and model."

"Rupert wasn't as surprised about the drug part as he should have been," I said. "I bet she was the one supplying Patrick back then."

"Vincent and I took Rupert back to the station, and he ranted about his wife most of the way there. Couldn't understand why she would deal drugs when they already had plenty of money."

"She was bored," I replied.

"That was my conclusion," Whittaker said and threw one hand up. The other was holding his coffee. "I suggested the idea to

Rupert. He said he'd rather she'd..." the detective checked himself, choosing his words before he continued. "Rather she had a relationship with the gardener to relieve the boredom."

"I'm sure," I responded. "Better than causing their daughter to hate them and someone else's daughter to die."

He nodded. "That was pretty much his explanation."

"Will McGinnis get away with having Patrick killed, sir?" I asked.

He smiled. "DNA from under Patrick's fingernails are a match for Brenda's henchman. That, along with the blood on the boat, and we'll have a reasonably solid case against him. I suspect he'll roll on her before it's all over with."

"Good," I muttered. "Did you have an opportunity to ask Henshaw about the cabin cruiser, sir?"

"I did, yes. Do you have a theory for that one?"

I took a moment to make sure I had my thoughts straight. "Was it with the house he rented?"

"It was, but it was out of the water, awaiting an overhaul," Whittaker replied. "Parked beside the house on a trailer since the owner purchased it nine years ago."

"So Henshaw launched it, picked up Chloe, then left it somewhere he didn't think we'd come across it, and Warwick happened to find it," I surmised. "Although he could have pulled the boat back out and parked it by the house as things turned out."

"That's partly correct," Whittaker confirmed. "He did plan on parking the boat back beside the house, but his plans changed," Whittaker explained. "He'd been chatting via WhatsApp with Chloe, but they'd never actually met. She seemed sympathetic to him and suspicious of her own mother as she'd witnessed her meeting with strangers at the house and other odd behaviour. But he did in fact abduct her in the boat. I think she told you that, right?"

I nodded.

Whittaker carried on. "But after reaching the house, they

figured out they genuinely wanted the same conclusion, so Chloe became involved in the scheme. With the boat being unregistered and not traceable to the house, they decided to scratch her message in the trim work and leave it somewhere it'd be found."

"North Sound Estates," I filled in for him.

"Exactly."

"But instead of it being reported, Warwick happened to stumble across it," I added.

"Which is why he couldn't tell you and Vincent precisely where it was. Warwick is being treated at the hospital. It appears he'd got his meds confused and missed some while doubling others. Poor man. Anyway, Henshaw dropped the boat, then walked about a mile to a small international college campus. He took a taxi from there to the centre of North Side. Then he walked to the rented house, so no one could report his exact location at either end."

We returned to sipping coffee for a while and I plugged all the new information into the case notes in my brain. I couldn't believe that what had begun as three separate cases all ended up being connected.

"What about the crew of the *Manannán*, sir?" I asked. "What's happening with them?"

"We have everyone in custody and will interview them as soon as we can," he replied. "So far, they've all requested the same solicitor who is flying in from Sint Maarten today via Miami. But it was one of the questions I had for you. Who do you think knew what was really going on?"

"That the boat was used to distribute cocaine throughout the Caribbean?" I asked, and he nodded. "The three men I originally met with for certain. The woman who went by Morar was either clued in or supporting them regardless, but that doesn't matter. She's dead."

Jazzy flinched, and I mentally cursed myself again.

"I couldn't say about the captain or first mate. But Siobhán, who did all the cooking and housekeeping, helped me in the end," I said, recalling her calling out a warning. "And I don't think Raven or Shandy knew about the drugs."

"Okay, that's helpful. Thank you."

Whittaker was ready to say something else, but I spoke first. "There'll be an enquiry into... what happened on the yacht, won't there, sir?"

He looked slightly confused.

"My role in the events at the end," I added, hoping he'd understand my point without me spelling it out in front of Jazzy.

"Oh, right. Yes, I'm afraid there will be. Standard procedure."

"I'll need Siobhán as a witness, sir. She saw everything from behind the bar."

A stuffy, judgemental *drittsekk* sitting around a conference table in Central Station could easily interpret my actions as overaggressive. But, in my mind, it was Lomond or me, and I could only hope Siobhán would say the same. My revenge-filled rage only meant I reached him sooner. And aimed for the kill.

"And my other question," Whittaker continued, "is whether you thought any of the clients were buying drugs on the yacht?"

I shook my head. "I didn't see any sign of that at the strip club, sir. My guess now is they were the importers."

"Strip club?" Jazzy asked. "Is that why you had those hoochie mama clothes?"

I looked at the kid and pantomimed a zipper across my lips. She rolled her eyes. But I'd slipped and would have to explain myself later.

"I also think Brenda had Patrick killed as a warning to the lochmen, or perhaps Rebecca," I hurriedly continued, "to not sell directly."

"That's probably correct," Whittaker agreed. "So am I right in saying, that from what you saw, the clients didn't actually break any laws?"

"*Ja.* And one man, David, but I don't know his last name, saved me from being shot by Lomond."

"What?" Jazzy blurted. "You were shot at?"

"I told you that was how Violet was killed," I said less gently than I wished I had.

Jazzy's expression had turned from excitedly curious hearing about the details to shocked and sad.

"I guess I got stuck on the Violet getting shot part and didn't think about you nearly being," she said. "I'm sorry."

"That's okay. I'm here because of Violet, so I'm happy you're thinking of her."

Jazzy took a deep breath and pulled herself together. "Will her funeral be in England?"

I looked at Whittaker, and his expression tightened. "Her parents weren't easy to track down. They're separated, and by what I could find out, not living in the best of circumstances. Her father's in prison for multiple counts of theft, and her mother has been in and out of various facilities for drug problems. I was able to speak with her this morning. Unfortunately, she told me she doesn't have the means to arrange transport of the remains or a service."

"Maybe we could do some kind of fundraiser," Jazzy suggested. "The car washes we do for school bring in hundreds of dollars."

Whittaker looked at me and I could tell he was trying to be delicate in front of the kid.

"Or we could have a service for her here," I suggested. "That way, her friends could say goodbye."

"I'd like that," Jazzy said, and smiled. "Violet would like that."

Thank you for reading *Missing Sommer*!

Would you like a little more time with Nora?
In return for joining my newsletter list, I've written a fun bonus
scene you'll find by using this QR code…

Don't forget to grab the next book in the series, *Hunting Sommer*

ACKNOWLEDGMENTS

My sincere thanks to:

My incredible wife Cheryl, for her unwavering support, love, and
encouragement.

My family and friends for always being there.

The character name Chloe is used in recognition of Chloe Frost
whose generous father, Chris Frost, made the winning bid to name
a character in this book from the Authors for LA auction benefitting
fire victims in the LA area. It is truly my pleasure to include Chloe
in this story.

My marvellous editor Andrew Chapman at Prepare to Publish for
his diligent work and wise suggestions.

Casey Keller, Craig Robinson, and Alain Belanger for their help
with all things Cayman Islands related.

My mate Alan Burgess for his Scottish slang advice!

Russell and Tuula Eacott for helping Nora with her Finnish!

Dive Rite, Shearwater Research, Reef Smart, Conch Republic
Divers, and Cayman Spirits for their friendship and support.

The Tropical Authors group for their advice, support, and humour. Visit and subscribe at www.TropicalAuthors.com for deals and info on a plethora of books by talented authors in the Sea Adventure genre.

My beta reader group has grown to include an amazing cross section of folks from different walks of life. Their suggestions, feedback and keen eyes are invaluable, for which I am eternally grateful.

Above all, I thank you, the readers: none of this happens without the choice you make to spend your precious time with my stories. I am truly in your debt.

LET'S STAY IN TOUCH!

To buy merchandise, find more info or join my newsletter, visit my
website at
www.HarveyBooks.com

If you enjoyed this novel I'd be incredibly grateful if you'd consider
leaving a review on Amazon.com
Find eBook deals and follow me on BookBub.com

Catch my podcast, The Two Authors' Podcast with co-host Douglas
Pratt

Find more great authors in the genre at TropicalAuthors.com

Visit Amazon.com for more books in the
Nora Sommer Caribbean Suspense Series,
AJ Bailey Adventure Series,
and collaborative works;
The Greene Wolfe Thriller Series
Tropical Authors Adventure Series

ABOUT THE AUTHOR

A USA Today bestselling author, Nicholas Harvey's life has been anything but ordinary. Race car driver, motorsports professional, adventurer, divemaster, and since 2020, a full-time novelist. Raised in England and resident in America for many years, Nick and his amazing wife, Cheryl, now base themselves in Grand Cayman from where they travel the world in search of new plots for his novels. He is the author of the Nora Sommer Caribbean Suspense series and the AJ Bailey Adventure series, along with multiple collaborations.

For more information, visit his website at HarveyBooks.com.